The Windlands Tales

John Ernest Briggs

The Adventures of Window Breesian

Part One:
The Path To The Northlands

Part Two:
The Search For The Northlands Treasure

Part Three:
The Search For The Angels Of The Very East

Some of these adventures may not have been true at the time they happened, but most of them are true by now.

THE ADVENTURES OF WINDOW BREESIAN
Part One:

The Path To The Northlands

By

John Ernest Briggs

Illustrations by the author

Including a Reference Appendix

Willowix Publishing

The Adventures Of Window Breesian
Part One:
The Path To The Northlands

Willowix Publishing
WillowixPublishing@gmail.com

ISBN: 987-1-7325181-1-7

Library of Congress Control Number: 2019905744

Printed in Century Schoolbook font

To my uncle

Bill (Breezy) Briggs
[Bill Breesian] –

Who taught me to tell stories by my listening
to him tell stories

THE ADVENTURES OF WINDOW BREESIAN
Part One: The Path To The Northlands

+++++++++

+++++++++

INTRODUCTION TO PART ONE

This is the story of Window Breesian, a young man who leaves his house and, as he walks down the road, kicks at a stone buried in the dirt. This is the start of an amazing adventure that takes him to far-away lands in search of adventure and fabulous treasures.

Along the way, Window encounters new friends, dangerous men, strange creatures, and fantastic places. It is a story of wonder, excitement, family, friendship, loyalty, mystery, exploration, danger, and love – a complex story with hundreds of characters, all intertwined, as Window travels far from home into the wild lands and beyond.

It was the year 147 of the Windlands Age. The settling and expansion periods of the Newlands were over. Since the Northern Wars of the 60's, the people of the Windlands had lived a happy and quiet existence. It was a very interesting time to be alive, and a very good time to travel to the Wilds.

Some of these adventures may not have been true at the time they happened, but most of them are true by now.

John Ernest Briggs

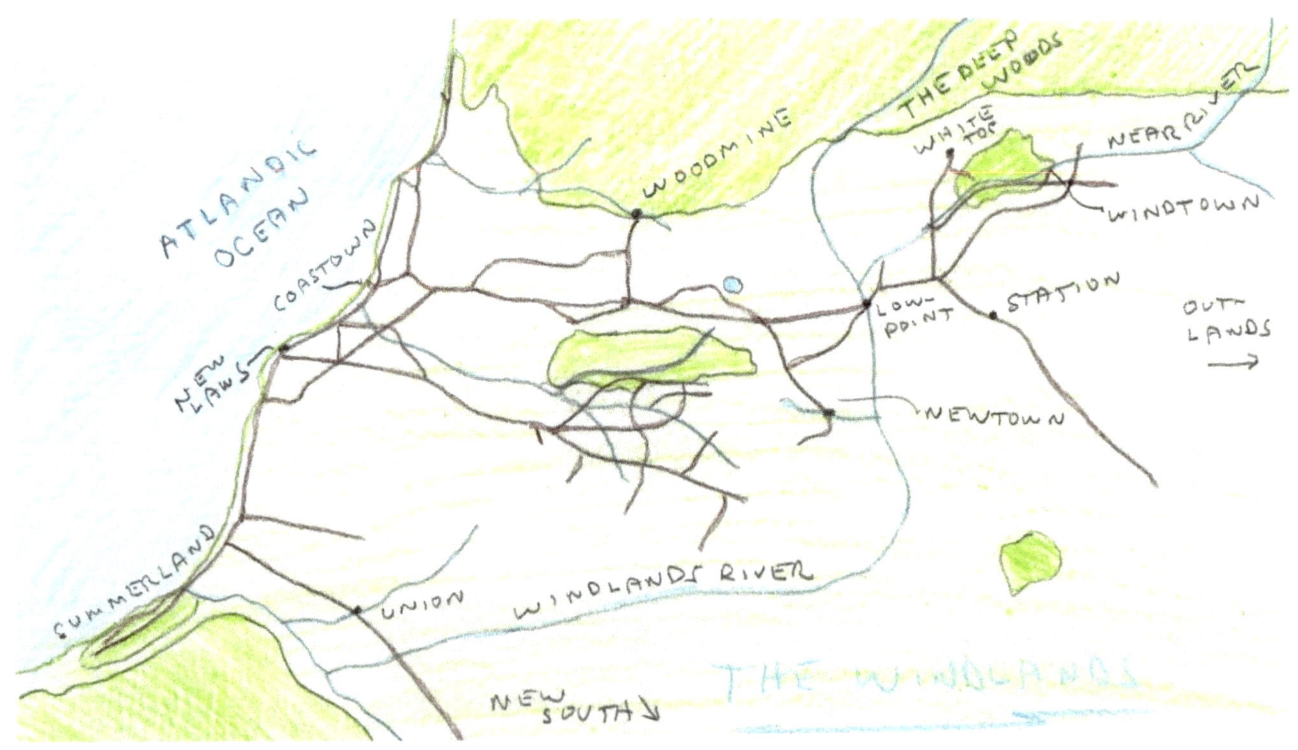

PROLOGUE

+++++++++

[FROM THE WINDLANDS TO THE WILDS]

Somewhere across the lands from the Windcoast, to the Northlands, and far to the Very East, the moon was shining, as it often did, into the bedroom window of Tresette and Vermillion. It was a tall, wide window with a rounded top, and was framed by soft curtains quietly moving in the warm summer breeze.

The breeze came in through the window and gently caressed the faces and ruffled the blonde-brown hair of the twin girls as they lay on their bed in their sleeping-shirts, waiting. The girls were now seven years old, and since they were five, their mother had often read them to sleep with pages of their favorite story. Tonight, they were ready to start it again.

"Hurry, Mama, please," pleaded Veri.

"Yes, hurry, Mama, please," echoed Tressi, her voice almost impossible to tell from that of her sister.

Their mother, moving easily in her silky-white night-dress, came over near the bed and lay the book down on the clothes-stand. The bright light of the table lamp reflected from the jeweled pin in her hair and flashed on the ceiling like stars in the warm night sky.

"Mama, I remember how the story begins. I remember the first line," Tressi spoke up.

"So do I, Mama. I remember the first line, too."

"Don't say it, Veri. I want to be surprised."

"Mama, I can't wait to hear all the nice parts again," Veri explained. "I like the parts where they find new, fun places and..."

"And I like the scary parts," Tressi shared. "But not the really, really scary parts," she quickly admitted.

"My favorite part is when Window first meets..."

"Don't spoil it, Veri. I want to be surprised."

"Oh, we've heard this story a hundred times, Tressi."

"We have not, Veri. Only... well... not a hundred. Besides, I like it when the travelers find..."

"Don't tell me, Tressi. Don't tell me yet."

Veri turned to her mother, who was patiently waiting for the girls to stop talking, so she could begin reading. "I like the parts that you are in, Mama."

"Mama, is it true?" Tressi asked, as she had done every other time her mother had read the book to them. "Is it really you in the story?"

"Yes, Dear, it is true. It really is me in the story."

"Can you tell us the words now, please, Mama? Will you tell us now?" the girls asked, almost together.

Their mother leaned over the bed and gently rubbed one hand across a cheek of each of her darling daughters. As she did, she whispered to each of them.

"Mae lorenne treselle," she whispered in Veri's ear, and "Traeso celvae coelanne," she spoke quietly to Tressi.

"Sweet dreams to you, too, Mama," Veri softly and contentedly replied.

Tressi looked up with big, happy eyes and smiled her response without making a sound.

"Okay, now, no more talking."

Tressi and Veri closed their eyes and settled their heads into their pillows.

Their mother pushed her hair behind her ears and picked up the book from the clothes-stand. She sat gently down on the edge of the bed and started as she had so many times before.

"The Adventures of..."

"We <u>know</u> the name of the book, Mama," Tressi quietly reminded her. Veri nodded her agreement.

Their mother smiled to herself and waited for both girls to get settled again. Then she carefully opened the book to Chapter One, gently rubbed her fingers across the drawing, and began.

"Chapter One, At the Summer Breeze," she read softly. As she did, behind their closed eyes, Tresette and Vermillion flew out of the window, across the miles to Windtown, and started, once again, on that adventure so far away.

Their mother sighed silently and thought back to those days long before – days that were so important to her. She loved those days and she loved this story. It was not only her daughters' favorite, but hers as well. So as she read it to the two girls, she was reading it to herself. And, like her daughters, she too remembered how the story began.

She sighed again, read the opening words, and started on the journey with them

"Window Breesian stood in the doorway of his house and looked out down the path toward the Town Road..."

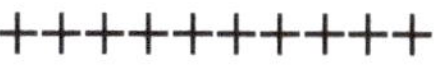

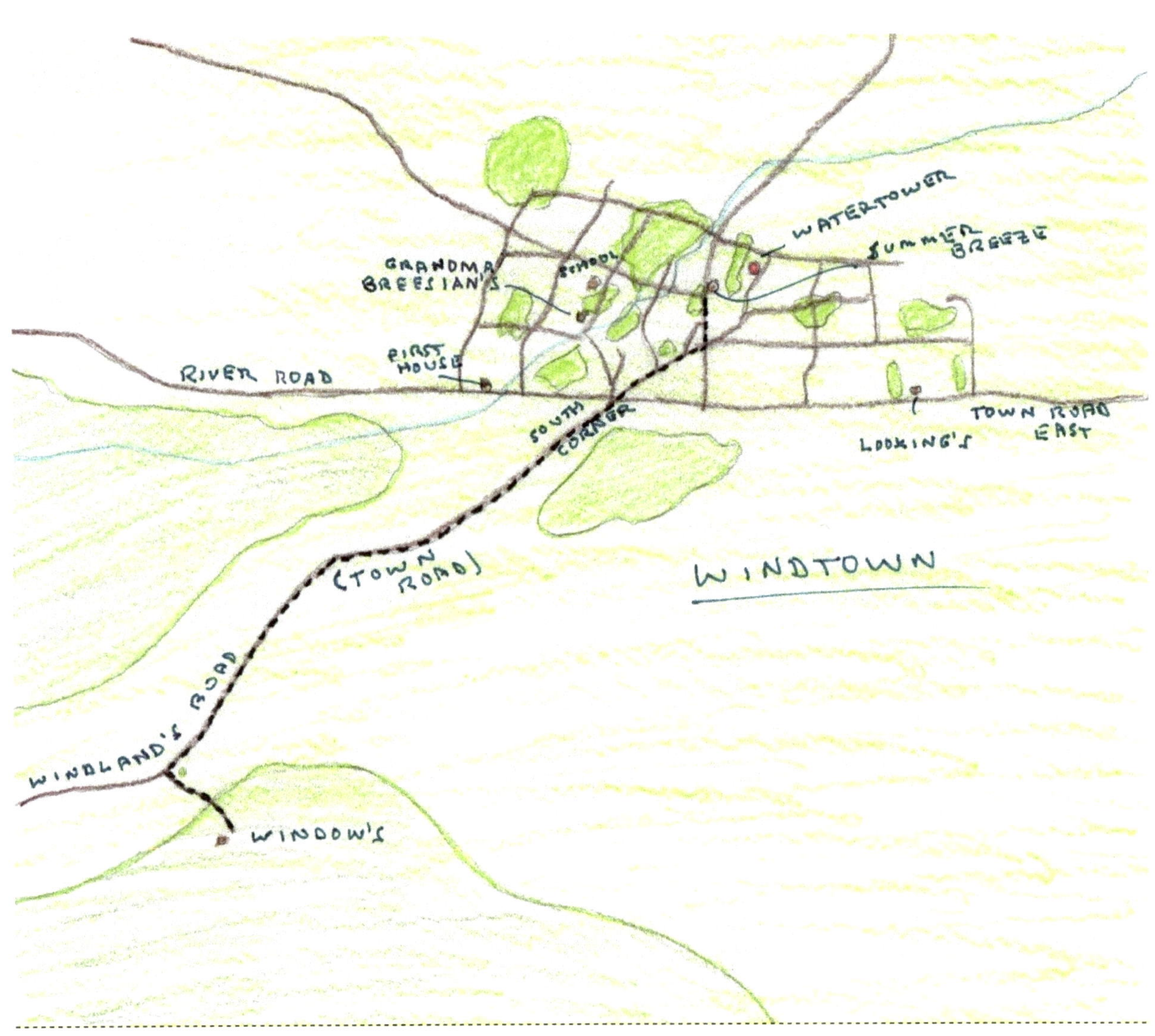

WATERTOWER
SUMMER BREEZE
GRANDMA BREESIAN'S
SCHOOL
RIVER ROAD
FIRST HOUSE
SOUTH CORNER
LOOKING'S
TOWN ROAD EAST
WINDTOWN
(TOWN ROAD)
WINDLAND'S ROAD
WINDOW'S

CHAPTER ONE

AT THE SUMMER BREEZE

Window Breesian stood in the doorway of his house and looked out down the path toward the Town Road. The bricks of the path were old and pale and almost buried beneath the leaves that the spring winds had blown from their winter resting place below the big willow trees that stood alongside the path. Window's eyes followed the curve of the path down the hill and across the bridge to where it met the Road, and then followed the Road as it peeked through the trees, all the way into Windtown. Above the Road, the sun shone brightly down from the midmorning sky. It had been a cold night last night, but today was warm, and a perfect day for an adventure.

Window stepped back into the house for a moment, grabbed his jacket from its place on the door hook, and picked up his key from the reading table. Stepping back onto the porch, he closed the door behind him and turned the key in the lock until it clicked. He shoved the key in his pocket and jumped off the porch, kicking leaves ahead of him as he walked down the path to the Road.

The sun was shining brightly overhead, but the trees above the path allowed only splashes of the brightness to slip through, striking a moving pattern upon the stationary pattern of the leaves and bricks. As Window came down the gentle slope of the hill and crossed the bridge, he saw two birds high above the forest trees on the other side of the Road. They dived together and then soared high again as they disappeared over the treetops to the

northwest. Window thought that they must be swinghawks out
for a late breakfast before returning to their nests by the river.

At the bottom of the path Window felt the warmth of the sun
on his face, as from there on, both he and the Road were without
any trees or shade most of the mile or so into town. He stopped at
the corner tree where the path met the Road and looked far down
to the left where it disappeared off to the west. Window thought
about where the Road went and how his parents lived at its end,
several hundred miles away in Coastown. They had moved there
five years before when his father, who had been in the Navy,
returned to captain a merchant ship to the Old Countries.

Window had never been to the Windcoast, but, as a boy, had
once traveled with his family as far as Woodmine to visit relatives.
He remembered too, a few years later, when he and some of his
cousins had walked to the bridge at Lowpoint and spent several
days exploring north up the river there.

Window turned toward Town and started down the Road. The
cool morning breeze brushed through his hair and refreshed him
as he went. His hair, dark and wavy like his mother's, was, like
hers, a little longer in back than on the sides. Like his father,
Window was almost six feet tall, and had deep brown eyes and an
easy smile. He had turned twenty-two just a few months earlier.

As he walked along, kicking at the dust beneath his feet,
Window wondered if any of his friends would be at the Summer
Breeze this time of the day. The day before he had completed the
woodwork in a new house in Town, so today he didn't have
anything he had to do. Window thought that maybe he would
spend a few hours in Town, and then go traveling down by the
river or perhaps walk to the Lake or to Whitetop Road. With
nothing he had to do and nowhere he had to go, it was a perfect
day for having an adventure. Maybe something would come up.

Just then, Window saw a rock lying in the road ahead and
adjusted his stride so that when he got up to it, he could easily
give it a kick. It was something he often did just for fun when he
went walking. He would try to kick a rock far out ahead of him
but have it still stay on the road. Then he would continue to kick
the rock and see how many kicks he could give it before it rolled

off into the grass. This time his very first kick sent the stone into some prairie-weeds.

As he continued to think about where he might like to walk to today, Window took a kick at another rock that was half buried in the dirt of the road, and watched it roll out ahead of him. At least, that's what he expected to happen. Instead, the stone just stayed there, sticking out of the dirt. He bent over and grabbed onto it and tried to pull it loose, but it wouldn't move. Next, he stood over it and kicked at it with the heel of his boot. This time he was successful and the stone came free. Except it wasn't a stone. It was a piece of metal, flat, and painted on one side with faded colors, light blue and silver. He picked it up and rubbed the dirt off that was still covering it.

It was some kind of medallion or emblem – about half the size of his palm – rectangular in shape, with slightly rounded corners, and had three raised, blue stripes diagonally across the front from the lower left to the upper right corner. Partially covering the stripes, in its center, was a circle with a star inside. In the two other corners, there were some other painted symbols that were too faded to make out. It was rusted quite a bit and looked very old.

"I wonder what this is," thought Window. "It looks like something military."

His mind jumped back to the pack of old uniforms and patches his father had given him from his Navy days. But none of the patches he remembered looked anything like the insignias on the medallion.

"Maybe it's from the Windlands Army or maybe it's even an Atlandan medal of some sort," his mind raced on.

Window knew quite a lot about the history of the Windlands. He had many books on Windlands history at home and had, of course, studied the subject when he was in the Town School. Numbers had been his best subject and learning about nature was a favorite, but history interested him most of all. He especially enjoyed the stories of the old days that his Uncle Breeze told. Of course, you could never be sure if those stories were true or not, but they sure were great stories. In any case, Window was glad to have found something that might be very old, and that had maybe even been, at one time, important.

He slid the medallion into his pocket and continued on his way into Town. The sun above made the trees to his left and those of the village ahead shine and shimmer. The air was fresh and the spring blossoms were in full bloom for the first time this year. A few feet away, in the grass to his right, he noticed a field rabbit nibbling and watching him as he walked by.

Just for fun, Window closed his eyes and walked on for a way as he enjoyed the heat of the sun on his face. Opening his eyes again, he looked up at a bundle of bright, white clouds that were drifting overhead. "What a great day this is," he thought, and then added, "I love this place."

As Window approached South Corner, he let his eyes scan over the treetops of Town. They formed a smooth, unbroken line against the sky with the exception of the watertower. The tower stuck up through the trees near the center of Town, its wooden water tank, round and white above the green of the willows and oaks around it. He was proud of the work he had done on the tower. Three years ago, just before his Grandfather Breesian died, Window had helped him build it.

It was the only watertower in all the lands east of the Windlands River. Window had done all of the woodwork in the interior of it's tall, cylindrical, red brick base, including the door that opened to the inside circular stairs that allowed one to climb to the top of the tower, as well as the stairs themselves.

Because he loved that type of work so much, Window had even gone to the trouble of including fine fittings and finishes, even though they certainly weren't necessary for such a structure. The little white framed window that opened to the outside near the top of the stairs was his own idea. From it, people who climbed the circular stairway could see almost half of the town from above the treetops. Window had learned all of his woodworking skills from his grandfather, and his grandfather had taught him well. Window missed working with him.

When he got to South Corner, Window stopped and looked down River Road to his left. He seemed to have always enjoyed looking down roads, wondering where they led to, and he would sometimes sit on his porch and spend hours imagining himself traveling to Coastown, or Ship's Harbor, or Summerland. He had always wanted to travel to the University at New Laws, and still hoped to go there someday, and on the way back, to see the bridges at Newtown. He often wondered, too, what was in the lands he knew nothing about, the Wilds to the north and east.

His eyes followed a short distance down River Road to the house where he was born and raised. His mom and dad had lived there from the time they were married, and Window had grown up there with his younger sister, Sally. The house was sold when his parents moved to the Windcoast in W.Y. 142, but Sally still lived nearby with her husband.

Besides River Road going off to Window's left, three other streets intersected at South Corner. The middle-left road, of course, went up the hill to Partridge Street and his Grandmother Breesian's house. That is where Window still kept his carpentry and woodworking tools, so he wouldn't have to bring them all the way to his house after a job was finished. There was plenty of room to store them in his grandfather's old workshop. Just north of his grandmother's house was the Windtown School and beyond that, on the right, was the park.

The Town Road East went off to Window's right and past Mary Looking's house on its way out of town. He missed her a lot. She had gone to live in Station a few months before and wasn't sure when she would be able to return. Her parents had moved and she had to go with them. At least her family still owned their old house and Mary was going to try to come back to live there as soon as she could. Window and Mary had been friends from the time she had moved to Town, and that friendship had grown into much more. He thought of the warm summer evening they had first sat on her front porch, watching heat lightning storms in the southern sky. They had held hands and talked half the night. Those hours together were the beginning of their close connection.

"Enough daydreaming," thought Window, and he started up the middle-right road to the center of town. He passed a couple of houses, turned left at the next street, walked by a couple of stores, and before long he was standing in front of the Summer Breeze.

++++++++

The Summer Breeze was a post tavern. Letters to and from anywhere in the world could be posted there, all delivered by the Windlands Mail. Window's mother wrote him often, and sometimes he would be surprised with a letter from Ameran or Atland which was written by his father while on board his ship, and posted when he was in port.

Window's Uncle Breeze ran the tavern and was also the local post carrier. Once a week, Breeze would load up all the posted letters and carry them to the people living between Town and River Bay. He would travel to the farms west of Town, then into the Near Woods, past the mill, and along the river. Yesterday was Post day, though, so Breeze should be here today, unless, of course, he had gone to the Post Inn on the West Road to spend the night.

Window loved Breeze's tavern, as did almost everyone else in Town. It was a great place to meet friends, have a drink, and talk of anything at all. When Breeze was there, the company was at its best. He was the greatest and wildest storyteller of all times, at least as far as the local folk were concerned. He had done some traveling for a while and had been in the Navy with his brother, Window's father. He came back home with a never-ending collection of tales, as well as the skill to tell them so that they were always believable, even if they were unbelievable. According to Breeze's stories, he had ruled faraway kingdoms and had otherwise been witness to the most wondrous events of recent history.

Window stepped up on to the wide wooden porch along the front of the building and glanced at the sign above the door. It read:

Bill Breesian
Owner and Proprietor

Below the sign, standing in the doorway, was his Uncle Breeze.

"Hi ya, Window," Breeze threw out, brushing his hand through his short, dark hair.

"Mornin', Bill," Window called back, and added a smile to his greeting. His calling his uncle "Bill" was something special between them. In all of Town and the Near Woods, only Window used Breeze's real name. His uncle had been called Breeze by everyone his entire life, but a few years before, when Window would visit Breeze's house and play cards with him and his wife, his wife sometimes kiddingly called her husband "Bill" as a joke. Window started calling him that, too. Now it was a bond between them. Breeze really liked it and enjoyed the friendship they shared.

"What's up this mornin'? I saw the new place over north," Breeze continued, referring to the house on which Window had just finished the woodwork.

"Yeah, it's all done, went really well. I took my tools back to Grandma's last night.

"What ya doing in town this morning?"

"I thought maybe Davey or Piper would be here. They told me yesterday that they had a day to wait 'til Dale got back from the crossroads, so they might be over early."

"What's up with you guys?"

"Hopin' they want to go to the Woods or something. Anybody been in yet?"

"Nah. It's too early. Come on inside."

Window followed Breeze through the doorway and headed right toward his favorite chair. He had spent lots of hours at that table over the years, and it still always made him feel good to sit down with a drink and some bread or crackers and pass the time. From there, looking out one of the tavern's big front windows, Window could easily see everything going on up and down the street, except that, right now, nothing was going on. Before taking his usual seat, he glanced up at the clock and walked over to the window to get a better look outside. He tried to see around the corner and up Middle Street but he couldn't.

"It's almost 9 o'clock," he thought. "I wonder if they will get here soon." Then he noticed that the letter posts were full.

"Hey, the mail's in!" Window exclaimed, mostly to himself. Breeze had gone into the back room to get them some water drinks and couldn't hear what Window had said.

Window left his chair still sitting under the table and went over to the near counter, glancing first at the letters pinned to the Windlands post, which held the outgoing mail. They were going to places all over the world, well, really, mostly just to places nearby. Most townspeople didn't know anyone outside of the Prairies and rarely had a reason to send letters very far.

Window always loved looking at the letters on the other post, the one holding the mail that had been sent to Town from other places, to see the stamps they carried. The different regions of the Windlands took pride in trying to design the most beautiful and colorful stamps, and a post day never went by without Window searching for a new and interesting stamp arriving on a letter from somewhere. Window's favorites were post stamps of ships or maybe important buildings in some place like Coastown or New Laws. In fact, he had a pretty nice collection of stamps at home. His mom always tried to send a new Coastown stamp when she wrote, and his dad sent strange ones from the Old Lands, and, of course, Breeze could get them from many different parts of the Newlands.

Just then, Breeze returned to the front room and set down a big glass of cold water for Window. It was freshly ladled from the bucket of water that was freshly pumped from the well out back of the tavern this morning.

"Got a letter for you. It's up," said Breeze, meaning it was on the letter post near the center window.

Window glanced at the column of letters and found it immediately. He gently pulled out the pin that held the letter and then returned the pin to its place on the post. The letter was from Mary Looking. Across the top of the envelope was a row of little hearts, each one red and perfect. In the middle was written:

Window Breesian
Windtown

Since there were only sixteen towns in all of the Windlands prairies, that was all that was needed to get the letter to him. Besides that, Windtown was well known because it was at the far eastern end of the Windlands Road that stretched hundreds of miles from the Coastlands.

In the upper right-hand corner of the letter was a two-penny stamp, which carried a picture of a heartflower. The stamp was marked with a post mark from the Station Inn. In the upper left-hand corner, in Window's favorite handscript, it said:

Looking for you

Window held the envelope and carefully slit open its top with a knife from the counter. Then he took the letter over to the window and leaned against the sill. He noticed a hint of Mary's perfume as he opened the folded piece of pink paper, and read:

Av. 16, W.Y. 147

My Dearest Window,

I miss you so much.

It's hard to tell you. Some days it seems easier not to think about you very much. I want to be with you, but I must wait even longer. Daddy is going to Union near the Coastlands to work on the river and I must go with him. After the snows next winter, he will return to his shop in Station and then I will come back to our house in Town.

I want you to be with me there.

I will be waiting for you.

My love is with you always,

Mary

Window stared at the letter in his hands, folded it back up, and then looked down at the floor for a moment. He felt the sadness he had been pushing aside for the months since Mary had left Windtown. He had been hoping she would be back this summer, but now it would be another year. His chest felt heavy, and for a moment, it was hard for him to breathe. He moved slowly as he walked to the table, pulled out his favorite chair, and sat down.

Breeze joined him. "What's the matter?"

Window handed him the letter and Breeze read it quietly. He handed the letter back but didn't say anything.

"Oh well," sighed Window. "I don't know if I'm really in love with her anyway." As soon as the words came out he wished he hadn't said them.

Breeze thought a moment then picked up his glass of water. "Ya know, Window, I always like to watch the little bits of iron and other stuff floating around in this well water. The water that comes through the tower doesn't have it in there anymore." He took a long drink and then looked out across the street at the leaves of a willow tree as the wind blew them about.

Window waited for his uncle to break into one of his great stories about love or well water or something, but Breeze seemed to change his mind and just sat quietly, thinking.

Neither spoke for several minutes. Each held his own thoughts as they looked out the window at nothing in particular, just the wind and the trees. They could feel the breeze as it blew in through the front door screen.

"Bill," asked Window finally. "Have you really been on lots of adventures?"

Breeze smiled and finished his water. His eyes brightened as he began to talk. "Many, many, Window. Big and small."

"When I was a boy, your father and I used to run all around Town together. When we got tired of that, we would go out in the woods or someplace else, just like you do. We thought everything we did was one big adventure. I found out later that it was, because we made it that way."

"When I was in the Navy, I sailed to ports in many places. Some were exciting and some not. If it wasn't an adventure, I would do what we had done when we were boys. I would make my own. I learned it's really not that hard. Even now, any day I want can be an adventure. I make my own adventures, Window." Then he added, "So could you."

Window ran his finger around the rim of his water glass. "I've always been good at little adventures, but I think I need a big one. I want to have adventures like you sometimes tell about, Bill – the kind that happen in faraway places, and with wondrous people. I don't want to always be just looking down roads and wondering. I want to live one of your stories, at least for a while."

Suddenly Window remembered the medallion he had found and took it from his pocket. "Maybe like the person who wore this medallion and lost it on the Windlands Road – maybe even before it was the Windlands Road."

"What do you have there?"

"I found it on the way in this morning. I think it's from the Continent Wars. Didn't the armies go through here? Or, maybe it was lost when the early explorers first came to the end of the Windlands. What do you think?"

Breeze took the medallion and looked at it carefully. "This is really something, Window. I'll bet this could be a hundred years old. It's got to be a military insignia of some sort. Where did you find it?"

"Right before the first turn coming in from my place."

Breeze pointed to the other side of the room. "Get the box that's on the top shelf of that cabinet, would you Window? I'll get us some more water."

In a minute Breeze returned with the water glasses full and sat back down. Window was waiting for him. "Look inside."

The shallow, wooden box had a hinged lid. It was old and worn, as though it had been halfway around the world a few times. Window lifted the lid. Inside were some of Breeze's navy patches, several well-used maps, and other items, including some small paper books. Breeze grabbed one with a flag on the front and quickly thumbed through. "Look right there, Window. Those

stripes are almost the same as on the medallion. It's probably a
Captain's insignia from the early Inlands Division."

Window took the book and carefully examined every page. The
stripes were similar to those on several of the crests and emblems
inside, but he really couldn't find anything else that looked like
the markings and colors on the medallion. Disappointed, he said
at last, "Well, maybe it's from somewhere else,"

Just then, the screen door flew open and Davey, Piper, and
another friend of Window's, Will, burst in.

"Hi, Window," called Davey. "Mornin', Breeze," added the
others.

"Hey guys," came the reply. "Look at this. Window found an
old army medal from the War."

"Well, maybe it is," said Window. "We're not sure where it
came from."

The boys sat down together and everyone examined the
medallion. Well, they weren't really boys. Davey, like Window,
was twenty-two, and the others were a year younger. They had all
known each other for as long as they could remember.

Davey grew up near Window's house and they all, of course,
had spent years together in school. Davey and Piper were both
married and worked together delivering, to the local area, supplies
and materials transported to Town from the Inlands by Sally's
husband, Dale. Those three men had supplied all of the glass,
pipes, metal fittings, and paint used in the house Window had just
finished.

Piper's name was actually Tanding. People had started calling
him Piper because he had spent months delivering all of the water
pipes to the town when the tower was built. The pipes had come
from the metalworks at Newtown, which was several days'
distance from Windtown.

Will sometimes helped the others with deliveries when he
wasn't working in his father's wagon and harness shop. Window
was glad that, apparently, Will wasn't needed in the shop this
morning. The four of them were good friends and often managed
to get away together to go camping or exploring. Now, maybe
today could be another such day.

"Do you guys remember learning which armies were in this area, even before Town was here?" Window began.

"All I remember is that explorers came this far in W.Y. 19, and that's why the end of the Windlands Road started here," Piper offered.

"The end started here?" jumped in Will, wiping his blonde hair from his eyes and tipping back in his chair as he always did.

"You know what I mean, Willow," Piper threw back. "They knew they were going to end the road here even before they decided where to start it from the Windcoast. Didn't you tell me that, Breeze?"

"Will you guys knock it off?" Breeze had pulled out another book from the wooden box and was glancing at a page filled with small maps. "During the War, the Atlandan army used an area a little northeast of here as its base for troops sent east around the Deep Woods. The Near River was used as a source of fish to feed the troops. They remained there until W.Y. 68, sending supplies to the north."

"Another possibility is that the medallion is from the Windlands army," Window reminded them.

"I don't think you should call it a medallion," offered Will. "It looks like some kind of insignia that was attached to a shield or a belt or something."

"Maybe it came from the North," said Davey, "from the Wilds."

"No Northlandan troops ever came to the Windlands, did they Breeze?" asked Piper.

"Nah," said Will, answering for him.

"Maybe it belonged to some people from the Wilds that we don't know about," suggested Davey.

That comment really got everyone interested. Even Will sat up straight in his chair to get closer to the conversation.

To the north and east of the Windlands were wild lands that no one knew much about. Most of what was known about these lands was mysterious and frightening. All across the northern edge of the Windlands, from the ocean to the Outlands, stretched the Deep Woods. It was hundreds of miles long and about a hundred

miles wide. It was a dark, deep, unknown place that no one had
ever really penetrated. Only the people at Woodmine lived even
near its edge. Men who tried to explore the Woods always
returned with stories of thick jungle-like undergrowth, impassible
terrain, and strange creatures. In fact, it was widely believed that
monstrous animals of all sorts lived deep in its interior.

In the years just before the Continent Wars, the people of the
Northlands, which were on the northern side of the Deep Woods,
began having lots of trouble with creatures that came from the
Woods and attacked them. Other strange beings were said to live
in the mountains still farther north. No one was sure just what
the truth was about these things and few ever tried to find out.

Since the destruction in the North during the war, and the
abandonment of all of that part of the world by the Old Countries,
the remaining people of The Northlands were cut off from the
outside world and surrounded by the Wild Lands. No one knew
what had gone on with these people for more than seventy
years. The wide lands to the east of the Windlands had never
been explored at all.

"Do you think some other people besides Northlanders might
live in the Wilds, Breeze?" asked Piper, as he took another look at
the medallion.

"They may, Pipe. There may be people living on the northern
plains as well as to the east near the mines that brought the
original settlers to the Northlands. If anyone lives beyond the
mines, or east beyond the Outlands, I have never heard."

"Do you mean, Breeze, that you have heard something?" asked
Will. "How could you have ever heard anything about who lives in
the Wilds?"

Breeze didn't answer because he was on his way to the kitchen
to get some jam for the bread Piper had just taken from the
counter. He returned with a new jar of raspberry.

"It may be too hard to ever find out for sure where the
medallion came from," Window admitted. Then he added,
"Wouldn't it be great, though, if it belonged to some people we
don't even know about?"

"If we don't know about them," asked Piper, "how could we find out if it was their medallion, and how could it have gotten here anyway?"

"Ya know, Fellas," broke in Breeze." There is a way that medallion could have gotten here from the north Wilds."

The boys stopped talking and sat back in their chairs. Whenever Breeze started a comment by saying "Ya know, Fellas" he always went into one of his stories. Everyone was so used to it by now that, as soon as they heard him say it, they settled back to hear what the story would be about this time.

Breeze went on. "A couple of summers ago a traveler stopped here at the inn. He looked about your age. He was tired and hungry, for he had been traveling a long way without food or sleep. He said he had come from the Wilds and had been searching for a trail through the Deep Woods.

"A trail through the Deep Woods!" exclaimed Will. "Nobody's ever been through there. Nobody would <u>want</u> to go through there."

Breeze continued, "He said he had been in the North exploring and trying to locate the old Northlandan gold and jewel mines. He wouldn't tell me where he was from or what he found, but apparently, he knew enough Freelandan to talk to some of the old Northlands descendants he came in contact with. According to him, they told him stories that, years ago, during the War, a path was cut south through the Deep Woods – a path all the way through to the Windlands. He searched for weeks but wasn't able to find it. Eventually he came along the east edge of the Woods and found his way here.

"Come on, Breeze," said Davey. "Where did you get that story?"

"From the chair you are in right now," answered Breeze.

"But the Woods is miles and miles... did he tell you anything else?"

"When I asked him if he was going back to the Wilds, he said 'There are many treasures to be found in the North'."

"What kind of treasures?"

"He didn't say."

"What happened to this mysterious traveler, Breeze?"

"Well, Dave, he finished his drink, bought some bread and meat from me, and then he left."

Well, Breeze had done it again. Another great story that was hard to believe. A mysterious treasure seeker and a secret path through the Deep Woods seemed very unlikely, but it was something they would all hope could be true. Even though it seemed impossible, they wanted to believe it. Breeze's stories always had that effect.

"Did he mention the Talkers, Breeze?" asked Piper.

Davey and Will smiled at each other. Piper loved to hear about the Talkers. Years and years before, stories and tales came from the Deep Woods of animals who could actually speak – creatures who could think like men. It was all a part of the mystery of the Woods and the danger people felt lie there. The Talkers were the favorite subject of nursery rhymes and children's stories throughout the eastern Windlands. All of the boys had grown up on the stories. It was the great myth of the lands, although few people believed such animals really existed.

Breeze answered, "No, Pipe. But he did say that, whenever he spoke to people about going into the Woods, they told him to beware of the dangers he might find."

"What do you think lives in the Woods, Breeze?" asked Davey. "Do you think there really could be monsters in the Woods, or Talkers?"

"I don't know," Breeze continued, "But there sure are a lot of stories and rhymes."

Will spoke up,

> "A Mallen went to Calisay
> To sit before the King
> The King was very gracious and
> He asked the guest to sing..."

It was an old rhyme they all knew, and they also knew that Calisay was the name of the ruling city of the Northlands. Each had his own idea of what a Mallen was. They began to think of other children's rhymes and old Deep Woods stories.

"I like 'Armies on the march, marching, marching'," said Will.

Window had noticed Mary's letter in his pocket and thought about her for a moment, but he forgot about her again and began to think of the rhymes.

"How about, 'Beware of the Owt'?" Piper suggested.

"Beware his big snout, Beware of the..."

They went on for some time, taking turns reciting or telling titles of stories they knew. While they talked and enjoyed their bread and each other's company, Breeze told a few rhymes they had never heard before. Davey accused him of making them up just as he went along. Window just listened and thought quietly to himself about what it might be like to visit the places and see the creatures they spoke of.

Window hadn't said anything for a long time. He finally spoke up. "Do you think what he said was true, Bill? Is there really a path through the Deep Woods?"

"I don't know, Window, but I think so. Of course, after all these years there wouldn't be much left of it. Still, it would connect us with the North."

"Nobody would want to follow a path into the Deep Woods anyway," said Will. "They would never come out."

"I would," said Window.

"Yeah, sure you would, Winner," said Davey.

"How could you find it if you wanted to?" asked Piper. "Who could know where it is?"

"Who does know, Bill, where a path through the Woods might be?"

Breeze glanced up at his nephew. "Maybe your grandfather."

"Grandpa Windowen?"

"Yeah, when he was young, he went with some Windlands troops to the North. They were scouting or something. So he's been there, in the Northlands. He might have heard of the path – maybe even looked for it."

"I knew he was a scout before he met Grandma, but I thought they only went into the Outlands. I never knew he went to the North."

Window went on, "Hey, guys, let's go ask him right now. We could be out there in an hour or so."

"Nah, let's don't go out there today," countered Piper.

"But I want to find out right away if he knows about the path."

"What's so important about it, anyway, Window?" asked Will. "Even if he knows where it is, we wouldn't be able to look for it until this summer. Besides, even then it would take days or weeks. And it's too dangerous to be near the Deep Woods, anyhow."

"Yeah, come on, Window," said Davey. "Let's go down to the river instead. We've got to go see Riller at the mill anyway. He wants us to help him make sure the lumber is ready for a barn they're building down near the back timber. And, we've got to meet Dale tomorrow early. He's bringing the nails, rope, hinges, and bricks from the crossing."

"No thanks, Davey. I don't think I'll go with you guys today. I was going to but I..." He was going to mention Mary's letter but he changed his mind. He was usually pretty private about personal things, except with Breeze. "Why don't you just go on without me this time?"

"What are you gonna do, Window?" asked Will.

"I think I'll go ask my grandfather about the path and if he recognizes the insignia on the medallion. Maybe I'll see you guys tomorrow."

The boys tried to talk Window into coming with them but he wouldn't change his mind. Breeze brought everybody a round of beer and another half loaf of bread. The conversation turned to the weather and the plan to rebuild a bridge on the Near Woods Road. Once again, Window just sat quietly and kept his thoughts to himself. He loved to go places with them, but today he would go on his own.

After another half hour and a couple of salt crackers each, the three were ready to leave for the mill. They paid Breeze for the food and drink and turned to go.

"See you, Window," said Davey with a big grin.

"So long," "Bye, Breeze," added the others and they were on their way.

"Goodbye, you guys," Window called after them as they stepped through the door on their way out. He had a strange feeling that he wouldn't see them again for a long time.

Window sat down and looked out to watch his friends as they cut across the street toward Davey's. He missed them already.

"Well, Window," said Breeze once they were alone again. Window couldn't tell if it was a question or a comment or just a kind of sigh, Breeze talking mostly to himself.

They were both quiet for a moment, then, Window spoke up. "Well, Bill. I'm going out to talk to my grandfather today. I want to find that path and go into the Deep Woods. I want to go where nobody around here has ever been and do something they have never done."

Breeze looked out the window at the trees again. "I've been to the Old Countries, up the Windcoast, to the Islands, and after that to parts of New South, but I've never been to the Deep Woods — even to the edge. It would be a grand adventure."

"I want to be like that traveler that stopped here, Bill. I want to be the traveler in somebody's story."

"Maybe you can even find a treasure or something," said Breeze with a smile.

Window's eyes lit up for a moment, then he thought out loud. "What about the monsters, Bill? Do you think the Woods is dangerous?"

"I don't know, Window, it could be. But if you want to be in somebody's story, you've got to do more than walk to the river. You don't have to go to the Wilds, though, or be in somebody's story, to find things that are important. Your dad used to say that we each hold the key to our own treasures, wherever we go."

They stopped talking for the moment. Window helped Breeze clean up the tables and put things away. It was a job he had helped with many times before, a job he never minded, especially today, as it gave him extra time to think.

"I guess I'll get going, too," said Window when they were finished. "Thanks, Bill," and as he looked at Breeze his eyes added, "for everything."

Window stopped in the doorway and looked back inside. He wondered how long it would be until he was there again.

"See ya, Bill."

"Goodbye, Window."

He stepped off the porch and turned up the street to the
right. The breeze was still blowing and the sky was clear. It was
a great day for an adventure.

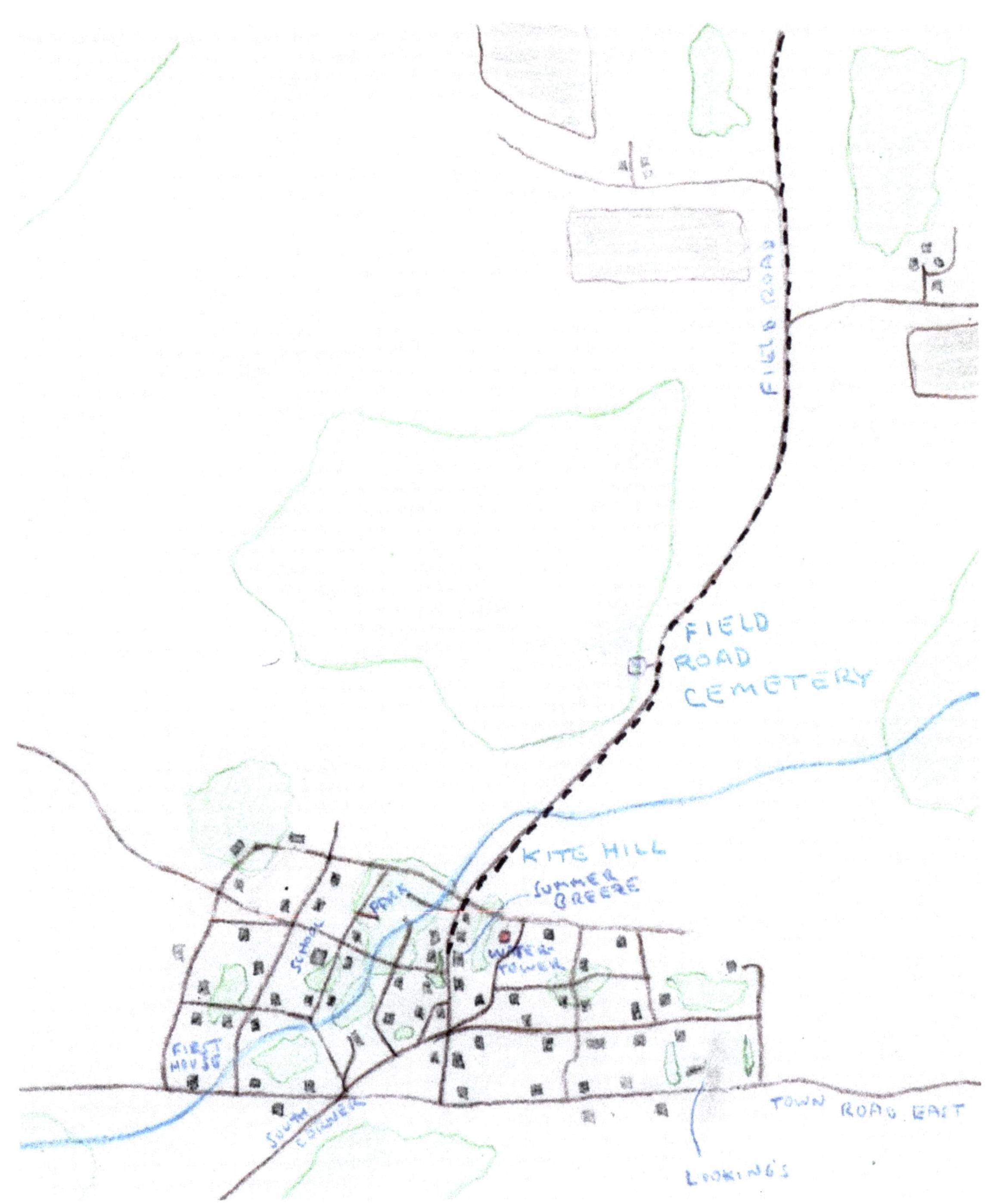
FIELD ROAD
FIELD
ROAD
CEMETERY
KITE HILL
SUMMER
BREEZE
SCHOOL
PARK
WATER
TOWER
FIRST
HOUSE
SOUTH
CORNER
TOWN ROAD EAST
LOOKING'S

CHAPTER TWO

TO THE FARM

As Window walked up the street past the few stores on his right, he glanced over and watched his reflection walking along with him in the big glass windows of Baker's Supply Store and The Windtown Journal. And, also reflected off of the glass, he could the hear voices of some children coming from the park farther up on his left. Then through the trees he could see them — young girls — two of them spinning the ends of a long jump rope and two others between them, jumping in time with the rope as it swung over their heads and under their feet. Hair and skirts were both flying wildly as girls went up and down and arms circled around and around.

As they jumped, the girls were singing a jumping rhyme and the spinners were counting the rope turns as the spinners always did. They sang and laughed and counted and laughed and jumped and laughed. Window couldn't make out, at first, which rhyme it was, but he felt sure that it was going to be one of the rhymes like those about finding gold or being chased by monsters that he had just been thinking about at the Summer Breeze.

As he got close to the head of Park Street, the singing and counting became clear. But the rhyme wasn't what he expected. "Ah, it's only the one about a princess jumping on her bed," he thought to himself. He was a bit disappointed, sort of feeling that the whole world should be thinking only of treasure and adventure like he was.

He stopped for a moment and looked up at the Windlands flag,
flying high above the circle of benches at the corner of the
park. The flag was light blue in color, with three tall white stalks
of prairie grass in its center. The grass stalks were standing at an
angle as though they were being blown to one side in the
wind. The sound of the flag quietly flapping in the breeze was
right in time with the counting and singing of the rope
jumpers. With the princess still jumping on her bed, he took one
more quick look at the girls, and continued up the street, the
happy voices fading as he started around the turn towards the
edge of town.

He passed under several big willow trees that grew over the
street and was soon completely covered in their shade from the
midday sun. He knew that as soon as he was beyond the trees
and the last house on the right, he would be able to see Kite Hill
and all of the colorful kites that would be flying there. In all of the
Windlands prairies, most people agreed that the best flying and
best looking kites were those made by the children from
Windtown. It was a long tradition passed down from the very first
settlers. They made plain kites, flag kites, dog kites, flower kites,
lace kites, diving kites, spinning kites, whistling kites, kites with
wings, kites with many tails, kites hooked onto other kites, and
windkites of every other description – each one wilder and more
colorful than the last. Of course, with the breeze nearly always
blowing in from the prairies, a spring day never went by that the
hill was not covered with kids below and kites above.
As he turned the corner, Window shielded his face from the sun
and raised his eyes to see what bright and fancy kites would be
aloft today, and if the highest ones were completely out of sight as
they usually were. He expected a hill-full of movement and color
but all he saw was the green of the grass and the clear blue of the
sky. He couldn't believe it. No one was there – not a single kid,
nor a single kite.
Then just as quickly, as he scanned the hillside, he heard more
sounds of happy children. He looked farther off to his right and
there they were – about a dozen or so boys and girls walking up
the street carrying their kites. Apparently, they had been at the

little shop next to the watertower working on them, improving the lift, replacing the paper or the cloth, or otherwise trying to create the perfect flying device. They were hurrying along, laughing and joking, soon to be sending their latest creations high above the treetops of Windtown.

Seeing the kids brought a smile to Window's face. He was glad that someone else was at least sharing part of his feeling of fun and adventure, even if their adventure was to be only on a hillside at the edge of town. "I wonder what they would think, if they knew where I might be going soon," he said to himself.

A few more steps and Window passed under the "Windlands Tree" at the very edge of town. It was very tall, very old, and very well known. Everybody knew that it was the very oak tree which John W. Near, the original explorer of the Windlands, had camped under as he came to the end of his inlands journeys. Of course, some people did wonder if it really was that same tree, since it was now 128 years since Near's expedition had been there. But Window's Uncle Breeze had confirmed it as fact to the people in Town, so, even if it wasn't true before, it was true now.

Above the Windlands Tree, the overhead sun lit the sky completely as Window started out the Field Road towards his grandfather's farm. As he walked, he put his hand in his pocket and outlined the medallion with his fingers. Then, almost out loud, he thought, "I hope Grandpa can tell me where this came from."

Window had gotten his name from his Grandpa Windowen. It was common practice in the Windlands for a first-born son to be given his mother's maiden name as his first name. Window's mother's maiden name was Kathryn Elizabeth Windowen and his father's name was Ernest Edwin Breesian, so he was called Windowen Ernest Breesian.

Along the side of the road the grass was sprinkled with spring colors of all sizes, shapes, and hues – dellflowers, cattails, and wild blueflowers – violets, bandi-barbs and moonflowers – bright yellow sun-petals and deep red firelights. The moonflowers were a favorite of Window's. They appeared a bit dull in the sunlight, but on a bright moonlit night seemed to almost come alive in a whole array of colors.

It was only a few minutes before Window was whistling to himself and was lost completely in thoughts of what flowers he might find if he were to go into the Deep Woods. A few more minutes and few more verses of "The Days of Alezan" and he found himself right in front of the town cemetery.

The Field Road Cemetery was another of the many places Window liked to visit. He always found it calming and relaxing to walk among the gravestones and read the names of people he knew and people he didn't. Of course, his Grandfather Breesian was buried there and his grandfather's brother, Kilian. Today Window was in a hurry, but still the shade of the cemetery trees looked inviting. He decided to stop for a few minutes and enjoy the quiet before going on to the farm.

As he slowly walked down the first row of gravestones Window read the names on them to himself. "Henree Liysenne, Maree Liysenne, Roxille Donning, O. T. Manner" – he was Windtown's first post carrier – "S. N. Layson" – Window's old neighbor – "Dannil West." Then he stopped. Looking up at him from the shiny dark-grey stone was the inscription "Elaine Breesian, W.Y. 110 – 145."

It was the grave of Breeze's wife, Elaine, who had died the winter before last. Window thought back. It was so cold at her burial – so sad. His aunt was such a friendly, happy person – and always ready with a smile and something nice to say about someone. And, she made the best sweet-water drinks in Town. Then Window realized – he hadn't played a game of Diamonds with anyone since the last time he and Will barely beat Breeze and Elaine by two points. That was just a few weeks before she became ill.

Window thought again of his uncle and how sad it was that Elaine had died. "No wonder Breeze took so much time now when delivering the post to the outlying inns, and much time visiting at The Summer Breeze – with her gone he had time to spend. I guess that's why he didn't have much to say this morning about me being apart from Mary until next year. I should have thought of that."

Elaine's grave was at the back edge of the cemetery, near the straight line of trees that separated the graves from the woods behind. As he thought of her, Window bent down and ran his fingers in the letters of her name carved in her stone. Then he decided to sit for just a minute before going on to the farm. He gently sat down on Elaine's gravestone and took a deep breath.

Looking three rows over to his left, he could see his Grandfather Breesian's grave. Window missed him too, and remembered the good times they had together when Grandpa Breesian was teaching him his woodworking skills. He wished he could tell his grandfather that he was going to the wilds to have an adventure. Grandpa Breesian would have liked that.

Overhead now the day-birds were flying. Window followed them as they soared and danced and skipped across the sky and the road in front of him. He could see thrushes, phoebes, cawbirds, and two willowix – the fastest birds in the Windlands. They raced back and forth, always side by side, always turning together and spinning to their backs as they started their quick trip returning to the other side of the field across the road.

Willowix were Window's favorite kind of bird. When he was a boy he used to imagine what it would be like to be a willowix and fly anywhere he wanted. That would be a very handy skill to have today.

Window's mother had taught him about every one of those birds. When he was little, his mom would feed the wild birds at their house, and, sometimes, she would take him and his sister on hikes to the Near Woods, where they would hope to see new types. He learned about the many colors of the swinghawk, the nests of the hedge sparrow, and the calls of different kinds of birds – too many to count. And, as he sat there now in the quiet shade, the sharp whistle of a hungry greywing floated through the air from above him. The thought jumped into his head, "I wonder what my mom is doing today."

+++++++++

At that moment, far away on the Atlandic Coast, Kathryn Breesian stood and looked out the doorway of her house on the hillside above the harbor at Coastown. Below, she could see the great ships loading and unloading their cargoes to and from far away places in the Old Countries and beyond. Out past the ships, the early morning sun sparkled on the bright water of the harbor, as above them, the gulls climbed in the sky over the light blue mast flag of the merchant "Wind of Briston."

Before her, spring flowers of white and pale red dotted the lawn in her small front yard. Just down the path below her house, the breeze was swinging the sign in front of the shop there. The fading paint on the sign faintly stated:

R. Sillson
Sailmaker
Flax and Cotton

She wondered if Mr. Sillson would be sitting on his bench in the sun again today, mending a sail as he so often did.

To the north and away on the top of the ocean ridge, stood the house of the Governor. Kathryn saw the bright white of its towers shining in the sun, surrounded by the light spring green of the tall oaks that shared with the tower the view of most of the city below and the sea that stretched out before her to the west. She knew that, from the Governor's house, one could look far to the north and see the Coast Road as it came into Market, and follow the road along the cliffs, through the Coastown harbor, and miles on to the south, until it finally disappeared on its way to the towns beyond.

Kathryn thought of her husband, far away once again. He was captain of the merchant ship, the "Kathryn B.," her namesake, which he sailed from Coastown to the West, carrying mostly leather, wool, hardwood, rope, and dried meat. In a few months, he would return to the Windlands with that cargo's place taken by cotton and cloth from Ameran; paper, paint, and ink from Atland; ale from Linder, and spices from the Greenlands. His letter from the port at Triston had told her that this month he would be sailing the Atland coast waters past the Channel Cliffs and on to the south.

Kathryn thought to herself, almost out loud, "Oh, my loving Ernest, how I wait to see you."

She took one more glance at the ships below and then noticed a few beautiful billowing white clouds beginning to fill parts of the sky overhead. She thought and wished, "Maybe the clouds blowing in above the harbor right now were over you only a few days ago." Then she added, " Please send me your love on the wind if you can."

Just then a little wingjay flew down from the linden tree and landed on the porch railing. Kathryn happily remembered, "Mora's coming." She stepped inside and looked above the counter. The note on her flower board said, "Mora today – 9 o'clock."

Kathryn was looking forward to seeing her friend and sat down on the bench at the front window table to relax as she thought about the day ahead of her. Mora and she often spent hours together up in the highland woods or walking through the grassfields watching for birds. Kathryn loved all of nature, but especially birds, and such times were a great joy to her.

She looked back at the counter, below the flower birds painted on the board, and noticed another letter that she had received a few weeks before. A smile came to her face as she suddenly thought about her son, "I wonder what Window is doing today."

+++++++++

Window felt the medallion through his pocket. It reminded
him – it was time to get going. As he stood up, he rubbed the
surface of Elaine's gravestone one last time – it was slick and
cool. He took another quick look around, stepped back to the road,
and started north again.

The walk was easy and enjoyable. Birds continued to fly
overhead and field animals of various types kept him company.
The breeze made the grass dance as it pushed on his back and
helped him along the road. A prairie hen and her chicks stood
silently as he walked by. A chipsquirrel jumped from his nest in
the grass and ran up a tree – chattering its displeasure at being
disturbed.

Here, each farm he passed had a windmill to pump water – just
like the one that filled the town watertower each day. The mills
were used by the farmers for other things, too – like sawing wood
and grinding meal – although most of that type of work was done
by "Riller the Miller." That's what everyone called the Mr. Riller
at the watermill on the Near River. He moved to the area a few
years before without a family and nobody seemed to know his real
first name or where he came from. He was well liked by the
townspeople though, and when Window was working on a house,
he got most of his wood from Riller.

As he passed the Field Road farms, Window sang to himself
and thought about the very old days. For a few minutes, as he
walked, he looked ahead and imagined a company of Atlandan
soldiers marching in front of him. He could hear their cadence
count in the clear midday air. As they stepped in time, they were
calling out the rhyme "Back to Calisay." Window followed them
singing along as he went.

After about an hour, Window could see his destination – the
gentle curve of the lane, the large faded red barn on the right, his
grandparents' house and workshop on the left – and above it all,
the silver blades of the windmill. The farmyard was surrounded
by wheat and clover fields on the west side, and a pasture on the
east, and, behind the barn, the beginning of Grandpa's
woods. Window knew the farm very well, having spent so many

summer and winter days there – as did many of his cousins. He
had happy memories of the big family picnics – the bonfires, the
games, the food.

As he walked up the lane and under the big elm tree that
welcomed visitors, Window was greeted by the two white ducks –
the very fluffy and soft Honk and Captain Peepers. He held out
his hand to touch them, but they ignored it. They just honked and
peeped as they followed him up to the barn. His grandfather was
just coming out, dusting off his hands.

Grandpa Windowen was tall and thin. His hair was almost
grey and his face was lined and friendly. "Hey, Window. Whatcha
doin'?" He closed the big white door behind him.

"Hi, Grandpa. I had some time, so I've come for a visit,"
answered Window, this time succeeding in petting the top of
Honk's head.

"Great! Your grandma's in the house. I'll be in in a minute."

"Okay."

Window turned and could see his grandma standing on the side
porch. She waved, and carried a basket of vegetables back inside
to the kitchen. Grandma Windowen was short and a bit roundy,
and was, as usual, wearing a print dress under her apron.
Window stepped onto the porch and followed her in.

"Hello, Window. I thought that you might be coming out here
sometime this week, after your last job. How did it go?"

"Oh, fine, Grandma. I finished yesterday and don't have any
jobs lined up for a while."

His grandma continued her work at the sink but she turned
and gave him a smile that could mean only one thing. At least he
hoped he knew what it meant.

"There's something in the cellar for you. Go on down."

"Hah!" He was right. Window opened the cellar door, and,
supporting himself with his hands on the rails, made it to the
bottom in two giant steps. The air was cool and damp – just as it
always was. And as Window had hoped, on the shelf next to the
jars of grape juice and canned peaches was his all time favorite
treat. He pulled the lid off of the round tin container and there
they were – a new batch of springcookies! The vanilla and lemon

scent hit his face and brought his mouth to life. He reached in and took out the top cookie. It was a tower one. At least that's what the picture was.

Every springcookie had a raised picture on it. The pictures were made by rolling out stiff, but unbaked, cookie dough, and pressing a carved wooden board onto the rolled out dough. On Grandma's springcookie board there was a tower, a bridge, some flowers, a kite, and eight other carvings. The dough pushed up to fill the carvings, and when the board was removed, the raised pictures remained on the dough. Following lines that were also carved into the board, the dough was cut into rectangular shaped cookies, with a different picture on each one.

By baking the cookies at a low temperature, the raised pictures remained – the cookies hard on the top and the edges but soft inside. Window loved the pictures and loved the taste. And, part of the fun of eating them was to pick out your favorite picture and chew around it as you ate. Grandma had said that they were called springcookies because, according to tradition, you were only supposed to bake them in the spring, and she had been doing just that for as long as he could remember. And she always made some extra ones for Window. Last year, she had made a whole batch just for him to take to one of his woodworking jobs.

In all of Windtown, and the nearby farmlands, no one else baked springcookies. Grandma said that was because they were an Amerand cookie, and, unlike her family, the ancestors of most people in Town came from Atland. Her mother had taught her to bake them when she was a little girl and she had made them ever since.

"Bring them up, Window," she called to him. He had already finished his tower cookie by the time he reached the top step. "Can you stay for supper?" she asked.

"Yes, I would like to. I want to talk to Grandpa about something. And thank you for baking these for me."

"Oh, I love to do that for you. I'm glad you like them so much. Why don't you take a couple more of them out on the porch with you? Your grandfather will be in soon."

Window reached into the tin and carefully selected a flag cookie and the one with the row of four small cannon on it. He placed the tin on the counter and glanced into the dining room. As always, there was a small vase of grassflowers on the lacey tablecloth on the table. Through the door on the other side of the room, he could see one of his grandmother's pale colored handquilts on the bed.

He stepped outside and sat down on the porch swing. Through the screen door he could hear his grandmother in the kitchen. She was whistling, as she always did when she worked. It was a soft, gentle whistle of seemingly no song in particular. Window loved to hear her. It was so calming and comforting. He had asked her once if she knew what song she was whistling but she replied that she didn't even realize she was doing it – and had no idea what it was.

Window was finishing up his third springcookie when he heard the shop door closing. Soon his grandfather joined him on the porch. He sat down on top of the wooden potato bin, hooked his heels in the opening in the front of the bin, and leaned back against the wall. They repeated their earlier greetings.

"What brings you out today?"

"I found something, and I would like you to look at it."

Window pulled the medallion from his pocket and showed it to his grandfather. "What do you think of this?" he asked.

Grandpa took the medallion and examined it carefully, turning it over several times. "Looks pretty old. Where did you get it?"

Window told him the whole story, all about his morning at The Summer Breeze, the conversations with his friends, and all about the mysterious traveler. His grandfather listened carefully. Like the others, he thought that the medallion looked military but could not be sure. Finally, Window asked the question that had brought him to the farm. "So, Grandpa. Is it true? Have you really been to the North?"

"It's true, Window. I have been there." As Grandpa answered, his face seemed to change. He got a soft, faraway look in his eyes, as though he was traveling back to those days in his mind. "It was a long time ago – almost fifty years. The Governor at

Coastown wanted to know the condition of the lands beyond the Deep Woods. There hadn't been any contact with the Northlands in years and our expedition was sent to see what we could find, and to report back to the Windlands Army."

Window's breathing took a sharp jump. "And what about a path through the Woods? Does one really exist?"

Grandpa continued, "Yes, Window, it does. Well, anyway, it did back then. During the Continent Wars, the Northlanders knew they were greatly outmatched by the Atlandan armies and Windlands volunteers. They placed all their hopes for resisting them on a plan to cut a path through the Deep Woods that they could use to intercept enemy troops marching around the edge of the Woods to the east. Having the path would also provide the Northlanders the opportunity to attack west through the Windlands. Come on inside, I want to show you something."

Window followed him into the house. They went to the little west room, as it was called, where his Grandpa kept his books and papers. Grandpa reached between some books in the bookcase and pulled out a worn, leather-bound notebook and walked it back to the dining room table. He opened the book and flipped through its pages. He found what he was looking for and slid the book over to Window. It was a handwritten page of notes in faded pencil. It read:

Members of the Windlands Army Northlands Expedition
W.Y. 98:

      Captain John R. Near   (Windcoast)
      Corporal W. Briggs   (Woodmine)
      Scout: William Windowen   (Windtown)
      Rayard Oldsmith   (Horselands)
      R. Kensing   (Reed)
      S. Rails   (Coastown)
      John Revell   (Newtown)
      Jess Lucette   (Summerland)
      W. Gravand   (Atland)
      S. Cassidan   (South Range)
      L. Canette   (Freeland)

R. Hollen   (Ameran)

"These are the men who went with me." Grandpa explained.

Window read down the list and up again, his mind wondering and imagining.

"Grandpa, what did you find in the North?" he asked, certain he was about to hear the most exciting answer of his entire life.

"We found that the Northlands had never recovered from the devastation of the war – even in Calisay, the ruling city – which was one of the few places not destroyed by the Atland Army. There was really nothing much else to report. We had planned to search for the gold and jewel mines in the east but we ran into serious trouble and never got the chance."

"Before trying to find the eastern mines, the one place we wanted to see for sure was Battleplain, the name given to the plain where the last big battle of the Northern Campaign was fought. Atlandan soldiers who were killed in that battle were buried right where it took place. We wanted to see if those graves were still there. And we had just found those gravesites, when we were attacked by a large band of wild men from the far-northern mountains. We were greatly outnumbered and one of our company was killed – Rails, our quartersman. We temporarily drove off the attackers but we had to retreat in a hurry. We quickly buried Rails in that same cemetery before we left to return to the South."

"And what about the path, Grandpa?" Window's thoughts rushed on. "Tell me about that. Where is it?"

"It enters the Deep Woods south of Calisay. We followed it all the way south through the Woods to the Windlands. In fact, its southern end is not too far from here. I am sure you could find it."

Window's heart jumped again, "How come no one has discovered it in all these years?"

"No one has looked for it. Besides, you have to know where to look."

Window was sure now. He had to go into the Deep Woods. This would be the adventure he had always dreamed of. He had to go there tomorrow. He would leave in the morning. Glancing

back at the notebook, he picked it up, and without thinking,
turned the page. There near the top of its other side he found:

Captain John Page – second row, third stone

"Who is Captain Page, Grandpa?"
"When we buried Rails in the Battleplain Cemetery, there was
no time to make him his own gravestone, so we buried his body on
the back side of Page's stone. And, one more thing, Window. Our
expedition had taken a large metal box full of Freeland coins with
us. We thought that the Northlands probably still used Freeland
money as they had ever since being settled by the Frees in the
early days. We hoped to use it to buy supplies or anything else we
needed, if we had a chance. But our horses had been killed and
we had to leave a lot of things behind when we left.
We buried the coins along with Rails. We placed them about a
foot down in the dirt, right on the back side of Page's gravestone.
If you want to look for a treasure, those coins may still be there."
Window's heart and mind were racing – adventure and
treasure! Then his thoughts slowed down a bit. "But Grandpa,
couldn't it be dangerous? Isn't the North still a dangerous place?"
"I would think that it is, Window. And that's not all. You
would have to watch out for more than just the Northlanders."
Grandpa turned another page of the notebook and there was a
list of words written down the left side of the paper. But not just
words – words, many of which Window recognized from all of the
old stories and rhymes. They were the names of wild animals and
creatures from children's rhymes.
"These are the creatures we saw or believe we heard on the trip
back through the Woods. We were not attacked, but we did stand
guard every night to be sure."

Window read slowly down the list:

Owts
Mallen
Revers
Tree Snats

Wild Ashdogs
Nakes
Racbirds
Vale-bears
Guyspiders
Ban-wallows.

His mind flew ahead. "Did you meet any Talkers, Grandpa?"

"No, but I do believe that they exist. The Deep Woods is a strange, mysterious place. You would need to be careful, Window, very careful – very, very careful."

Window slumped back in his chair and closed his eyes. He was going. He was going on his adventure. He didn't care about the danger. He was going to find a treasure. He would find where the medallion came from. He would become the traveler in someone else's story.

"Who do you think that the traveler at Breeze's could have been, Grandpa? He seemed to know a lot of things about the North."

"Well, I would guess that he learned about the North from someone who had been there – someone he knew or was related to. Since Breeze thought that he was about your age, maybe, like you, he was a grandson of one of the members of my expedition."

Window looked at the twelve names on the expedition list again, "Who could it be, Grandpa. Whose grandson do you think he might have been?"

"Well, besides me, there were eleven others. Rails was killed – and was too young to have had a family, so that leaves ten. Also, two of our group returned to the North two years later – Oldsmith and Revell. They wanted to look for the treasure of the Northlands King that was lost when the Kingdom was destroyed, and try to find the gold and other mines in the east. I have never heard if they returned. And I feel certain that if they had, they would have stopped here and told me about it. I don't know what happened to them. They may have been killed in the North."

"I would guess that the rest of the men returned to their homes when their military service was over. I am not sure – except for Captain Near. I heard that a few years later he was Commander of an Army post in New South. You know, he was the grandson of John W. Near, the explorer who came to this area in W.Y. 19."

"The man from the Windlands Tree and the Near River?"

"Yes, that's him. So maybe the traveler was his great-great-grandson."

Just then, their conversation was interrupted. Grandma called in from the kitchen, "It's ready."

He hadn't noticed before, but now Window could smell the sweet aroma of sugarbeef and the salty smell of the gravy. They left the notebook open on the table and stepped to the kitchen.

"We'll eat in here tonight. I didn't want to bother you while you were talking at the other table. Of course," Grandma went on, "I was listening to you two in there. That's quite a story, Window. And it sounds like a great adventure. I'll help you get ready tonight so you can leave early in the morning." She gave him a quiet smile and he returned it.

Window was so surprised he was almost shocked. He had expected that his Grandma would be against his traveling into the dangerous Wilds, and probably try to talk him out of going.

She didn't show it, but she <u>was</u> very concerned for him. She knew that it would be difficult, and probably dangerous, especially because Window was going by himself. But, while Window and Grandpa were talking about Window going to the North, it brought back strong memories from years before, when her family had come to Windtown.

She was a young woman then, and hated that she was to be living on a farm in the Windlands prairies, instead of, as she had originally planned, in Coastown, which even then, was a city of about 20,000 people.

But, one thing changed her mind. She met a man who captured her heart and spirit – Window's grandfather. He was young and bold and exciting. She marveled at his stories of his adventures in the Northlands. She loved how he was not bothered by little things in life, and instead, faced any work or problem without fear or complaint. Grandma felt that his expedition to the North had contributed greatly to his being such a strong, capable man. And through their years together, she could always tell how very important the memories of that expedition were in his life.

Grandpa had admired her strength of character and joy of life. They fell in love and built their house and farm and family together. And now, they had been sharing that particular adventure for many, many happy years.

So, Grandma <u>was</u> concerned for Window, but understood his need to go. And she hoped he would come home from his journey safe and happy, and, like her husband did, even more confident and thoughtful than she felt Window already was.

++++++++

As always, Grandma's meal was delicious. Besides the meat and gravy, there was warm milk, fresh bread with sweet butter, and peaches – all followed by more springcookies. Those cookies had never tasted so good to Window.

After supper, Grandpa got out his boot knife, some light rope, a water tin, and some matches for Window to take with him the next day. Then he drew Window a map of the way to the Northlands cemetery. Window would need to follow the path north through the Deep Woods, then, once out of the woods, pass to the west of Calisay, and go as far as the Northway, which was the main east-west road in the North.

The Battleplain Cemetery was just across the Northway. It would take several weeks to make the journey. Window planned to take most of the food he would need with him, however, the wild spring redberries were ripe, and they should help keep him fed. Grandma packed bread, some apples, dried berries, and lots of dried meat – and, of course, all the springcookies he could shove into the pack that they found for him in the barn workroom.

Grandma also gave him a light woven blanket to sleep under, an extra shirt, and a few other items – including a regular pencil, three coloring pencils, and a little notebook she found. She wanted Window to keep a journal of his travels, and draw some pictures and maps of things he saw and places he went.

As they were finishing up the packing and the planning, Window asked, "Is there a key to the treasure box, Grandpa?"

"Well, Window, there was, but I'm sure that Captain Near had it. Besides, the box is probably rusted away by now so only the coins would remain. They were silver and a few gold. And just like finding the path, the real key to any treasure is knowing where to look."

They had no Northlands coins for him to take with him, but Grandpa gave him three silver Windlands coins – a new Windmill Dollar and two Kitepieces. On the back of each of those were three prairie grass stalks blowing in the wind, the same as on the Windlands flag. Window also had a silver Willowix piece and two copper Prairie Hen one-cent pieces in his pocket – those were the coins which people called p-hens or pennies. It wasn't a lot of money, but he was happy to have it, just in case he might need to trade for something.

After all seemed ready, Window took his letter from Mary Looking from his pocket, read it two more times, then gave it to his grandmother. "Will you please keep this until I get back," he asked. "I want to keep it safe." Then he remembered, "Oh, yeah," and handed her his house key too.

Next, he asked his Grandma for a piece of writing paper – and an envelope. He went off by himself to the extra bedroom and wrote Mary a letter. He began, "My Dearest Mary."

He wrote to her of his plans. He wrote of his hopes. He wrote of how his heart belonged to her and what a treasure she was to him – and he answered her declaration by repeating it, "And I will be waiting for you, too, when you return to Windtown. My love is with you, as yours is with me, Window."

He let out a deep sigh and sealed the letter in the envelope. He carefully addressed it and brought it out to his grandfather. "Please give this to my Uncle Breeze. And please ask him to be sure to put a windflower stamp on it, and post it. He will understand – and know what to tell Davey and the guys."

"Okay," said Grandpa quietly, and felt the sadness in his grandson.

Grandma had been sitting at the kitchen table, examining the medallion, and thought she thought of something. She was remembering a rhyme that seemed to describe it.

"A star for the old countries and three stripes for the new
A flower to grow and a ship..." She saw Window come into the room.

"I guess you might soon know where the medallion came from. I hope you find out."
"Thanks, Grandma. Say, is there anything you would like me to look for while I am gone?"
She thought for a moment. What she wanted to say was "Look for the way to get out, as you go into any dangerous situation. I love you, Window, and need you to come back to us safely."

What she did say was, "Well, here's something you might try to find – the bird that has been your mother's favorite ever since she was a little girl. Why don't you look for a red-winged flower wren? We haven't noticed one here on the farm in a long time. She would love to hear that you saw one."
Window smiled at the idea, "Okay, I will, Grandma, I will," he replied as he remembered the trouble he had saying that bird's name when he started in first grade at the Town School.
"And Window," she added, "come back home when you have found everything you hope to find – but not before."

"How about you, Grandpa? Is there anything that you would like me to look for while I am in the Northern Wilds? Anything else you wanted to find but couldn't?"
"When we were in the North, I heard of great beasts that roam the wild plains – tall creatures with silky fur and very long necks."
"Like that animal on the springcookies?" replied Window, recalling the strange looking animal on a cookie he had eaten earlier while he was loading his pack.
"Well, I guess that could be the same one."
"How could a creature from the Wilds get carved on an Amerand cookie board?"

"I don't know. But I always wished I had seen one of those creatures – if they really exist."

"I would like to see one of those too," Window replied. "Grandma, where did you get that springcookie board?"

"It was my mother's, and she got it from my grandmother. I guess it is very old."

"Like my medallion," Window thought, and then he thought, "Maybe just one more cookie." He reached into the tin on the counter and pulled one out as Grandma smiled at him. It was one with the picture of a tower.

Everything was ready for the morning. They went out onto the porch. Window sat on the little bench. Grandpa and Grandma sat together on the swing. As they slowly moved the swing back and forth, it squeaked in a constant rhythm. Grandma started to quietly sing an early days hiking song in time with the sound. Window joined in but Grandpa just listened.

> "The road is long and winding
> The day is bright and clear
> The way back home behind us
> The way ahead is here
>
> We look back for a moment
> We think of those behind
> We turn again and look ahead
> To wonders we might find"

The three of them sat up late into the night – Grandpa mostly telling stories and Grandma mostly mending socks – Window mostly listening. It was a beautiful spring night but getting cool. Window pulled his jacket tighter and then covered up with another blanket Grandma had gotten him from the porch cupboard.

Eventually everybody stopped talking and all three of them just sat quietly and listened to the wind chimes that were hanging from the edge of the porch ceiling. The chimes seemed to be telling a story of their own – sometimes speaking loudly, sometimes softly, sometimes quickly, sometimes slowly. It was a beautiful story of magical places and wonderful adventures.

Window closed his eyes. His thoughts flew far away and back again. Finally, he stretched his arms and slowly stood up. "Well, I'd better get to bed. I've got a big day ahead of me tomorrow," he smiled.

The three of them said their goodnights, and then his grandmother added, "Window, what will you dream about tonight?"

Window smiled again. Ever since he was a little boy, whenever he slept at the farm, she would put him to bed with that question. Never before had it meant so much to him.

"I don't know, Grandma, I'm not sure. I'll tell you in the morning."

Window's room was dark as he slipped into bed. He closed his eyes but knew he could not sleep. Thoughts were racing through his head – images of terrible creatures chasing him – of finding rooms full of gold – of sailing great ships to faraway places. He lay quietly and then he began to hear, through the slightly open window, the wind chimes from the porch. They were soft, but clear – the night breeze gently playing them for him.

He opened his eyes. The room was no longer dark. The moonlight was streaming in the through the window and reflecting from the other side of the room. Over on the clothes chest he could see the faded blue stuffed rabbit that Grandma always gave him to sleep with when he was little. Its whiskers were all worn off but it didn't seem to mind. It looked so calm and peaceful – its quiet eyes sparkling in the moonlight. It didn't move but just looked back at him. Window closed his eyes, and this time, went to sleep.

NORTHLANDS
GALWAY
THE DEEP WOODS
WHITE TOP
THE FARM
NORTH RIVER
WINDSTOWN
WINDLANDS PRAIRIES
LOW-POINT
STATION

CHAPTER THREE

INTO THE DEEP WOODS

Window opened his eyes. The moon was gone. The early morning sun was just beginning to lighten the room as he quietly slipped from bed. He didn't want to wake his grandparents. He quickly pulled on his clothes and – wait – he smelled something – something really good. It was bacon frying.

"Well, okay, I guess Grandma's already up," he thought to himself as he opened his door and walked to the kitchen. There she was, standing at the stove, turning the bacon once again, as she glanced back at him.

"Good morning, Window."

"Good morning, Grandma. Would you like me to wake Grandpa?"

"I don't think that will be necessary," she replied, as just then, the screen door opened and her husband came in from the barn. "He's been up for a while."

Window smiled at himself and hoped that Grandma wouldn't tell Grandpa.

"Hey, Window," Grandpa greeted him. "It's a beautiful morning – should be a great day to travel."

"Hey, Grandpa," he threw back. What's going on out there?

"Chickens all fed. That's about it."

They sat down to eat, Window taking the chair by the wall where he always sat when he ate with them. Grandma had put a clean tablecloth on the table and brought in some windflowers from beside the house. She served the bacon and Grandpa passed the hot rolls. As they ate, Grandma spoke for a minute about the new white corn she had planted in the garden the other day. Nobody said anything after that. All three of them quietly finished eating, thinking their own quiet thoughts, each of them unsure of what to say.

"Well, I'd better get started," offered Window as they pushed away from the table. He lifted his pack from the jacket hook by the door and Grandma helped him pull it on. Then she took a cloth bag of food and another of springcookies from the counter and pushed them into the pack.
"Be sure to come back with some good stories to tell at The Summer Breeze, and don't forget to draw me some pictures of things you see."
"Okay, Grandma."
"And here is that tin for your matches."
"Thanks, Grandma."

Window checked in his pocket for the map Grandpa had drawn for him. He checked in the other pocket for the medallion. Finding each in its place, he nodded that he was ready and they went out onto the porch. The screen door slammed shut behind him as he pushed past it. The early morning sun was just coming over the trees down by the road.

Grandma took Window's hand in both of hers and looked into his eyes. "I hope you find everything you are looking for, Window." Then with a smile on her face added, "Have a nice adventure."
Window smiled back at her, "All right, Grandma, I will."
As he started down the porch steps, she added. "May the Angels watch over you and keep you safe until I see you again." Grandma always said that when someone was leaving her house, and she had never meant it more than she did at that moment.

Window turned back to her. "Grandma, why do you always say that? Do you really believe in Angels?"

"Well, no, I guess not, but it seems like such a nice thing – to have someone to watch over you and take care of you. It's just an old saying, I guess."

"Angels are from the old stories, aren't they Grandma, from the days when the Windlands were first settled?"

"I think that's right, Window, and many people thought they saw them. And there is that Angel on one of the springcookies."

"Yeah, Grandma. It's one of my favorites."

"Well if you do see an Angel, Window, tell her that I said 'Hello,' okay?"

"All right, Grandma, I will."

All this time, Grandpa remained quiet. He usually let his wife do the talking for him when he was feeling serious.

Grandma kissed him on the cheek. "Goodbye, Window. We'll see you in a couple of weeks."

Window looked back in her eyes and answered, "Well, maybe in a couple of weeks." Then saying "Goodbye" to them both with a nod, he stepped off of the porch and onto the grass.

As he walked past the chicken yard next to the house, Window glanced through the wire fence. The chickens were scratching at the ground and pecking at the corn Grandpa had strewn there earlier this morning. Window remembered how, when he was a boy, he always enjoyed helping his grandfather feed those chickens. Back then, Window thought that he might grow up to raise chickens someday. Some people didn't, but Window had always liked the smell of the chicken house.

Only one chicken noticed him and bothered to look up. She fluffed her feathers and stretched her neck in Window's direction. "Goodbye, you guys," he called to them, but they didn't seem to care. And he didn't care that they didn't care. "I love this place," he thought to himself.

As he passed beneath the windmill, Window looked up to watch the blades spinning in the morning breeze. He could hear the slight whir as the blades followed each other around in a never-ending circle. Then he noticed one of the pigs in the pigpen rooting around in some trash by the side of the barn. As the pig stopped rooting for a moment, an old piece of newspaper from the trash that had been thrown up into the air settled down right in front of him. The pig stood still looking at it. For a moment, it looked as if the pig was actually reading the paper.

"Well, but pigs can't read," Window thought. Then he thought about what he might find in the Deep Woods and said out loud to himself, "Well, at least pigs around here can't read." Then he thought again, "At least I don't think so." He looked back at the pig. The pig looked up at him, gave a big snort, and turned back to his rooting.

A few more steps and Window was beneath the two big willow trees on the far side of the barn. One of them was the tree on which he and Mary had carved their initials two summers before. And there they were. He remembered that day well, and all the time he had spent watching her smile and the sun reflect from her smooth, light brown skin.

Window stopped and looked back at the house. His grandparents were still on the porch. He waved and they waved back. Then he turned, walked between the trees, and was gone. His adventure was beginning.

Grandpa was right. It was another beautiful day. The sun was out. The breeze was blowing and there were just a few clouds overhead – a great day for a hike across the back fields. Window had done this many times before – often with Davey and the guys. But this time it felt completely different. It <u>was</u> completely different. He walked along the fence by Grandpa's clover field, cut into the woods, crossed the creek near the back fence, and climbed the hill at the back edge of the farm.

Pushing out of the farm woods into the far clearing he stopped. This was it – the end of Grandpa's property and the beginning of the Northside Wilds, as they were called. From here on, the way was over lightly wooded hills and across grass fields until the next woods was reached – in about five miles Grandpa thought.

Window had never been past this point before. He and the guys had sometimes talked about going farther this way but none of them ever had. There were no more farms or roads or houses. Just quiet land covered with wildflowers below and birds flying above. "This is a beautiful place," thought Window, and stopped under a tree to check his map. There really wasn't much to check. All he had to do was keep heading north until he reached the Deep Woods. Grandpa had drawn a dashed line to show where he thought Window should go, but it was only a rough idea. Grandpa had admitted that he had not been out this way in all of the years since his expedition to the North.

By the time the sun was overhead, Window had already walked about ten miles. He stopped for a few minutes under a big oak tree to take a short break. He opened his pack and pulled out his water tin and a springcookie. It was an Angel one – a woman in flowing robes with wings sticking up behind her. "I guess it <u>would</u> be nice to have an Angel to take care of me," he thought, as he took a bite that took off one of her wings.
He didn't want to take very much time to eat because he wanted to get to the Woods before it got dark. Suddenly the day didn't seem so bright. It was such beautiful country and weather that he hadn't thought about where he was going – where he was going to be in a few hours. "I hope I can find the path okay," he quietly said to himself. "I hope it is still where it was." Grandpa had been quite sure of where Window would find it – if things hadn't changed too much.

He hiked along, watching the birds diving over the trees, enjoying the feel of the sun on his face. Then he decided to sing a marching song, but then, decided not to. He wasn't feeling too much like singing. He was feeling very quiet. For a few minutes he just listened to the sound of his own breathing as he worked his way up another small grass covered hill.

By late afternoon, Window knew that he was getting close. He was about two miles beyond the wide creek that Grandpa had mentioned. The ground started to rise steeply – as though the whole world was slowly going up into the sky. He felt his legs ache as he climbed higher and higher – and his heart beating excitedly in time with his legs. He could only see sky above the grass in front of him as he took one step after another, each one more difficult than the one before. And then he was there!

He reached the top of the rise and the ground in front of him dropped off suddenly. Down below and across a narrow band of grass, Window could see the Deep Woods spread out before him – for as far as he could see. Far to the east on his right and far to the west on his left – bright green sunlit trees spread out to the horizon. And ahead of him – miles and miles and miles of treetops moving in the breeze like waves on an ocean – that is what it was – an ocean of trees, for as far as he could see.

Window felt an excitement that he didn't remember ever feeling before. The Woods below him was an entire new world. He looked out over the trees and wondered if this was how his father felt when going out to sea. The expanse of trees and their movement in the breeze seemed to mesmerize him. He just stood still and watched in wonder for several minutes. Then he reminded himself that he needed to look for the path. He wanted to rush down and immediately enter the Woods but he needed to find the one place in all of the miles of trees where the path began.

Grandpa had told him what to look for – Signal Hill. When Window had asked him why it was called Signal Hill, Grandpa had replied with an uncertain, "Nobody knows. Maybe the Northlands soldiers used it."

Window's grandma had been listening to that part of their conversation. "Some say that the Angels used to live there," she called from the next room.

Hearing those answers, Window's mind had come alive, thinking of the possibilities, but he responded with only an, "Oh," and a sheepish smile.

According to Grandpa, Signal Hill was the only high ground within the Deep Woods near this part of its southern edge. It was about a quarter mile into the Woods and stuck up about as high as the treetops. The path was located just east of the base of the hill. All Window had to do was find the hill and look for the entrance to the path at the treeline just to the right of it. Those years before, when Grandpa was there, all of the trees had been cut from the top of the hill so spotting its top was easy. By now it was probably overgrown with trees again, but it should still be easy to see, as those trees would be sticking up higher than all of the rest.

Window took out his map and studied it. When he had crossed the wide creek, it was running from east to west, so he knew that he was very close to where he wanted to be. He may not have to search for miles up and down the edge of the forest. Perhaps he could see the Hill from where he was right now.

He held his hand up to his eyes to block the sun and followed the edge of the Woods from his far right to his left, searching for a high spot in the trees. He found none. His spirits sank as suddenly he thought that perhaps he might not be able to find the path. He had never before considered that. He squinted against the glare and looked as far as he could see to the horizon of trees straight ahead. As his gaze returned to the treeline in front of him he saw it.

There it was – almost directly in front of him – not covered with trees or even much grass, but just a small brown spot near the top of the waving trees. It disappeared and appeared again as the treetops waved back and forth around it.

Window's heart jumped, he was so close. He stuffed the map back into his pocket and looked for a way down the slope in front of him. He slid down a tall embankment and climbed down some more sloping hillside and quickly reached the open space below. He looked up and realized that from here he could no longer see the Hill – but he didn't care. He would find the path – searching along the forest edge until he did.

As he looked at the trees in front of him, he couldn't see any entrance or any sign of the path. He wasn't surprised since Grandpa had told him that the entrance to the path was never marked and the path was never cut all the way to the forest edge. Besides, that had been many years before, so certainly, even if it had once been easy to find, things would have changed by now. He just hoped that the path still remained at least enough to follow north.

Window decide to enter the Woods up to his right, go into the trees several hundred feet, and then move back to his left until he found the path. So he angled to the east across the grass that surrounded the Woods, and reached the forest edge. As he looked into the trees a thought struck him – he had never before seen woods so dense. He turned around for a quick look back at the high rise he had just come down from, took a deep breath, and slipped beneath the trees into the shade of the forest. He was in the Deep Woods!

Immediately he felt the cool of the complete shade. No sun was leaking though the branches high overhead. He pushed low branches and bushes out of his way as he went straight in. After a few hundred difficult steps through the thick underbrush, he turned left and worked his way west towards the direction of the Hill. It didn't take long. In just a few minutes he found it – the path through the Deep Woods – the hidden way to the North!

The path was covered with grass but otherwise hardly overgrown at all. It would be extremely easy to follow. And it was much wider than he expected – not a narrow one or two-person path, but wide enough to allow four or more men to walk side-by-side. "I guess that the Northlands Army brought wagons with them on their way to the south," Window thought to himself.

To his left, he could see the trees covering its end and almost see the sunlit grass outside the Woods. To his right, the path went straight north, with branches arching overhead, like a tunnel into the dark green of the trees. He let out a quiet sigh as he adjusted his pack and took his first step on his secret way to the Northern Lands.

His immediate plan was simple – find Signal Hill and climb to its top. He stared as far ahead as he could up the path. It seemed safe. It looked as though it hadn't been used in many years. That was okay with him. He didn't really want to meet anybody – or anything.

All of a sudden, Window felt very happy. He was on his adventure. Everything was going fine. He even let out a couple of whistles and then put them together into a little song. He stepped through the grass and weeds that covered the ground and moved ahead quickly up the tunnel of trees.

Before long, he was at Signal Hill. The path passed right by its base. It seemed odd that such a hill was there in the Woods. It looked as if someone had built it, the way it stuck up among the trees. Then Window was reminded of some pictures of Marsene jungle temples he had seen in his geography books.

 As the path touched the base of the hill, he could see the steps. Starting from the level of the path, wooden steps were built into the hillside. Climbing to the top would be easy. The steps appeared in surprisingly good condition as he took each one slowly. As he worked his way upward, he wondered why they had survived so well. And why did the trees on the side of the hill grow shorter and shorter as he climbed higher and higher?

After about a hundred steps he reached the top. The peak of the hill was flat, and about the size of a big room. There was a bit of grass, but it was mostly bare dirt. In the center of the top was what was obviously, at one time, a fire pit. Around it were several tree trunks lying on their sides. They had been cut and placed there as seats around the fire.

"Well, here is where the signal fire was lit," he thought. He sat down and looked out. He was at the level of the treetops – as though he were a bird sitting on the highest branch of a tree. It was an odd but beautiful sight. He was surrounded by a deep green, moving carpet. To the north he could see the Woods disappear into the sky. To the south he could see the high ground outside the Woods that he had looked down from just a short while before. In front of the rise he could follow the edge of the Woods east or west. All around him the sea of trees waved and twisted and sighed in the wind.

He decided that it was time for a little something to eat. He took his pack off and reached a piece of dried meat and a piece of bread from inside. Each bite was satisfying as he took his time eating and washing it down with some of Grandpa's well water. He felt very pleased with himself – a bit like he had just discovered a new land somewhere. He wondered if the owner of the medallion had ever been in this spot. He wondered who had kept the top of the hill free of trees. He wondered about back home, his friends, the members of Grandpa's expedition, the traveler, monsters, the Talkers, the Northland and its treasures.

He wondered what his father was doing right now.

Window closed his eyes as the late afternoon sun warmed his face.

+++++++++

[IN THE SOUTHERN WATERS]

Halfway around the world, Ernest Breesian stood on the bow of the Kathryn B. and peered off into the distance. The stars overhead were clear and bright with not a cloud to cover them. Galloway was somewhere out ahead but the lights he was searching for were still hidden by the night. In less than an hour the sun would be up, but by then it would be too late. A storm was coming. Not a storm of wind and rain, but the storm of the Linden naval ship, Gesselle.

Captain Nomanie was not a man to trifle with. He had warned Captain Breesian that if his ship was found in Linden waters after sunrise that his cargo would all be confiscated and his crew taken. He would be allowed to remain with his ship, but with no one to man it, it would be left drifting in the Southern Waters, lost and waiting to be boarded by Zentani pirates. Breesian had dealt with them once before, and was fortunate to have survived with his life.

So this time he was running from two ships. The Gesselle was less than an hour behind him, and, to make things worse, according to the warning of a clipper captain, the Zentani Rayolt was fast approaching from Tilrann waters off his starboard side.

How did he always seem to get into fixes like this? Perhaps, this time, it was because he didn't like the idea of sailing 200 miles out of his way, around New Rochelle to the east, just to avoid a possible meeting with the navy patrols or with the latest ship of trade-lane pirates from the port at West Reanne. Besides, two years before he had sailed through these waters without meeting a single vessel larger than a bob-water skimmer.

But this time was different. He and his crew of 27 had made it to Hearte without any incident more exciting than an encounter with two days of fog, but this time, just by chance, the Gesselle was in port when they arrived at Nadine. Of course, that made it impossible to load any tar or honey or any of the many other specialties of the outer Linden Colonies. The locals didn't mind selling to the Newlands ships but the government insisted on collecting taxes and tariffs on every item loaded. The last time the Kathryn B. was in these waters, Captain Breesian had conveniently forgotten to pay the required fees and left port in a hurry. He had outrun the smaller Linden naval skiff-vessel but this time he would not be so lucky. His hold was half filled with Hearten metal and tools for the Northern Islands, and the Gesselle carried 17 sails.

As he searched the horizon once again for a sign of Freeland safe harbor, Breesian's bridge officer, Anders, approached his long-time commander without bothering to salute. "The signal fire on the Gesselle is in sight, Captain. We will not reach Galloway in time. What is your order?"

Captain Breesian did not have much time to think. He did not have any time to think. He was only sure that being boarded by either vessel would be the end of his beautiful Kathryn – the end of his command he loved so much.

"South-south west, Mr. Anders, quickly." The thought rolled off his tongue at the same time it sprang from his mind.

He did have a chance, but not much of one. Certainly the Linden Navy was under orders to pursue pirate vessels as well as fee-delinquent tradeships from the Newlands. His idea was either brilliant or stupid. A course of south-south west would sail the Kathryn B. directly between the other two ships. When they each saw his mast flag, they would certainly take chase. If wild luck was with him, the duel chase would bring them right towards each other, as he, luck allowing, would pass across the paths of them both. And then, instead of the other ships overtaking him, they might confront each other. The Rayolt would quickly turn to run, but the Gesselle would catch her. It would take only a quick cannon battle to cripple the Rayolt, but boarding her would take the day.

The stars were beginning to fade above him. Breesian glanced to the east as the sun began to send its light from below the distant sealine. He glanced west and south and strained to see the mast flag of either ship. "Well, my dear Kathryn, I hope you have a beautiful day today." The words slipped from his lips before he realized it. He wasn't sure if he was speaking to his ship or to his wife in faraway Coastown, but perhaps to both. And his plan could work – but it probably would not. Either way, he would know soon.
As the Kathryn B. twisted to turn about in the Atlandic wind, Ernest Breesian hurried back to the ship's tower. His mind was still racing. The first ray of morning sunlight caught the tip of the massive mainsail. The stiff sea breeze pushed against his face. The spray of the water dampened his deckcoat. It was the start of another great day in the life of a Newlands seacaptain.

+++++++++

Window opened his eyes. It was time to get going. He wanted to get as far as he could up the trail, and set up a camp before nightfall. He shoved his water tin into his pack and lifted it to his back. "I wish I could find something here to take with me," he thought. He quickly scanned the ground around the fire pit looking for anything that may have been left there by the Northlanders or by Grandpa's expedition. He kicked at the dirt a bit but found nothing. He was just about to give up when he saw it – sticking up from the dirt next to one of the logs. He reached down and picked up what he thought was his first treasure – but it was just a small rock – like millions in the world. "Oh, well," he said aloud, and, standing up, threw it as far as he could into the ocean of trees to his left.

Window took one last look across the treetops in the direction he would soon be traveling. Above the trees, barely visible, he noticed something – a large group of birds circling about a particular spot. They circled, then, dove down, disappearing for a moment, then reappeared again. "I wonder what is going on over there?" he thought. "I guess I'll find out soon enough."

He took the steps down the hillside slowly, one at a time, thinking about what lie ahead. Then, turning to his left, he concentrated on moving quickly up the trail. His pace was steady.

At once he began to notice things – things that he didn't notice before. The Woods was very quiet. He heard no birds or breeze or anything. He saw no squirrels, no rabbits, no sunlight. It seemed as though he was all alone – as though something had scared everything else away. All he noticed was the coolness of the air and the straightness of the path. It stretched out ahead of him, the trees arching overhead, the grass beneath his feet short and easy to walk over. Here, no trees and few weeds were in the pathway. It was as though someone, or something, had kept the path clear all of these years. But, still, the path itself didn't look as though it had been used recently. There were no bare spots or marks on the ground. Along the edge, Window looked for the remains of the trees that the pathbuilders had cut down, but he could find no evidence that the path had not sprung up naturally all those years before.

For a couple of hours he pressed on. Eventually the straightness of the path gave way to an occasional gentle curve. He crossed a shallow creek, and had to climb a small rise, but it was still the easiest hike he had ever made. After a few miles, the trees began to thin out just a little. He could sometimes see the sky open above him, and then he began to notice flowers along the edge of the path – types of flowers he had never seen before. There were cute little white ball-shaped things, big green flowers with fuzzy petals, wispy blue bunches of extremely soft tendrils.

Although he couldn't see it, he knew that the sun would be setting before too long. He knew, too, that he had better find a place to spend the night before it got dark. And probably, darkness would come very quickly in the Deep Woods.

He began to look off to the side of the path to see if he could find a small clearing to build a fire in. He could have slept right in the middle of the path, but he knew he would feel better if he could set up a little camp to the side. It only took a few hundred steps before he found what he wanted. Off to the right there was a clearing in the forest of trees. It was much larger than he expected to find. Perhaps it had been cleared by the Northlanders and used as a camp during the war. Then he remembered – Grandpa had mentioned something about the Northlanders' "last camp." This was probably the spot. It could easily have held the tents of a hundred men.

The light was already failing as he set his pack down on a fallen log near the back of the clearing. He quickly collected some twigs and dry branches and scraped out a bare spot on the ground near the log. In just a minute and one of Grandpa's matches later, his little corner of the Deep Woods was bright and alive with a friendly, crackling fire.

While the fire lighted his world, Window unrolled his blanket and sat down to eat something. He had another piece of dried beef, an apple, and a springcookie. It was another Angel one. "I guess the Angels are looking over me," he thought. He had had no problems, and not a single thing seemed scary or dangerous. "I hope it stays that way," he spoke aloud as he added some bigger sticks to the fire.

"I wonder what those birds I saw from the Hill were doing earlier," he remembered. Then he realized – he still hadn't seen any birds or animals since he started on the path. He didn't want to see any big creatures, but what could be the reason that there were none at all?

Suddenly he didn't feel so safe and secure. His walk had been so pleasant that he had almost forgotten that the Woods might be dangerous. He sat quietly and listened – still no birds singing their night songs, no chipsquirrels chattering, not even any insects buzzing and clicking. It all seemed very strange. A chill went up his back. He leaned closer to the fire. Overhead, above the branches of the trees behind him, he could see the night sky.

Somewhere out of sight, the moon must be up because he could see
its light on a few clouds far above him. He just sat and thought
for a long time. There really wasn't anything else to do. He
watched the fire flicker and flame before him. He began to
imagine seeing pictures of things in the flames – creatures and
faces and eyes. A rhyme jumped into his head. He sang it aloud
to himself:

> "If you find a two-toed Zumbler
> Knocking at your door
> Please remember what I tell you
> And what Zumblers are known for
>
> Stay in bed and lock the windows
> Keep your feet well off the floor
> Close your eyes and make your wishes
> Don't get up to do the dishes
> Keep your shoes on tightly or
> That two-toed Zumbler will soon have four"

He followed that with:

> "A rumbling stumbling tumbling Zumbler
> Rumbled and stumbled and tumbled along
> A rumbling stumbling tumbling Zumbler
> Couldn't turn right and he couldn't turn wrong
>
> A rumbling stumbling tumbling Zumbler
> Went for a walk and..."

Window went on for a few more verses of Zumbler lore. Then
he let out a big sigh. Singing those rhymes from his childhood had
made him feel a lot better. He glanced back into the fire but this
time all he saw was fire – no creatures or faces to think about.
Overhead, the clouds drifted apart and, high above, the full moon,
glowing bright white against the dark sky, shined its light down
on his little camp. It brought a smile to his face as he was
reminded of other nights camping with his friends – sitting,

telling stories, and singing songs with them half of the night.

Window looked back at the fire and then beyond it towards the path. His heart froze. Standing in the moonlight, about forty feet away, was a shadow. Not the shadow of something – but a dark shadow, shaped like a man, standing still, and not on the ground, but above it! Window could look though its shadowy shape and see trees beyond it. His body tensed, his breathing almost stopped. He reached down to the side of his boot and pulled out his knife. He quickly looked around to see if there were any more of the shadow-men but saw none. As the moon went behind a cloud, he looked back at the creature. It was gone.

Had he imagined it? He was sure he hadn't. He didn't know what to do. What could he do? Slowly he took all of the remaining branches he had gathered and put them on the fire. The flames blazed brightly. He looked again but the shadow was not there. What could it be? Surely it must have been a moonshadow of a man but it couldn't have been. It was not attached to anything but seemed to be floating just above the ground. His mind reeled, grasping at ideas to explain what he had seen.

Maybe it wouldn't come back. Maybe it would stay away and leave him alone. Maybe it was only in his mind, inspired by the fire and the years of stories about Deep Woods creatures he had heard. But no story every mentioned a shadow creature. This was impossible.

Then he changed his mind. He wanted the shadow to reappear. What kind of story could he tell back at the Summer Breeze if he didn't have more to tell? He pictured himself around the big table with his friends telling his story, "And then I saw this shadow thing." What kind of story is that? If he was going to have an adventure, at least he wanted to know what his adventure was.

"Maybe it's not dangerous. Maybe if the moon comes out again I will be able to see it." He laid his knife down on the log next to him. He knew that the fire would only last for a short time. He needed more to burn. He decided to get some larger pieces of wood. He couldn't imagine that he would go to sleep tonight. He would probably sit up all night, afraid to close his eyes.

Without going too far from the light of the fire, he was able to find some larger branches to pull across it. As the flames jumped upward, sparks and embers rose high above him, twisting and turning up to the top of the trees. Suddenly, he realized that he was now sending a signal to everywhere for miles around, "I am here. Come get me. I am easy to find. Just follow the light."

"Well perhaps I will not have to walk for miles to the North after all. Perhaps I will get no farther than this." He felt foolish. How could he have thought that traveling into such a dangerous place was a good idea? Why couldn't he have stayed home and stayed safe?

His thoughts were interrupted. The clouds uncovered the moon again. Its bright light once again shone down before him. He looked at the spot where the shadow had been. And there it was again in the moonlight, a dark shadow, in the shape of a person, tall and very thin, with a head, arms, and legs. Well, at least the outline of a person, like a silhouette, just standing before him. The shadow sometimes drifted slightly out of shape and then reformed itself again. Window got the feeling that maybe the figure could have taken different forms, but took the shape it did just for his eyes.

The moonlight left again and the shadow disappeared as Window was looking at it. Almost immediately, the moonlight returned and, with it, the shadow creature.

After a couple minutes of watching it just stand there, Window's fear of the shadow began to fade, just as the shadow itself had faded without the moonlight. It didn't seem dangerous any more. It just seemed to be watching him, although it didn't have any eyes that Window could see.

"Okay," thought Window, "Before the moon goes behind another cloud, I need to do something."

"Want to come join me by the fire?" Window called out to it. "Want to listen to some old stories about the Deep Woods and have a couple of laughs? Do you live around here?"

The shadow remained the same, quietly standing and seemingly watching. Window pulled the medallion from his pocket and held it out to the creature. "Have you ever seen this before?" he asked. The shadow remained still then flickered a bit as a slight breeze passed through the clearing. "Is watch people all you do?" Window was starting to enjoy this mysterious visitor. So when the moon again went behind a cloud he felt disappointed, but soon it returned and the shadow with it.

Window decided to just keep talking. Once he got up and slowly walked towards the shadow but it moved away, so Window returned to his fireside log.

Things stayed that way long into the night. As the moon moved slowly across the night sky above the clearing, Window told old stories of the Deep Woods, stories of Windtown, stories of faraway places. The Watcher, as Window called the shadow, gradually moved a bit closer to the fire, but still kept about thirty feet away. Window marveled at being able to see right through its shadowy form, wondering and wondering how such a thing could be.

The Watcher seemed to enjoy Window's stories. It sometimes drew still closer as if looking forward to a certain part of a story. Sometimes it would start to drift apart a bit and then pull itself back into the shape of a man again. Always it stayed quietly, watching and listening.

"If you like these stories," Window told it once, "you should come back to the Summer Breeze with me and listen to the stories my Uncle Bill tells. His stories are a lot better than mine. We could sit on the porch out in the back on a moonlit night and have a great time. Davey and I would grill catfish for everyone. You could pass the rye bread around or – well, maybe you could just watch and listen. I am sure that the guys would love to have you there. It must get lonely out here all by yourself."

Then Window realized that that is what he thought – the shadow seemed lonely. It seemed to want to be close to him but was unable. Window wondered again what it was, and where it could possibly have come from.

Overhead, the moon had passed beyond the opening in the trees. The edge of its light on the ground was working its way across the clearing to where the shadow creature stood. Very soon the moonlight would no longer shine down on any of the campsite. Window knew that the Watcher would be gone then too. Would he ever see it again? As the last ray of moonlight began to disappear behind the trees, he took one final look in the shadow's direction. "I hope to see you again sometime. I would like that." The Watcher seemed to answer as it shimmered in the fading light and was gone.

For a long time Window sat on the log and stared into the fire. "What a story to tell the guys back home! What a story to tell Uncle Bill! I wonder if they will believe me." Thinking of his friends, Window felt happy, and then he felt very sleepy as his long day and night caught up with him

The fire had died down to a few glowing embers. Window dragged the ends of the burning branches into the fire and it burst back into flames. He lay down on his blanket in front of the log with his head on his pack and pulled part of the blanket over him. The cold, spring night was upon him but he felt warm and comfortable in front of the fire.

He felt safe and secure, watching the flames as they sparked, and crackled, and jumped high above him. Then Window noticed – the night insects were singing. They buzzed and chirped and hummed. It was as though, at last, the Woods was welcoming him.

Then, the bugs quieted for a moment. He could hear the branches of the trees rubbing against each other, as they were moved by the wind. Over just beyond his fire he heard a little chip-squirrel ruffle some leafy grass as it rushed behind a downed log. The world had come alive with sound. Window wasn't alone in the Woods after all. He was a part of it.

The buzzing of the insects filled the air again. They sang him a sleeping song as his mother used to do so long ago. The tired young traveler's eyes closed as he imagined he was standing before a golden castle in a faraway land. And then, with just one deep sigh, Window Breesian fell asleep on the first night of his adventure in the Deep Woods.

CALISAY
THE DEEP WOODS
CIRCLES
WINDTOWN

CHAPTER FOUR

ON THE FOREST PATH

It was cold. Window woke up shivering. The fire had gone out hours before and a damp chill filled the air. The sun may have been up somewhere, but none of its light added any heat to the ground or to Window's blanket. He threw the blanket off and climbed to his feet. Stretching the stiffness out of his arms, he ran his hands through his hair and surveyed the clearing. Everything seemed okay.

He grabbed his pack and sat down on the log. Breakfast was going to be in a hurry. A piece of bread and some dried berries later, Window rolled up the blanket and was ready to get started – then he noticed them.

All around him on the ground, there were little paw prints in the dirt – prints of little padded paws with very long claws. Window shuddered, but not from the cold. Apparently, he had had visitors in the night after he had gone to sleep. Around the fire pit, the prints formed a perfect circle. Apparently, some little somethings had spent part of the night enjoying his fire.

Window imagined what it must have been like – how the creatures must have examined him – smelling him, and maybe even touching him. He was glad that he had slept with his pack under his head. He had been going to hang it from a tree, but certainly, the paw-creatures could climb trees. "I guess I got lucky, this time," he said to himself – then he drew in a short breath and repeated, "This time."

Window examined his pack more closely. Across one side, in the heavy brown cloth, he found four long, fresh scratches. It was probably the side of the pack that was exposed as he slept with his head on it. The paw-creatures had been all around him. And probably, a bite or a slash by one of them could have been poisonous or deadly. He could easily have been hurt or killed.

Maybe they had never seen a campfire before. Maybe they liked it and thought that if they disturbed him, the fire would go away. Whatever the reason, he felt very fortunate. His first night in the Deep Woods could have been his last.

Then it hit him – he should just turn back and leave the Woods. He had had his adventure with the Watcher. He had a great story to tell back at the Summer Breeze. He hadn't found any treasure, but finding treasure was a childish idea. It would be foolish to go on any farther.

Suddenly the Woods seemed too quiet. Then he thought he heard something – something moving behind him. He shuddered again and quickly turned to look. Nothing was there. He tried to see into the trees but it was impossible to see very far. His muscles tightened with a fear that he had never felt before. He was in danger – creatures could be anywhere, watching him, ready to attack.

The shadow visitor of the night before seemed almost like a dream to him now. Now he had to be careful. He was in the Deep Woods. He had heard all of the stories – some people don't ever come out.

Window sat quietly for a minute, listening for more sounds and trying to decide what to do. He heard nothing else and started to relax a bit. Maybe he had imagined hearing things, or, maybe, it was just some harmless little animal out for a morning stroll. And if the paw-creatures had wanted to hurt him, they easily could have.

Just then, a small many-shaded blue bird flew down from a tree and landed on the ground by him. It had spied a breadcrumb that Window had dropped while eating, and pecked at it, and then

swallowed it. The bird looked up at him and chirped a quick
melody that seemed to say, *"It's okay, it's okay."*

Window relaxed further and whistled back at the bird, trying to
imitate its call. The bird whistled again and took off into the trees
behind him.

"I guess that no bird would fly into a bunch of monsters," he
thought. "I guess nothing is hiding in those trees."

The words of his Grandma flashed to his mind. "Come back
home when you have found everything you hope to find – but not
before."

"Okay, Grandma, you're right." he answered to himself, and
then he continued. "Bill was right, too. If you want to be in
somebody's story, you've got to do more than walk to the river."

Window felt better. He would go on as planned. He would find
the treasure in the Battleplain Cemetery. He would just be very
careful from now on. The first thing to do was to make a weapon
to defend himself. He had his boot knife but it was pretty small.
He wished he had brought the hand ax that Grandpa had
suggested, not to use as a defense, but to help him cut a heavy
stick.

He quickly searched and found a dead tree that had fallen near
the forest edge and tugged and twisted on the straightest branch
he could find until it came loose. After carrying it back to his log,
he spent about twenty minutes cutting and carving and smoothing
it. He was really quite pleased with how it turned out – a heavy
walking stick, standing about chest high, perfect for fending off
something or whacking something over the head. It even had a
knob up near the top that would serve as a handle. "This will be
enough if I get into trouble," he comforted himself.

Then he was ready to go. Window shouldered his pack and
started across the clearing to the path. As he walked over the
ground where the Watcher had stood, he examined the grass but
could see no sign of anything having stood there. "I hope to see
you again," he called out to the trees, and started back up the
trail.

++++++++

The trek continued to be a fairly easy one. The ground was
level and the grass was short. It was odd that the path had not
become overgrown but he saw no signs of anything dangerous.
Occasionally the trees thinned out but then soon covered the path
again. Window sometimes poked his defense stick into the ground
as he walked and sometimes swung it by his side.

The morning was cool and comfortable for walking. As he
finished another mile or so, Window began to enjoy himself again.
He noticed several different birds whose type he could not
identify. More and more flowers appeared – each more colorful
and beautiful than the last. He did not see any of the spring
redberries he had expected to find but there were other berries of
various colors and sizes – bunches of small green berries, pink
pods of others, and deep purple juicy looking berries that he really
wanted to try – but decided not to, just in case they were
poisonous.

Window hiked on – reveling in the amazing flowers and
particularly the birds – enjoying their many calls and songs. The
path took a few slight turns but mostly continued straight to the
north. Then, far ahead, he saw something – a light brown shape
in the path. It was large and completely covering the green of the
trail.

He slowed his pace, and, ducking low by one side of the path,
carefully moved towards the object. If his way was to be blocked
by any creature, he would be ready. His right hand held tightly to
his walking stick as he got closer. His breathing became rapid but
he forced himself to steady it.

He couldn't make out what it was ahead – it was just large and
– then he loosened his grip on his stick. What he had seen was
not an animal or an object of any kind – it was the path itself!

As he approached the colored "object" he discovered that,
starting rather suddenly, the grass of the path was worn away,
and it was now a path of dirt. From this spot on, the path actually
looked like a path – the grass was obviously worn away by the feet
or paws of something.

Window carefully examined the dirt beneath his feet. There
were no tracks he could discover, but it was certain – Woods
creatures used this path, and used it often. He would need to be

even more alert from now on. He could not afford to be surprised
by anything that might be harmful to him. He considered moving
off into the trees to the side of the trail and to follow it that way,
but that would not work. The forest was too thick. He would not
be able to travel except on the path itself.

So, there was only one thing to do – keep going. He thought
about singing as he went, but rejected that idea. It was only the
middle of the morning and he still had most of the day before him,
so he would just keep moving. Maybe the path would change
again, as quickly as it just had.

Window walked on, carefully watching and listening as he
went. The path crossed a stream. He was able to step on rocks so
he didn't get his boots wet. On and on he walked – and then he
heard them. Ahead, on the trail, birds were cawing and cackling.
The path took a slight curve to the right, and he could see them.

Ahead, something was lying in the path. It was the remains of
an animal. He did not know what is was, but it appeared to have
fur of light brown and white stripes. It was dead and its body was
in pieces.

The remains of the animal were surrounded and almost
completely covered by about a dozen of the biggest, blackest birds
Window had ever seen. They were bigger than even a Windlands
prairiehawk. They were wildly attacking the body of the dead
animal – pulling strips of flesh from its carcass – devouring it
while they screamed out.

The birds continued their attack relentlessly. Window gripped
his heavy stick and approached slowly. He would scare them
away and simply pass by the carcass. As he got closer, suddenly,
one of the birds noticed him. Then they all noticed him. He held
up his stick and moved forward. He let out a loud yell and raised
the stick above his head as he advanced.

Anywhere back home, this would have been a fine plan, but
here in the Deep Woods it was not. The Caw-birds turned his way
but did not move. They did not fly away. They only opened their
blood-covered beaks and looked at him with large white eyes.
Fear shot through his body – their beaks were filled with teeth –

long, sharp-looking teeth – teeth that dripped blood and pieces of
the dead animal. Several of the birds held up the claws of one foot
and swiped them toward him. The claws were long and sharp and
covered in glistening red.

There was no time to think. He could only attack them before
they attacked him – and try to get away. He would have to kill as
many of them as he could before they could reach him. Window
walked toward the birds, holding his stick ahead of him. As he
did, the birds let out a new sound that he had never heard from a
bird before – a squeal so high pitched and loud that it hurt his
ears.

The Caw-birds came at him, bearing their teeth and claws. If
they reached him, he would probably be killed. He could see the
hate in their eyes.

Window swung his stick at one of his attackers – the advancing
Caw-bird easily dodged the intended blow. Then, to Window's
great surprise, the birds stopped their attack immediately and
retreated into the trees on each side of the path. He could hardly
believe it. He was safe. The terrifying Caw-birds had given up so
easily. He hurried past the bloody remains of the animal on the
trail and quickly walked on a short distance. Then he turned back
to see if the birds might follow him.

Immediately, Window understood the reason for the Caw-birds
change of heart. Standing over the carcass on the path was
another creature – an ugly, furry, dirt matted, monster! It sniffed
at the dead body and then looked toward Window. It was about as
tall as Window's chest and was standing on its two crooked hind
legs, and large, padded back feet. It had short front legs that it
was using like arms, and long fingers that made it look like a
hairy, misshapen man. The monster's gaping mouth was
enormous – and filled with rows of jagged teeth that could easily
tear the arm off of a man.

It all happened quickly. The Teeth-monster let out a low growl
and started toward Window. There was no time for him to escape.
Window raised his walking stick above his shoulders, and braced
himself. The creature dropped to all fours, raced at him until he
was about ten feet away, and, with a terrifying growl, leaped

74

through the air. Window reacted. He swung his walking stick at the creature and hit it squarely in the face. Falling to the ground, the monster let out a loud yelp, and then a louder growl. Deep red blood was spurting from what appeared to be its nose.

The creature wiped his face with his filthy arm and roared his disapproval. From far back down the trail came a roar in answer. Another creature was on its way!

Window turned and ran. The bleeding monster chased after him. He could hear the course breathing of the creature and the scraping of its claws on the hard dirt of the path behind him. Window fearfully glanced back – the monster was gaining on him.

There was no hope of escaping. He could think of nothing else to do. In desperation, Window turned and wildly flung his stick at the advancing savage animal. The whirling stick struck the creature in the legs – it tangled between its front legs and one of its back feet and the running monster tumbled to the ground. Its bloody face smashed into the dirt – furious, it jumped immediately to get up. It could not. Its foreleg would not support its weight. Its leg was broken!

The creature once again let out a terrible roar of anger – its mouth wide – its teeth slashing in Window's direction. The horrifying roar was answered by the other monster – closer than before, but not yet in sight.

Again Window turned and ran – this time without thinking, without stopping, without looking back – deeper into the Woods. The dirt of the path passed beneath his feet in a rhythm that matched his pounding heart. Escape was his only hope.

He ran on and on – up the tunnel of trees to the North. He kicked dirt ahead of him as he ran. He crossed a narrow clearing, and raced back under the canopy of trees. He splashed through a creek that crossed the path and startled a young deer-creature that had stopped for a drink – it bounded into the trees as he passed. He forced himself to go on long after the pain in his chest and his legs told him to stop. Finally, miles from where he had started running from the Teeth-monster, he stumbled on a root sticking up in the path, and fell. Window slammed down hard onto the dirt. He could not get up. His body would not respond.

Window Breesian lay on the ground on the Deep Woods path. His mind was clear but his body exhausted. He would have been still terrified by what had happen to him, but he realized that would do no good. He would just have to take care of himself. He would have to continue to the Northlands as quickly as he could.

Slowly, Window dragged himself to his feet and started up the path again. Then he felt his pack still strapped to his back. He hadn't even thought about it as he ran, and was so glad that he hadn't, or he probably would have tossed it aside and would now be without anything. Wow, what a story to tell Bill and the guys! What a story! And, now that the danger seemed to be past for the moment, he felt a bit proud of himself. He had faced the creatures and survived. He was still on his adventure through the Deep Woods. He was sore and tired but not really hurt. It made him feel pretty good to think about it. He took a deep breath and smiled to himself as he went on.

++++++++

The miles continued to pass beneath his feet. He stopped for a lunchtime meal and enjoyed another springcookie for desert. He started out again, deciding that any Deep Woods monster that wanted to, could easily find him, so he didn't try to hide himself. He sang as he went – songs and rhymes of armies marching and monsters monstering.

He passed fantastic flowers and walked under the tallest trees. He saw little Deep Woods animals of every kind – wood-mice, treedarts, quick, little rock jumpers, and slow moving branch squirrels. The day was clear and the path easy.

The afternoon sun had moved across the occasional opening in the trees above him. The spring air turned a bit cooler as the path was once again totally in the shade. Still Window walked on, mile after mile. He marveled at the birds and animals and plants of the Woods. Once he came upon a furry, water creature that looked a lot like a large ground otter, but saw nothing that seemed dangerous.

Window had tired of singing. He had tired of walking. He had tired of watching out for danger. He had eaten again and then just slowly continued along the path. A breeze blew across the top of the trees above him and the leaves rustled together. He listened to them for a moment, and as the leaves rattled against each other, Window imagined they were singing to him.

Then he heard a sound that confused him – the sound of a real melody coming through the trees. The sound of high voices somewhere ahead – voices singing. He hurried up the trail. How could it be? There was no mistake. Off to his left through the trees, Window could clearly hear the voices. It sounded like a choir of children – high, clear voices, singing different parts – singing in Atlandan!

He recognized the song. It was a spring field song about Windlands farmers planting their crops. He had even sung it himself, when he was in school.

"The fields do sleep until the spring…"

It was impossible. He had to see who was singing. Who could it be?

"Winter snows are far from sight…"

He could not image who it could be.

Window turned off of the path and pushed into the forest. The song ended and another one began – again, a chorus of high, children's voices, singing in perfect time and harmony. It was a summer holiday song from the Middle Prairies. He climbed a small rise and looked down to the clearing below.

Across the open space before him, Window could see the singers. They were not children, but scores of the oddest animals he had ever seen. The singers were about four feet high and stood upright in groups of ten or twelve on the opposite hillside and under small trees in the depression below him.

The creatures were entirely covered in what appeared to be silky fur, with only their eyes and mouths easy to discern. Their heads looked rather like that of an owl or, perhaps a sea pannier. They had only slight shoulders so the fur flowed smoothly from their heads down over their bodies. As a few of them moved, Window could see arms and legs, but they were so covered with their long fluffy fur, that the arms and legs disappeared into the rest of their fur as the creatures stopped moving.

The singing creatures were in groups of a rainbow of different colors. One group was those whose fur was colored dark brown. One group was light grey, another blonde. Others were pale orange, light blue-green, yellow, and one group was almost bright red.

Window stood in awe and watched and listened. These singing creatures had to be Deep Woods Talkers! It was true – there really were talking creatures in the Woods, just like the old songs and stories said. And, somehow, they knew his language and his own songs!

As one song would end, a different group would start the next one. Everyone would then join in. It was a beautiful, joyous sound, sailing across the clearing and into the woods – high, sweet voices of innocence and charm. Window was captivated by the music. As groups of the singers stood closely together and sang, they gently swayed back and forth, their silky fur blending together. It gave the impression of one big, living creature, with many mouths and eyes. Their mouths all opening and closing in perfect harmony.

Suddenly it all ended. One of the singers called out and pointed in Window's direction. Within a few seconds, they had all scattered across the clearing, and hid in bushes and behind trees and on the open ground. Well, they were apparently trying to hide, but Window could still see most of them. They were easy to see – their colors contrasting greatly with the greens of the forest. Some of them lay very flat against each other in low places, and made what seemed to be colored carpets on the ground.

Then, as the fur-creatures' scrambling for cover had finished, Window heard another voice. Off to his right, about half way up the hillside, was a single creature – still singing. Unlike all of the others, this singer was covered entirely in bright, white fur. His eyes were closed, and from his mouth came a happy song of a happy singer. He had not heard the alarm, and didn't realize that the others had stopped singing, and had run away to hide.

Window felt a bit sorry for the white-fur creature. He didn't appear to belong to any of the colored-fur groups, and he looked lonely singing all by himself.

The singer ended his song and opened his eyes. He looked around for his companions and his eyes met with Window's. He didn't run, but looked back at Window curiously.

"Hello," Window called over to him.

"Hello," came the reply, in a clear, calm, high-pitched voice.

"I know that song, too." Window hoped that the singer would not run away.

"Where are you from?" asked the creature.

"I have come up the path from the Windlands in the south."

"I have been to the south once."

"Have you ever been to the Windlands?"

"No, but I would like to go."

Window wondered what to say next. "Would you like something to eat?"

The creature thought a moment, "Yes I would. Yes, I would."

Window stepped down the side of the hill nearer to the singer, and sat on the grass. None of the other creatures moved. They remained in their multicolored piles and groups, seemingly melted into the ground. They shimmered in the sunlight as the breeze gently moved their fur.

"What's your name? My name is Window."

"My name is Circles," came the answer in perfect Atlandan, as the Talker sat next to him.

"Would you like an apple, or some bread? Or a springcookie?"

Pulling off his pack and reaching inside, Window retrieved a cookie and handed it to Circles.

"Oh, a kite!" squealed the Talker, as he saw the picture on the cookie, "I love kites!"

"Do you have kites here in the Woods?"

"No, but they have them in Calisay."

"Have you been to Calisay?"

"Just to watch the kites." Then he added quietly, "Well, not really – but I want to go."

"I didn't know that there were kites in Calisay."

"Oh, yes, I have heard all about them."

Circles took a bite from the springcookie that removed the kite's tail. What Window was sure was a smile came to the Talker's face – well, at least to his mouth. Window couldn't really see his face – just delicate, smooth, fluffy, feather-like fur, slightly moving in the breeze. The Talker had small teeth and two little dents below his eyes that seemed to mark his nose.

Circles' eyes opened wide. They were perfectly round and solid black against bright white – a really dramatic look that made him look very wise – sort of like a prairie owl.

"Have you ever seen a man before?" Window asked.

"A few times."

"I hope I didn't startle you."

"I knew that you were there all the time. I just wanted to see what you would do."

Circles closed one eye half way – in a sort of a wink. Window smiled at him and dug in the pack to retrieve a cookie of his own. It was one with a flag on it.

The two new friends sat and talked for a long time. Window told Circles about his journey up the path and shared more of his food. Circles listened carefully – his eyes fixed on Window in great interest – especially when Window told him about the treasure of Freeland coins he hoped to find. The other singers slowly got up and drifted away, as they tired of waiting for the man to leave them alone. After a while, Window and the Talker were all by themselves, lost in conversation and good spirits.

Circles explained to Window about himself and the other singers. They were a type of Deep Woods Talker that the other Talkers in the forest called Woots. They lived mostly in this part of the Woods, and only rarely traveled far from their homes. They lived in shallow caves or tree-houses, eating wild tree-fruit, berries, roots, and wildflower leaves. Woots were very friendly, happy creatures – enjoying each other's company – hiking, playing games, and singing – especially singing.

Also, every Woot had a special skill or talent – some were good at finding food or building shelters or something simple like climbing trees or drawing pictures in the dirt. Discovering one's special skill was important to the Woots. It gave them an identity within the entire group.

"I can't decide what I really am. My real name is Runner, but others say that, not knowing what my specialty is, I just run around in circles trying to find out. So, they just call me Circles."

"I'm really not too accepted around here. That's why I was off singing by myself. Also, I am very late getting my color. By now I should be turning, but so far, I haven't started. I won't really feel like I belong until I do. Until then I won't know what family I will belong to."

"What do you think it is that is special about you?" Window asked, hearing the sadness in the creature's voice.

"I don't know what I do best. I can sing pretty well, and I am good at wondering about things. And I am friendly. But, perhaps, so far, I am best at listening and looking. My hearing is very good, and I can see far things better than anyone. I am a good talker too. I know how to speak Atlandan <u>and</u> Freelandan.

"How did you learn to do that?"

"The Olds teach us when we are News. We have school in the morning until we learn our languages. I listened very carefully. And, besides singing, we Woots are very good at speaking clearly."

"But I don't really know what I am. Nothing I do seems to feel just right to me." Circles stopped talking for a moment and looked at the ground. Then he raised his eyes and looked right at Window.

"What are you, Window, do you know?"

"Well, back home I am a builder and a woodworker – but now – I guess that I am just a traveler."

"I wish I could be a traveler. I would love that."

"Where would you like to travel?"

"I want to see the ocean – and the mountains – and the kites of Calisay. I haven't ever seen the kites – well, only in my dreams. But I have heard all about them. They sound wonderful."

"Are you going to the ocean, Window? I wish I could go to the ocean."

"No, I am traveling to the lands a bit past Calisay."

Circles' eyes opened wide. There were tears behind them. His voice started to get lower in pitch and it shook as he continued.

"Window, even when I am with the others, I am lonely here. Every day I dream of going to the south or to the north, but no one will come with me. No one wants to be a traveler. Everyone feels right at home here, but I am sort of lost. Maybe if I went searching, I could find out who I really am."

"Window, could I be a traveler too – with you? Could I go with you to see the kites at Calisay?"

Window already really liked Circles and felt a connection to him. He was touched that the Deep Woods creature must have felt the same way. He sighed quietly to himself and answered carefully. "I am sorry, Circles, but I am not going to Calisay. It may not be safe for me. I plan to pass by the city on my way farther north."

"But you <u>could</u> go to Calisay, Window. Don't you want to see the kites – and the towers? And, I could help you, Window. I can speak Freelandan. And I know how to stay safe in the Woods, too."

"You do?"

"And I could help you find the treasure."

"Are you sure you want to be a traveler, Circles? The road ahead could be very difficult and dangerous."

"I am not afraid, Window. I am tougher than I might look. I once was almost caught by a Thasher, but I escaped by hitting him with a rock. And, another time, I went for almost a week without eating anything but tag-roots. Have you ever tried that?"

"No, I have never done that," replied Window, chuckling inside and liking his friend even more than he did before.

"Please, Window. May I go with you to see the kites at Calisay?"

Window looked deep into Circles' eyes and smiled. He <u>was</u> happy to find a friend to walk with – to share an adventure. It would be a lot more fun with someone. And, besides, he <u>would</u> like to see the Northlands city, although he wasn't sure it was a very good idea.

"Okay, Circles, we will go to see the kites at Calisay – you and me. We will both be travelers, together."

The young Woot smiled in return and jumped up. "I'll be right back, I'll be right back," he explained, and went running across the clearing and up and over the hill on the other side – his fur flying as he ran. In only a minute he returned, out of breath, and happily said, "Okay, I'm ready."

"Aren't you going to bring anything with you?"

"I am bringing <u>everything</u> with me. This is all I have."

"What is all you have? All I see is you."

"That <u>is</u> all I have, Window – me."

Window smiled again, and felt as if his new companion was perhaps the richest person he had ever met. "Okay, Circles, I am ready too, it's time for an adventure. Let's go see the kites!"

"Let's go see the kites, Window. Let's go to Calisay!"

Window pulled his pack over his shoulders and they started out at once. A few Woots had gathered together and waved as Circles waved goodbye in return. The two travelers climbed up the hillside and made their way back to the path, where they turned, and headed north up the tunnel of trees.

++++++++

It was late in the afternoon but there would still be lots of time to travel before it got dark. They made a very interesting pair as they walked side by side. Window was tall and steady, and wearing dark pants and jacket. Circles was short, and kind of

wobbly, and bright white. Circles liked to kick the dust as he
walked, but he never got dusty. Woot fur was so slick that dust or
dirt or even mud or water wouldn't stick to it.

They talked as they went – taking turns listening and sharing
stories about themselves. Circles was very interested in
everything about Window and his home. Window wanted to learn
all about the Deep Woods.

Circles had heard about the shadow creatures before. He didn't
know where they came from, but knew that there used to be a lot
of them in the Woods, but something must have happened to
them, because no one had seen them in a long time.

"What should we do, Circles, if we meet another Teeth-
monster on the path – like the one that was chasing me?"

"I know what to do, Window, if we see one – but we won't.
There aren't any dangerous monsters in this part of the Woods.
But tomorrow, farther north, we might meet one."

"Are you sure you know what to do to keep us safe? Are you
very sure?"

"Yes, Window, I know what to do," and then Circles added,
"You will see."

The two passed under hundreds and thousands of trees as they
continued to the North – and colorful flowers brightened their
way. The day was pleasant – the conversation was happy. "May I
have another springcookie, please?" asked the Talker, as they
stopped for a brief rest.

Window bent down, and Circles reached one from the pack.
The cookie held the picture of the strange, long-necked animal
from the wild Northlands. "Hey, this looks like a Silkie! I have
always wanted to see a Silkie. Could we go see a Silkie, Window?"

"I don't think so, Circles. I don't know where they are."

In a disappointed voice, Circles answered simply, "Oh."

They hiked on. Window explained how to make springcookies,
and showed Circles the medallion. Circles taught Window which
of the wild berries were safe to eat and the names of the flowers
along the trail. Time and distance passed quickly and as the sky

started to get dark they decided to stop for the night. Circles
picked a spot under the trees and they quickly made a little camp.

As their campfire blazed into the sky, Window got out his
notebook from Grandma and wrote down a few things. Then he
showed Circles the names he had copied from his grandfather's
papers – the men who had been in his grandfather's expedition.
"What are these words, Window?" asked Circles as he pointed
to the first name on the list.
"That is the name 'Captain John R. Near.' He was the
grandson of the man from the Old Countries who first discovered
the Newlands. And, if John R. had a grandson, I wouldn't be
surprised if he was the mysterious traveler who told my uncle
about looking for treasures in the North.
"Do you think he did, Window? Do you think that Captain
Near had a grandson?"
"I don't know, Circles, but if he did, that grandson is probably
off somewhere, right now, having a grand adventure."
"Not an adventure as good as ours, I bet."
Window smiled, and closed his eyes, as he tried to imagine
what that young man might be doing at that moment, wherever
he may be.

+++++++++

[AT THE UNIVERSITY AT NEW LAWS]

*John E. Near stood at the top of the dormitory steps at the
University at New Laws, and looked down into the Center
Yard. The evening sky was still glowing behind the Class
Hall building to his left. On the walkways below, students
hurried from their last hour classes in hopes of getting back
to the cafeteria in time for the end of the supper hour. John
had eaten early and had something else on his mind.*

*On his mind was the meeting he had planned earlier in
the day. He had forgotten all about the History of the South*

World Explorations, the Mathematics of Motion, and the Writing of Persuasive Argument. He didn't care that his laundry needed to be done, or that he was several dollars short of what he needed to buy his mechanical drawing materials. He was thinking of other things.

John took the twelve steps down to the walkway two at a time. He turned to the right, and quickly moved past Landers Hall in the direction of the East Gate. The breeze from the ocean blew his hair, and across his face, as he looked toward the University Hall which, like the other buildings, was built of the pale stone from the quarry across the river. The Bell Tower stood out against the fading sky, standing high above the oak and elm trees at the end of the Yard. Then, glancing up, he noticed that the lights were still on in the Library, which meant that, in his enthusiasm, he had left his room too early for his meeting.

On his left, he passed the main gymnasium. He knew that, inside, the huge ball courts were empty for the night, and decided to step in to spend a few minutes alone as he sometimes did this time of night. He easily pulled open one of the heavy front doors and slipped inside.

The six courts, side by side, stretched from his far left to his far right. They were quiet and nearly dark, lit only by two small lamps on the east wall. The contrast with the daytime was strong, as then, scores of players would be running back and forth, catching and throwing and dodging the dull red colored balls used to play towerball. The slaps of the players shoes on the hardwood floor and the smacks of the balls hitting the endwalls would echo off the far side of the great room, travel high into the arch of the ceiling, and noisily mix together to fill the whole building with continuous sound. Now, however, the room was empty and quiet.

John sat on a sidebench for a moment and listened. The only sound he heard was the soft whirl of a ceiling vent turning as the night breeze spun its fan blades high overhead. The quiet was soothing and made him feel very comfortable, as it always did.

Without thinking about it, he gently whistled a few notes of no song in particular and was surprised to hear how the sound seemed to fill the great hall. He glanced from side to side as if searching to see if anyone had heard him, but he was alone. Then he noticed a new sound – the sound of his own breathing joining that of the overhead fan. He thought to himself, "I love this quiet."

He looked around again, straining to see the far ends of the hall. Then the sound of his breathing reminded him of his other love.

In a few minutes, he would be on the steps beside Rayard Hall, beneath the willow trees, and in the arms of his girlfriend. They had met just a few weeks before, but John knew that they were falling in love. She was always in his thoughts or very near to them. Every night, for the past eight nights, they had met in the quiet dark and held and kissed and talked – the hours with her speeding by like minutes as their hearts blended into one.

Unable to wait any longer, John listened one last time to the quiet around him, and then happily slipped through the doors, and into the now almost dark world outside.

He walked past Wells Hall and toward their meeting spot when his heartbeat suddenly jumped. He could see Julie leaning near the lamp against the side stone wall, the silhouette of her body outlined, her brown hair gently moving in the warm night breeze. The flickering light caught her eyes and lips and her beautiful smile.

Julie stood quietly without moving her body, or moving her eyes from him, as John climbed the steps. Then she slowly reached out to take his hand and pulled him tightly against her. As she closed her eyes, she let out a deep sigh and softly whispered, "Hello, my love."

+++++++++

Window opened his eyes. Circles was quietly staring into the campfire flames. The fire was failing a bit, but they could still see by its light. Circles looked again at the list of the Expedition names.

"Woots don't know how to read, Window, but I wish that I could. Could you teach me to read? I would like that."

"Sure, Circles, I will teach you to read."

"And I could teach you how to write songs and how to rhyme. We Woots are very good at that. How do you like our songs?"

"What songs?"

"The Deeps Woods songs the children sing in the Windlands."

"What do you mean your songs? And how do you know all of those songs, anyway?"

"I mean that the Woots made them all."

"All of them?"

"Well, many of them – a lot of the ones about the Deep Woods and the Northlands, anyway. Some of them were made by other Talkers, too – we all love singing and storytelling and rhyming. Many of them were made in the North when the Woots lived up near there. After the Wars, we moved to this part of the forest with our Talker friends, the Owts."

"Now, as you may know from the stories, Owts never live in one place very long. The Owts even liked to leave the Woods sometimes, which other Talkers rarely did. They would often visit Windlands shepherds who tended flocks just beyond the southern edge of the Woods – to the west of where you live, Window. There wasn't much for the shepherd children to do out on the grasslands, so they enjoyed trading songs and stories with the Owts."

"So, the Owts would bring new Windlands songs back with them to the Woods, and, in the winter, when the shepherd children would return to their homes, they would teach the new songs and stories they had learned to the village children. The songs were one of the very few things that the shepherd children had which the village children did not, so the shepherd children kept it secret where they had gotten the songs. Eventually, after many years, every child in the Windlands prairies knew them – but only the shepherds knew where they had come from."

There it was – a story even Breeze could be proud of! And, it was just wild enough to be true. All those early stories and songs and rhymes came from the Talkers – it was fantastic! The Deep Woods Talkers were a big, big part of life in the Windlands, and no one even knew about it. What a story! What a story to tell the guys back home!

Circles continued. "And here's a new song you have never heard. I made it myself, just a few days ago. I will sing it for you."
The Deep Woods singer stood up and stretched his arms. Then he took a deep breath and opened his mouth. What came out was the sweetest song Window had ever heard. It was a captivating melody, rising and falling in perfect steps, and sung with crystal clarity. It told the story of a young princess in a far-away land. Circles' voice was beautiful – his song was beautiful.
Window listened in amazement, and watched his friend as the final notes of the song sailed across the clearing and up into the trees.
"That was wonderful, Circles. I don't think I could ever make a song like that. I see that you are a Woot of many talents. I hope you will sing again for me sometimes."
"Sure, Window. We can sing as we travel."
"I would like that, Circles."
"So would I, Window. So would I."

Window returned the notebook to his pack. Then he dragged the rest of the wood they had gathered onto the fire and it once again blazed bright and hot. It was so hot, that when he opened up his blanket to sleep for the night, he lay down a bit away from the fire, but still close enough to keep warm. Circles' could sleep anywhere, since his special fur would keep him comfortable, with or without a blanket or a fire, but he came and sat by Window, wanting to be close to him.
"Thanks for letting me come along with you, Window."
"I am glad you are with me, Circles. We will have a fine time."

Circles scooted closer and put his head down on the edge of the blanket. "Window, could we go see the Silkie, too. I would really like that."

Window smiled and took a deep breath. "Maybe, Circles. Maybe we'll go see the Silkie, too."

Circles closed his big round eyes and settled against Window's leg. Window could feel him breathing – a slow, soft, quiet rhythm in time with the forest breeze. Soon Window's breathing matched that of the Talker – soft and gentle and resting. He felt the heat from the fire on his face as he followed his friend's example and closed his eyes, too. Before long they were both asleep – the sky was clear above them – the moon would soon be out. It was a beautiful night on the path through the Deep Woods.

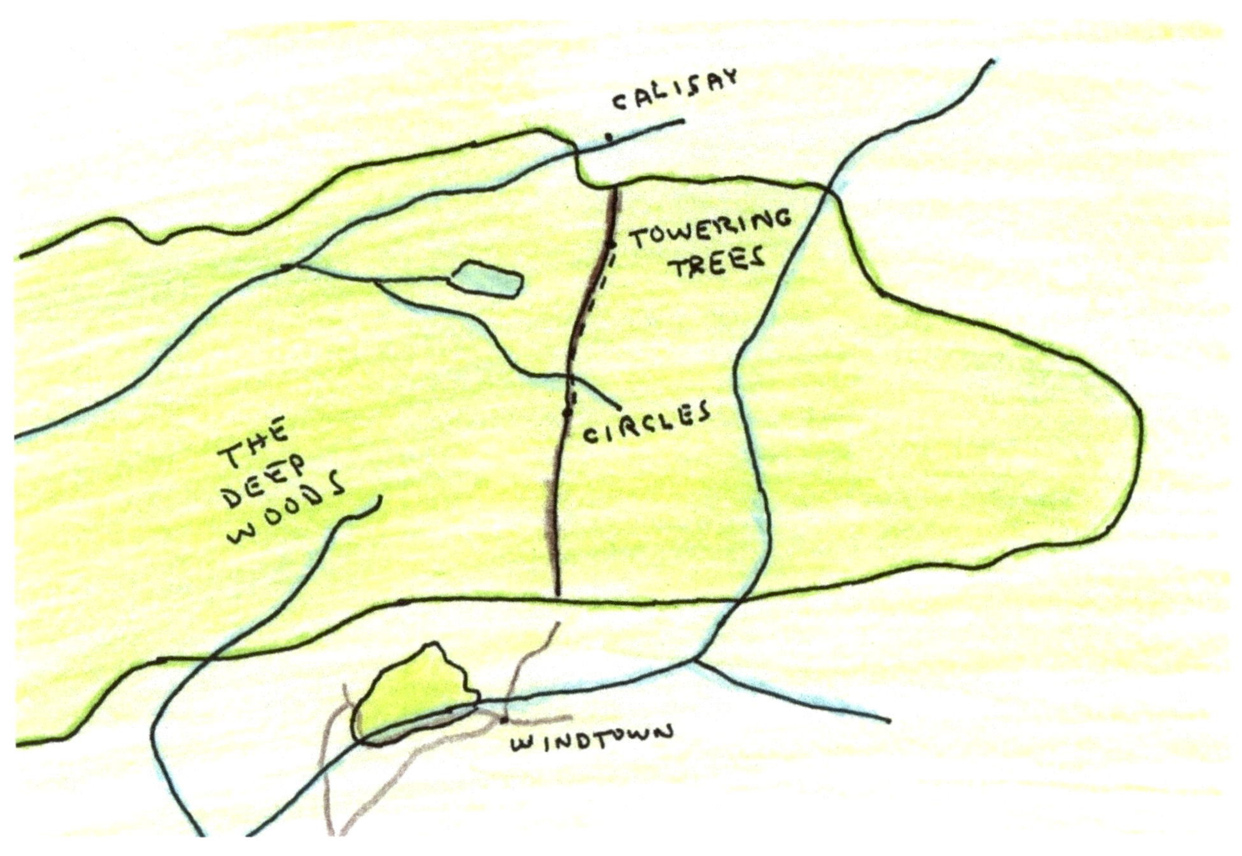

CALISAY
TOWERING TREES
THE DEEP WOODS
CIRCLES
WINDTOWN

CHAPTER FIVE

TO THE TOWERING TREES

"Window, Window, wake up – but don't move." Circles was whispering, and gently poking his sleeping companion.

"Circ..."

"Ssshhh. Don't say anything – and move very slowly. I want you to see something."

"What is it?"

"Ssshhh. Quiet! You'll scare them."

Window opened his eyes. It must have still been the middle of the night – the moon was eerily glowing from behind some clouds. There was a mist in the air that gave everything a frightening look of danger.

Circles was still pushed close to him. About fifteen feet away, their fire had died to a bed of glowing ashes.

"Look over there." Circles nodded toward the trees about twice that far to their right.

Window stiffened in fear. Looking back at him from behind trees and between bushes were glowing yellow eyes – pairs of eyes – unblinking, watching, seemingly attached to no bodies. The eyes were not reflecting light, but each shone with a light of its own.

"Don't move," Circles warned. *"You'll scare them."*

"Scare them?" Window replied as quietly as he could, *"What about us?"*

And then, as Window and Circles lay quietly and watched, out from the trees they came – one by one, in a single row – furry little animals with huge glowing-yellow eyes, walking on their hind feet – and each dragging a small, dead, tree branch behind it!

The line of creatures came right over to the campfire and circled it, just a few feet from the fire-pit. They were the paw-creatures – eight of them – each about two feet high, with dark ragged fur, and horribly long, sharp claws – claws that Window thought could easily slice across his face or cut right through his jacket. Their eyes burned brightly with a look of evil and hate. They gazed straight ahead without a glance to the side as though they were hypnotized.

Window held himself stiff – afraid they would notice him. As they approached, the paw-creatures moved in unison – their feet slowly stepping together in perfect harmony. Even their sickening, raspy breathing was exactly in time with the others.

The animals dragged their sticks in a circle around the fire pit a few times, then stopped and faced the dying ashes. They raised the branches they were dragging and, all at once, tossed the branches into the fire pit. Then they leaned forward toward the fire and blew their breath at its base. The ashes came to life, and within a minute the fire was blazing brightly again – the burning branches crackling and popping as the flames jumped high.

Then the creatures sat back on their hind legs and held their front paws out to the fire. Their claws, glistening in the reflected firelight, looked like sharp knife blades slashing at the fire. Then the creatures began rocking side to side – clicking their claws together in a horrible scene of apparent viciousness.

This scene went on for several minutes. Then the moving back and forth stopped and some of the paw-creatures began humming. One of the creatures looked over toward the two travelers as though he had heard something. Window whispered to Circles as quietly as he had ever whispered in his entire life. *What should we do?*

"Watch this," came the reply.

Circles sat up straight and spoke out loud toward the ring of animals, "Hi, guys."

The creatures' reaction was immediate and dramatic. With piercing squeals of fear, they scampered in all directions into the trees – scrambling as quickly as possible to hide, in what appeared to be complete and absolute fear. Several of them tripped as they ran, and tumbled and spun in their wild escape.

Window was surprised and stunned – having been certain the two of them would be attacked. Circles' reaction was quite different.

He broke out into a loud chattering sound that confused Window completely. Circles flopped back down to the ground and his body shook. He was totally enjoying the moment. Window quickly realized it was a joyous laugh – Circles was uncontrollably laughing.

"Okay, okay. Thanks for telling me what to expect," Window exclaimed sarcastically over Circles' chatter as he let out a deep relaxing breath. "What are those creatures? They look so horrible. Aren't they dangerous?"

"Only if they knock you down while they are trying to run away when you startle them," replied the still-chuckling Woot. "They are really very gentle, and eat mostly fruit and berries and roots – like me."

Window let out a laugh of his own. Circles went on to explain.

"We call them Fire-claws. They love to just sit and enjoy any fire. Since they don't find fires very often, they probably followed you all the way up from your first camp. Sometimes they just dance in the moonlight. All of the Deep Woods Talkers see them from time to time, and we always enjoy a bit of fun at their expense. They will probably be back tonight when their courage returns. They know that a Woot would never hurt them."

"In the old days, some of them would travel with men from the North. Fire-claws can see very well in the dark, so the men would let them accompany them, to help warn of dangerous animals. The paw-creatures aren't Talkers, but they would run away when any monsters came near, so the men would be alerted and could be prepared.

"Yes, the way they ran away, I thought perhaps they learned to do that from the Woots!" kidded Window.

"In the Deep Woods, there are two types of creatures – those who run and those who die," answered Circles, completely seriously. "Especially if you are as colorful as Woots are." Window regretted what he had said.

"Well I'm glad that they are not dangerous. I thought that we were in serious trouble."

"Not this time. Not this time."

Circles was right. In a couple of minutes, the paw-creatures appeared again at the edge of the clearing. Circles waved to them to come back, and one by one, they returned and sat down by the fire. The color in their eyes had lightened a bit, and now the animals looked warm and friendly, instead of fierce.

Window didn't speak to them, but Circles sang the creatures a song. They rocked backed and forth with the song, and Window wished that his camping friends back home could see the sight.

It was a happy song about a Woot and an Owt who were friends, and who went walking together. When the song was over, Circles told their guests, "That's all for tonight – time to go." The Fire-Claws stood up, all bowed together, and quietly went back into the trees.

Window was amazed – his traveling partner had surprised him again. He wondered what other surprises his new companion might have in store for him. He was glad again that Circles had joined him on his trip to the North.

The early morning sun was already beginning to lighten the sky above the trees, so the travelers decided to stay up and not try to sleep any longer. They shared a quick breakfast and soon were headed north once again. Circles thought that it would take five or six days to reach Calisay – as he put it – "If we don't have any trouble."

++++++++

They were now in the center of the Deep Woods – where the most dangerous of the monsters lived. Circles had been through this part of the forest once before and knew that the chances were good that they would encounter more creatures – but this time, creatures who would not run away at the sight of two lone travelers.

Here the trees grew even thicker and closer together. The sky was completely hidden by the heavy leaves and overhanging branches. Dark tendrils of vines hung from the trees and underfoot the path was no longer free of grass and weeds. The air became damp and cold and seemed to wrap itself around Window and slow him down. The tree branches reached farther out into the path and Window felt as if they were trying to grab him as he pushed by them.

Circles walked next to Window and they quietly talked as they went. They hiked on and on – the miles passing beneath their feet. The sun was now overhead but they could not see it. They were deep within the heart of the Woods. They began to notice the bones of animals along the trail – not lying as though the animals had just died there, but strewn about as though they were flung around by whatever killed them.

Still they walked on – carefully listening and watching for anything – but they saw and heard nothing but the gloom of the trees and the sound of their own breathing. Then, in the dark of the afternoon, Circles reached for Window's hand. He didn't say anything, but just squeezed the hand and stopped walking. Window could feel the tenseness in the touch of his friend.

The air was still. Window could hear nothing. Then, from behind them, he heard breathing – deep, hoarse breathing. They slowly turned to look back down the path, and there they saw the source of the terrifying sound – a huge, four-legged monster following them.

Window had never imagined the existence of a creature so enormous. It had the look of a wolf or a creyont, but was many times larger – probably eight feet high – with shaggy fur, a long, pointy snout, and beady eyes – and teeth, scores of short little spikes, neatly fitting together when it's mouth was closed, and

dripping disgustedly when the monster stretched his jaw towards
them.

Window held tightly to Circles hand – they would never be able
to escape it. Circles squeezed Window's hand again and then let
go. "Stay here," he instructed, and boldly walked towards the
waiting creature.

The monster growled loudly and just watched as the little Woot
approached it. Window was too frightened to say or do anything.
Circles' bravery was unlike anything Window had ever seen.

At the edge of the path, between Circles and the monster, was
a large rock – about as tall as Circles. He scrambled up the side of
the rock and stood on top of it. The creature came right up to the
rock and bent down slightly as it thrust its horrifying snout in the
face the young Woot. As Window looked on, he imagined that
Circles' white fur now had a touch of red in it. The monster
sniffed at Circles, snorted loudly, and stretched open its huge
mouth.

Circles stood and directly faced the deadly creature. And then,
inches away from the jaws of the monster, Circles started to sing –
a high, clear melody in a language Window did not recognize. The
monster closed his mouth and backed away from the rock – from
Circles – from the singing. Window watched, again amazed by his
young friend. The monster – the huge savage monster, towering
above Circles – was retreating. Circles continued to sing – the
creature continued to back away. Suddenly it turned and ran –
down the path and out of sight.

Window hurried over to Circles and lifted him down from the
rock. He was shaking a bit as Window hugged him tightly. "I am
so happy that you are alright, Circles. You are a very special
Talker, indeed!"

"I am glad you are alright, too, Window. I would be lonely
without you."

The two travelers held on to each other for another moment
then Window said, "Well, okay, let's get going." They each kept
their other thoughts to themselves, as they turned and once again,
headed to the Northlands.

As they walked, Circles went on to explain about the creature's reaction to his singing. Many of the most dangerous Deep Woods monsters hated to hear singing. They hated it so much that it would drive them away when they heard it. Since they had come to the Deep Woods, the Woots had learned the very best songs to sing to drive away many of the different monsters. It seems that certain pitches and sounds affected each of them a bit differently. The Tarrille they had just encountered disliked "At The End of the Day" the most, so Circles knew that all he had to do was sing that song if they met up with one. Circles admitted he was so frightened that he had forgotten to sing it in Atlandan, and was really glad that the monster didn't like to hear it in Woot either.

And so, Window learned an even greater respect for his fellow traveler. Of course, if a monster attacked quickly, or caught them sleeping, it could still be deadly, but Circles explained that his hearing, and sense of smell, were so good, that he would easily be awakened when all but the quietest monster was nearby.

The next few days on the path, nothing quite so spectacular happened. The travelers passed through the darkest part of the Woods and were pleased when the trees began to thin out a bit. They camped each night and finished up most of the food Window had brought along. They each saved one springcookie for, as Circles put it, "when we really need them."

Circles taught Window more songs to sing as they walked. Window especially enjoyed some nonsense songs Circles taught him and even started to learn one in the Woot language, which was particularly happy sounding.

All one afternoon they had to walk in the rain – a drenching downpour that rolled right off of Circles' special fur. Window got soaked and had to dry all of his clothes by the fire that night. Circles sang a song about summer rain as the fire died down, and Window closed his eyes to sleep.

The next afternoon, they passed what seemed to be a stone-covered path going off to the side of the main path. Circles explained, "The Owts say that there is a lost, abandoned, stone

city in the Woods somewhere near here, but I have never seen it.
I have never been this far north before."

Another time, Window noticed that Circles had no difficulty
handling rocks and sticks and food or anything, and asked how he
could hold on to things so easily. Circles replied, "I can climb
things, too. Look at my hands and my feet."
Circles showed him the palms of his hands and the bottom of
his feet. They were each covered with a rough, but soft, skin that
almost stuck to things that touched it. Circles explained, "I can
easily run across wet rocks without slipping."
"Why would you want to do that?"
"Well, I don't know," and then Circles added with a smile, "but
if we come across any need to run across any wet rocks, I can be
the one to do it. And, who knows, it may come in handy when I
help you look for treasure."
"You may be right, Circles. You just may be right."

Each night as they camped, Window taught Circles more
letters to read. Window wrote all of the Atlandan letters on a
page of his notebook and taught the Woot how to pronounce them.
Circles learned quickly, and so Window next taught him a few
words to read.

Circles wanted to learn to write, too, so Window happily gave
him scripting lessons. Circles had no trouble holding Window's
pencil, and working very slowly, in the firelight, his letters were
really pretty good.

On their fifth day together, while they were stopped for a rest,
Window took out his notebook and was again looking at the list of
names from his Grandfather's expedition.
"What name is this one?" Circles asked, joining him, and
pointing at the second name on the list, trying to read it but
needing help.
"The name is 'Corporal W. Briggs' from a Windlands town
called Woodmine. He was the second in command of the
expedition."

"Tell me about Woodmine, Window. Have you ever been there?"

"When I was very young, my father took our family there to visit his uncle and some cousins. My Dad's uncle was a builder like his brother, my Grandpa Breesian. It took many days by wagon to make the trip. I don't remember much because I was so young. But Woodmine is well known because it is the only place where Beamwood is found – at the edge of the Deep Woods. Beamwood is very strong and beautiful. It is shipped all over the world from the Windcoast. I would like to work with that wood someday."

"Do you think that Corporal Briggs had any grandsons, Window – a grandson who was the traveler in your uncle's story?"

"I don't know, Circles, but I hope to find out someday. Maybe you and I can go there together."

+++++++++

[BACK TO WOODMINE]

Will Briggs was tired. It had been a long three weeks since he and the rest of the crew had left Woodmine with the spring shipment – six hundred of the biggest, straightest, heaviest lumber-trees on the continent. It was enough beamwood to keep the shipbuilders and wood-millers on the Windcoast supplied for months. The logs would become the hardest, most beautiful building beams in the world, and they would be shipped to near and far places as soon as the millers had cut them to size.

Two months before, after the forest crew had ventured once again into the edge of the Deep Woods to harvest the trees, Will had decided that, as he did last year, he would again be a rider. He would join with the rest of the Woodmine riders and make the fifty-mile trip to the coast – but these riders didn't ride horses – they rode the beamwood logs.

The Falls River ride was the only way to transport the massive, beamwood logs to the coast. The river was fairly gentle as it wound under the bridge at Woodmine, so the first part of the trip was easy. But, as soon as the river passed the rocks at Waterdell, things changed quickly. The River took on the speed of a racehorse as it made the long, steep drop to the shallow falls. And the jam only slowed a little, as the river leveled out and started to widen beyond the last curve.

Years ago, the twenty miles of rocky shallows that extended to the coast beyond the falls had been bypassed by the Falls Canal. So now, the logs were sent by river as far as the falls, and then through the canal the rest of the way. But, getting more than a million pounds of quickly moving wood to go where they wanted it to go was not an easy task for the riders. The jam had to be directed towards the canal, and caught on the levee near its entrance. Any wood that went beyond the levee to the falls would be lost on the rocks beyond, and would be unable to be retrieved.

And this time, unlike the shipment last autumn, the beamwood decided to make things a bit more interesting. The lead strap of lumber got caught on a sidebar and ripped away from the main pack. Of course, the pack didn't slow down just because it was coming apart. Will had to jump from the twisting jam to keep this trip from being his last.
But the riders were lucky and the main jam was saved. The wood had been delivered – well most of it – and now the riders were returning home. Will's flatboat rounded the last river turn before the town. He finally saw the Woodmine Bridge, and knew that his journey was almost over.

Return day was a time for a holiday in Woodmine. On the bank, and on the docks at the landing, just beyond the bridge, he could see the waiting townspeople. Soon they would carry each of the log-crew riders to the park for a celebration. The riders would be seated at the massive beamwood table under the trees, and the festivities would begin – games, songs, dancing – well, except no dancing for the exhausted guests of honor – and most of all, the bread and pies.

The day that the riders left on their journey, the town's women, and remaining men, started preparing for their return. They gathered the ingredients for the bread and pies they would bake. In Woodmine, everyone loved bread – all kinds of bread. Each family in town had their specialty, and so a different kind of bread was baked by every family.

There was twisted bread, round bread, flat bread, square bread, tall bread, long bread, and bread with jam – all kinds of jam – bread with meat – all kinds of meat – bread with butter, bread with salt, bread with sugar – hard crusty bread, soft chewy bread, bread with lumps, bread with bumps, and bread with holes – bread with cheese, bread with seeds, bread with candy baked inside – bread with dried fruit, bread with berries, bread with...

And, the people of Woodmine also loved pies – lots of pies – all kinds of pies – pies with...

Will's wife, Loren, was the first to reach him. She pinned the flower ring to his shirt and welcomed him with a kiss – then another. The Briggs family aunts, uncles, and cousins all cheered, and everyone sang the traditional welcome home song, "On The Canal."

Will Briggs was tired – but he didn't mind. As he sat with the others from the crew, he enjoyed the happiness of the townspeople spread out before him. It had been a very good trip. And now, it was a grand ending to a grand day. He was home. He was safe. He was tired. Will Briggs would sleep soundly tonight.

+++++++++

Window closed his notebook and put it away. "I hope that we can find some food in Calisay. I am getting tired of dried meat and berries." Then, remembering that he didn't have any Freeland coins, he added, "Did you bring any money?"

Circles answered immediately, "I am in charge of running on wet rocks – you are in charge of money."

They both laughed and started up the path again.

The miles continued to pass by them. The thick, dark, trees of the deepest Woods were replaced by taller, lighter, trees that let more sunlight through. The weather was very pleasant and the path was easy. They couldn't be certain how much farther they had to go to reach Calisay, but felt that they must be within a couple of days of the edge of the Woods.

Late in the afternoon, as the travelers had stopped for another meal, they were confronted by another Deep Woods animal. It was a large, wild, ground rodent of some kind – about three feet long with four short, thick legs. Its two front teeth were large and dangerous looking. As he had done before, Circles walked right up to the snarling creature and started singing. To Window's surprise, the creature listened for a moment, then jumped at Circles with its mouth wide and tried to bite his leg. Circles ran back toward Window as the creature chased him.

Window quickly grabbed a short stick from the ground and hit the creature a few times, trying to keep it away. That only made it angry. There was nothing else to do but run. "Quick, up the trail!" shouted Window, trying to hold off the creature as Circles got away.

Window grabbed his pack and took another swing at the animal with his stick. The massive rodent grabbed the stick in its mouth and pulled it from Window's hand. Window gave a kick towards the creature, and turned and ran after Circles. The animal chased after him, barking and snapping its teeth at Window's legs. He and Circles both ran up the path as fast as they could – which for Circles wasn't very fast.

Fortunately, the creature wasn't built for running. With its short legs moving beneath it, it looked more like a fast waddle

than a run. Window and Circles quickly outdistanced the creature
– but it wouldn't give up. They would run ahead and stop to look
back – the creature would still be coming after them. It wouldn't
give up its chase. They were running and laughing at the same
time. Circles was getting pretty tired.

Finally, Window quickly opened his pack and reached for a
strip of dried meat. He threw it back towards the rodent and it
bounced on the path in front of it. The advancing animal stopped,
sniffed the meat, picked it up in its teeth, and trotted off, back
down the trail.

Window turned toward Circles with a questioning look on his
face as if to say, "What happened – wrong song?"

Still trying to catch his breath, Circles answered with a smile,
"Well, it doesn't always work. It doesn't always work." Then he
added, "I guess that some animals like my singing!"

Window kidded him about it the rest of the afternoon.

++++++++

The traveler's sixth day together started with more beautiful,
spring weather – warm and clear. They sang as they went,
enjoying each other's company, and looking forward to reaching
the Northlands. Circles talked about the kites he had heard about
and Window told him all about the different types of kites back
home in Windtown, and how they were made. Window sometimes
thought of the difficulties they might have with the Northlanders,
but would quickly put those thoughts out of his mind.

Late in the morning of that day, the travelers came upon an
area of the Deep Woods where the trees were the tallest they had
seen – giant trees that towered high above them. And, these trees
had few branches near the ground. Most of their branches were
high, near their tops. They had small, thin, pale green, flat-circle
leaves that let light shine through them. The path became wider
in places and it often seemed as though the travelers were
walking through giant rooms with majestically high ceilings of
light-green colored glass. The mid-day sunlight on the high, pale
colored leaves gave the effect of bright windows high above.

Below, the path was smooth, and sprinkled with the same small, light-green leaves.

As they entered one of these wide, room-like places on the path, under the tallest trees yet, the effect of the sunlight shining through the ceiling of leaves above was stunningly beautiful. They started through this room under the trees, when suddenly Circles stopped, and took Window's hand to keep him from going on.

"Someone is near, Window – a human." Circles listened carefully and sniffed the air as his eyes scanned ahead.

"It is a human female."

Window quickly glanced from side to side but couldn't see anyone.

"I see her, Window. There she is, off to the side, near the end of this open space."

Window followed the tip of Circles' finger and could just make out a slight figure standing a couple of hundred feet away, beneath the trees, at the far end of the wide room.

"Is she alone?" asked Window.

"Yes, she is the only one."

They slowly walked forward. The figure moved slightly towards the trees nearest her. Window and Circles continued across the leaf-strewn floor until they had covered about half of the distance across the room.

From there, Window could see the young woman in the shining, mid-day light. She was somewhat tall and rather slender – maybe twenty or so. Her hair was long, straight, and the lightest blonde. She was wearing a very short skirt of wide, vertical stripes – stripes that had once been light blue and white, but the skirt was now so dirty that the white stripes looked almost grey.

Above her waist, the girl wore only a sheer underblouse that left her shoulders and arms completely uncovered and the rest of her upper body seemingly so. Her legs were bare, except for what appeared to be a chain or bracelet on one ankle, and she was wearing no shoes. It looked as though pieces of cloth were wrapped around each of her feet and tied there.

As Window and Circles walked closer toward the girl, she turned as if she were about to run away.

Window stopped approaching her, and held out his hand for Circles to do the same.

"Hello," Window called out to her. She didn't move.

"Wae nasenne no kae, fentae," Circles spoke to the girl in Freelandan. Window had never studied Freelandan and could not understand what Circles had said.

The girl seemed to understand, though. She didn't answer, but she moved away from the trees and stood facing them with her arms straight down at her sides. Her hair briefly fluttered in the breeze. It looked as if she was waiting for them to say more.

"Why don't you see if you can get closer and talk to her, Circles," Window suggested. "Here, maybe she would like this." Window dropped his pack to the ground and dug out his extra overshirt. He loudly tried to shake the wrinkles from it and then handed the shirt to Circles.

As Circles slowly walked toward the girl, he held out the shirt so she could see what it was. *"Sae nas trentae, saelle akanesse."*

The girl waited, without moving, until Circles reached her, then bowed her head slightly. She held out both of her hands for the shirt. *"Wae tou centette arontae,"* she spoke as Circles placed the shirt across her open hands. Her voice was calm and clear.

Circles continued, *"Sae na meree Circles."*

"Sae na meree Panni," came her reply, as her face relaxed a bit.

She held out the shirt by its sleeves, wrapped it around her chest, and tied the sleeves behind her back – keeping her arms and shoulders uncovered. The grey color of the shirt almost matched the once-white stripes of her skirt.

She was a beautiful young woman. Her eyes were bright blue, and her face and lips were smooth and gentle. Her hair hung straight down to the middle of her back, except, well, not all of it was so straight at the moment. It was tangled and dirty. Her face, arms, and legs were hidden beneath grime, as though she had slept on the open ground. Wherever she came from, she must have left in a hurry, as she had no overshirt or jacket or shoes.

Window was very curious about where she was from and what had happened to her, but realized that now was not the time to ask those questions.

The girl again bowed slightly to Circles. *"Mae sette wille fondaerone. Wae meree daselle?"*
Circles replied, *"Wae meree, Window."*
"Lisone maesae, Window," she called to him. *"Se tae ontelle sanretee. Tae callarae fentosaelle."*
"Hey, anytime," Window called back, not understanding a bit of what she had said.
Circles joined in, "Her name is Panni, and I'm sure she is hungry, Window. Let's have lunch."
"Okay, sure. Bring her over. I'll cook."

Window spread his blanket on the flat, smooth ground. Somewhat reluctantly, Panni followed Circles over to him. Window watched her as they approached. She was striking in her beauty.
Panni knelt on the blanket, and sat back with her legs beneath her. Then she held out both her hands to Window, palms up. He wasn't sure what to do in response, so he simply, lightly, touched her palms. Panni slightly moved her hands as if she were going to pull away from Window's touch, but she held them there until he removed his.
"Mae wen aeselle, mae hartasette," she addressed him quietly and respectfully. As she spoke, she first gazed straight into his eyes, then looked down, then again sent her eyes straight into his. *"Oen trene sae meree, Window."* Her voice was soft and sweet – her words spoken as though she was choosing them carefully.
Window only guessed what she was talking about and replied. "I am happy to meet you, Panni. I hope you will join us for lunch. We are having the finest things I can dig from the bottom of my pack."
Circles chuckled a bit, and then, so did Panni. Along with her quiet laugh came her first smile – a gentle smile of warmth and acceptance. She was already becoming comfortable with them.
Window emptied all of the remaining food from his pack and

laid it out in front of Panni on the blanket. There was a small tin of redberries, one piece of dried meat, one apple, and the last two springcookies. Then, realizing that she was probably thirsty, Window offered her the water tin – which had been freshly filled from a stream just a few hours before.

Panni started to reach for the tin quickly, then stopped herself, and carefully took it from his hand. Closing her eyes, she drank from it slowly, and repeatedly.

After she finished her drink, Panni gently touched each of the food items, and chose both the apple and a springcookie – the one with a kite picture on it. Window chose the dried meat stick, and Circles chose the berries. Window used his boot knife to slice the apple for the hungry girl. She watched with great interest as he let each slice fall onto the lid from the berry tin that he used as a small plate for her.

As they ate, Circles and the girl spoke quietly in Freelandan. Panni ate slowly and carefully as though every bite had to be done perfectly. Window just watched and listened.

And, as Panni spoke to Circles, she would occasionally look towards Window, as if to politely include him in the conversation, although Circles had told her that Window could not understand what they were saying.

Window didn't mind. He was enjoying the beautiful day, this beautiful place, and the quiet company of his lunch companions. He briefly closed his eyes and just listened to the rhythm and flow of the Freelandan conversation. It had a very relaxing sound – almost a quiet melody of words that he enjoyed just listening to.

After Panni finished her apple slices, she carefully examined the springcookie. *"Sen nae tou setenne aeresse,"* she spoke with a smile, and pointed to the sky. Then she slowly ate the cookie, obviously enjoying every bite. Window thought that his Grandma would be happy that someone from the wilds appreciated her baking so much.

Circles turned to Window, "May she come with us, Window? She told me she has run away from her home and has nothing."

"What will she do with us, Circles? What will we do with her?"

"We can take her to Calisay, and get her some clothes and food. After that, I do not know."

Then, as if trying to convince Window to let her come along, Circles added, "Maybe she is good at finding treasure."

Panni seemed to know what Circles was asking. She looked calmly and confidently, straight into Window's eyes, waiting for his answer. He had realized the possibility of her coming with them as soon as he and Circles had first seen her. They certainly would not leave her alone in the Woods. She didn't have to wait very long for his answer.

Window smiled at her, "We would love to have you come with us, Panni."

Circles explained, "*Non lesae mellelise.*"

Panni returned Window's smile broadly, leaned forward, and kissed his cheek.

"*Sae maetille, Window,*" she added to the kiss.

Window picked up the last one of the springcookies and returned it to his pack. "I hope we get to Calisay, soon," he mentioned to Circles, and then added, "and I hope you brought some money for food."

"Money is your responsibility, remember Window? I am in charge of running on wet rocks."

They both laughed as Panni looked inquisitively at them. Window wondered to himself how they were going to get food, and clothes for Panni, in the Northlands city. At the moment, he had no idea what would happen to them there.

Window rolled up the blanket and tied it to the top of his pack with the closing straps. "Well, let's get started. Let's go to Calisay!"

"Okay, Window," agreed Circles. "Let's go."

"*Okay, Let's go,*" Panni repeated as best she could.

The three unlikely travelers turned to the North. They walked together, towards the opening at the end of the light-filled room beneath the towering trees.

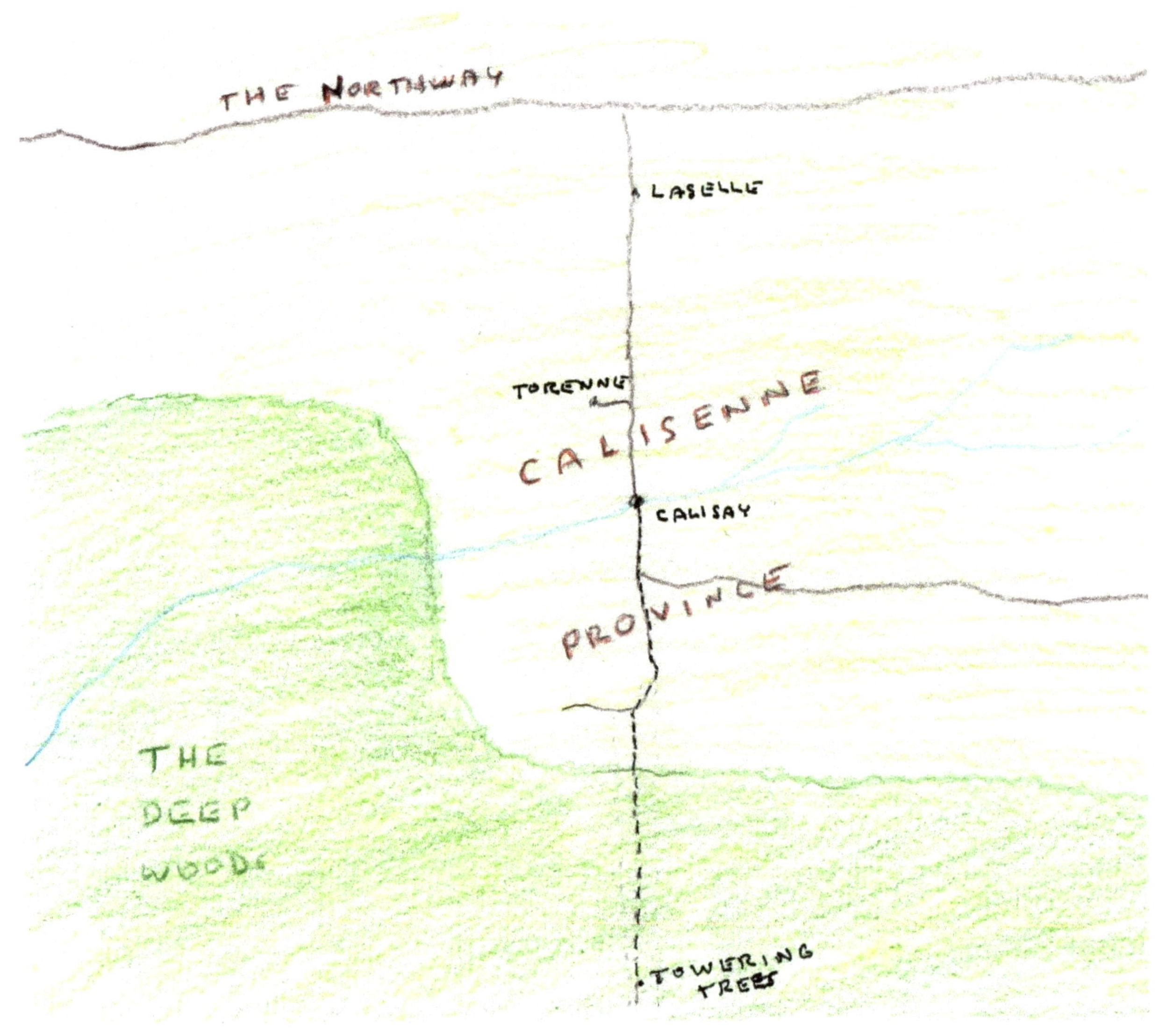

THE NORTHWAY
LASELLE
TORENNE
CALISENNE
CALISAY
PROVINCE
THE DEEP WOODS
TOWERING TREES

CHAPTER SIX

ON TO CALISAY

The three travelers walked side by side by side beneath the trees up the path to the Northlands. Most of the time, Window just listened as Circles and Panni talked to each other in Freelandan. Sometimes they would laugh about something – once Panni seemed to get tears in her eyes and talked very quietly. Then they walked on for a while without conversation.

After an hour or so, Panni seemed to cheer up and even sang a soft little melody to herself. Twice, she spoke to Window. Once she pointed out a beautiful, blue, feather-bird high in a tree overhead, and once, she offered him a few of the handful of bell-berries she picked after Circles told her they were safe to eat. Window noticed that Panni was walking with some difficulty, trying to step rather carefully.

They came to a wide, slow-moving stream and decided to stop for a while. Window filled the water tin, and the other two rested on the bank.

Panni sat quietly – straight and tall – with a slight smile on her face and a calm look in her eyes. The midday sun peeked through the trees and shone on her face, and brought it to life, even under the dirt that covered it.

Window sat down next to Circles and, as they rested, Circles explained to Window all that Panni had told him about how she came to be as she was, alone in the Woods.

Her name was Pantine Tresette. She was from a poor village in the Northlands region of Traepellen, near the edge of the Deep Woods, many miles to the southeast of Calisay. Traepelle was one of the many now-independent areas in the North that were once part of the Northlands Kingdom. She had been taken from her family several years before by the local ruling nobles and forced to live with other women-servants in a castle that was damaged in the Northern Wars and abandoned by its owners.

Her usual servant duties were cooking and tending the gardens, but then, a year ago, the castle-lord chose her to be trained as a dancer for the court of the ruling noblemen of the area. She had no choice, and was taken from her domestic-servants room and moved to a section of the castle where she lived with the other dancers. She was not yet considered old enough to perform with the others, but was forced to practice with them, dancing for hours every day – and was also taught strict behaviors of dress, conversation, and deportment.

When she reached her twentieth birthday, Panni was to be required to join with the other dancers, performing in the court of the fief-owner. She would be expected to entertain the self-proclaimed noblemen and their guests, serve them, and pay them the strictest attentions – and her twentieth birthday was in two days.

Panni hated her forced servitude, and would not accept her future of performing for the nobles. She was determined to escape before her birthday. Three days ago, late at night, she climbed through a high chamber window, wearing only her night skirt and blouse, and lowered herself down vines to her freedom. To discourage escape, the women in her part of the castle were not allowed shoes. So as she fled, barefoot, through the forest, her feet had become badly scraped and cut. Eventually, to help protect them, she tore her sleeping blouse in half and tied the pieces around her feet, but that had done little good.

Panni could not go back to her family – she would be discovered and returned to the castle, and her family would be punished. So she could only run away. She had no possessions – only a jeweled bracelet, welded around her ankle. It identified her as belonging to the servant class, and as being the property of the noblemen.

If her ankle band was seen by someone who was a member of any of the various ruling families and classes in the North, she would be held, and returned to her owner. And she wanted only to be free – to decide for herself how she would live – and, someday, to return to her family.

"And, Window," Circles explained to his friend. "Panni's name, 'Tresette', is the Freelandan word for 'heart.'"

Window looked over at the beautiful, young woman. "I wonder what hers is like," he thought to himself.

As Window listened to Panni's story, he knew he wanted to help the Northlands girl, but had no idea how he possibly could. Well, there was one small thing he could immediately do for her.

Window dug into one of the little pockets on the inside of his pack and retrieved a small, soft, cloth that was wrapped around a bar of flower-soap. His Grandma had added soap for him at the last minute, thinking that Window would enjoy clean hands and face once in a while on his journey.

Panni's bright eyes became even brighter as she excitedly, but politely, took the soap. She thanked Window twice, and waded in the knee-deep water to a large, flat-topped rock that stuck up slightly from the middle of the stream. She sat on the rock, carefully folded Window's shirt and her underblouse and placed them neatly beside her on the rock. Then she dipped the soap and washcloth in the water, and cleaned herself.

She washed her face, neck, and shoulders first, gently, taking time and care. Then she covered her arms in lather and slowly caressed them with the cloth. Next, she gently soaped her back and upper body, rinsing with the cloth as she finished each part. Even though the water was somewhat cold, Panni didn't mind.

She seemed to enjoy every moment as the dirt of her escape washed from her. It was as if she was washing her past and her servitude away.

Finally, lifting her short skirt out of the way, she cleaned her legs and feet – all slowly and carefully, still taking time as she gently covered them with the bubbles and lather. Window offered his small towel for her to dry herself, but she declined with a shake of her head, and let the sun dry her, as she pulled her legs onto the rock and closed her eyes. Washing her hair would have to wait – until when, Window could not guess.

Although she did not mention them or complain, Panni's feet were obviously very sore from the cuts and bruises they had sustained in the woods. Window had no medicine or bandages to offer her. Those were two things that Grandma had not thought of including in his pack. He tried to think of a way to make her some shoes from his blanket, but Grandma had also not sent any needle or thread with him.

When Panni finished drying in the sun, Window had another surprise for her – a small hair-comb Grandma had included with the soap. He threw it out to her and Panni smiled broadly when she caught it. Then she spent many happy minutes combing and straightening her beautifully long hair. Finally, she succeeded in untangling it and let it flow freely over her shoulders – except for a large section in the back that she braided. She tied the end of the braid with a long thread that Window retrieved for her from the frayed edge of his blanket when she returned from the rock.

"Senne kae matinelle lasae," she exclaimed proudly as she had finished her grooming. *"Lae masee, Window?"* She smiled at him and made a little bow toward Circles.

"You look very nice, Panni," Window responded. It made him happy that she obviously felt better being somewhat clean. He spoke to her, knowing that she could not understand most of what he was saying. "I hope we can soon find you some new clothes. Have you ever been to Calisay?"

Then Window remembered what was in his pocket. "Have you ever seen this before?" He held out the medallion to Panni. She took it and rubbed her fingers over it, examining it carefully.

Without any comment, she handed it back with a smile, but no indication that she knew where it was from. He held it for a while before returning it to his pocket, as they resumed their journey to the North.

That night they camped next to a small hillside along the edge of the path. Circles had found some bell-berries that he offered to the others for supper, while he dug up a bangle-root for himself.

Later, by the fire, Window used his boot knife and cut the large top flap from his pack. He cut the flap into two pieces – to be made into a pair of shoes for Panni. She stood on the pieces as he used his pencil to outline her feet on the canvas.

Then Window cut a wide strip from one end of his blanket and used the cloth to make several layers of padding that would be placed inside the shoes. Next, he cut long, narrow strips of cloth, and used the strips to go through holes he made in the edge of the shoes. Panni sat in front of him as he placed the padding and shoes around her feet. Pulling up the sides of the material with the strips, and tying them across her feet, and around her ankles, gave Panni the shoes she so badly needed.

"Sil no sae collessa, kalenne!" Panni thanked him. She walked around the campsite several times, trying the shoes out, still stepping carefully, but obviously with much less difficulty. Then she sat, admiring her feet in the firelight.

Finally, Window used one of the strips of cloth he had cut, to pull the top of his pack shut. There weren't too many things left in the pack, but he especially wanted to keep his notebook protected as best he could.

It was a happy evening for all of them. As they sat around the fire, Circles sang, then Panni sang, then she taught Circles a song and they both sang together. She had never heard Atlandan before, but had heard a bit of a couple of languages from the Deep Woods Talkers. Apparently, there were Talkers who sometimes passed through sections of the North and visited with the humans there.

Window gave Panni the blanket to sleep under. She had not slept much the last three nights – without a blanket or jacket she had been exceedingly cold and lay on the ground shivering most of each night she was alone in the Woods.

Panni lay down close to the fire and pulled the blanket around her. She would have a warm and pleasant night tonight. Circles pushed up against her to help keep her even warmer. She fell asleep almost immediately and Circles joined her.

Window watched them lying by the fire, the flames lighting their faces – Panni's smooth skin contrasted by Circle's soft, furry face, gently moving in the slight evening breeze. Window was glad to have them to share his adventure. He already felt a closeness to both of them – a closeness he felt would never leave him.

Window opened his notebook and wrote for a while. He hoped that Grandma would enjoy reading the account of his adventures – then he wondered when he might ever get home. His planned two-week journey was probably going to be much longer.

Window turned the notebook to the page of his Grandfather's expedition members. He glanced down some of the names on the list: Oldsmith, Kensing, Rails, Revell, Lucette, Gravand... Maybe Gravand was the one with the treasure-hunting grandson. Maybe his grandson was out searching for more treasure right at this moment.

+++++++++

[UP THE WINDCOAST ROAD]

Rell Gravand stopped at the corner. Or, I guess you could say, he started at the corner. In any event, he was there – at the signpost that marked the beginning of another long trip up the Windcoast. He leaned against the post and relaxed.

Above his head were nailed two wooden signboards, each bearing the name of a destination, and each pointed on the end like an arrow. One arrow pointed to the southeast, down the New South Road to his hometown of Union, and one arrow pointed north, up the Coast Road.

Three years before, he had thought that maybe it would be fun – start at the corner of New South Road and walk north, the entire length of the Coast Road – through Coastown and all the way to Treetop. Now, this would be the fourth time he had made the journey.

He would start early tomorrow morning. It would take about three weeks, but he didn't care. He loved the walk and the people he met along the way. Tonight, he would stay at the South Road Inn. Tomorrow he would make his way up the coast.

He would pass King's Straight Road, where he would see the oldest of the giant Windlands windmills. From there, on up the coast, the road would pass through the little sea towns of Nickelle and Newgarden, and he would see the lighthouse at Candalenne. Then he would reach the university city of New Laws, and go on past Wire and Redhall and Book's End before getting to the great harbor at Coastown.

Beyond Coastown, the road continued on through Market and Brickyard and, farther up the coast to Windport. Finally, he would pass the shipping docks at the end of the Falls Canal, the little port of Ship's Harbor, and reach Treetop – the northernmost settlement on the Windcoast. And, all along the way, he would meet new people and visit with them. That was his favorite part of the trip.

Two years ago, as he crossed the Midlands River at Book's End, he met a young woman painting the bridge – well, not the bridge itself, but a picture of the bridge. She was sitting in the shade, on the south side of the bridge, and was just finishing a beautiful painting of blues and whites and browns that perfectly displayed the structure. Well, actually, her painting made the old bridge look much better than it really did.

Last year, as he passed the harbor at Coastown, he discovered a woman who was just standing on one of the port docks, staring out to sea. He was going to ask her what it was that she was looking for, but she seemed so lost in her search of the horizon, that he decided not to disturb her.

On each of his trips, he had met scores of interesting people to talk to. This year, who knows whom he might meet? – perhaps a fearless knight or a runaway princess, or, more likely, a couple of fishermen displaying their day's catch at a seaside market. It didn't matter to him. He would have a great time.

Rell Gravand looked behind him, down the Coast Road to the south – towards Summerland. Maybe next year he would go that way. He had heard the fabulous stories of the wealthy people who lived there – their wonderful mansions and beautiful grounds. But, that was next year. This year, he was headed in the other direction.
He rapped on the signpost for good luck and looked out into the ocean. A warm sea breeze brushed his face. It was a beautiful night tonight, and tomorrow he would be on his way.

+++++++++

Window closed his notebook and put it away. He pulled the last of the firewood onto the fire and looked again at his new friends. Then he sat down, leaned against a tree, and closed his eyes. It was another clear night in the Deep Woods.

The early morning sun woke the three travelers. Panni's eyes were still sleepy, but she happily folded the blanket as they prepared to start again for the North. She combed her hair and, having no pockets of her own, slid the comb into the little pocket on the outside of Window's pack. Her constant smiles told the other two that she was thrilled to be free of her servitude, and to have found friends, after her three terrible nights and days alone in the Woods.

There was no food left in the pack except one springcookie, so they each had a quick drink of water, and began walking. Panni was sure that they were very close to the edge of the Woods. She had entered the forest to the east of where they were now, and had not gone too far in toward the interior, having mostly traveled to the west.

The Deep Woods path continued to be straight and even, with no sign of any dangers for the travelers. Window was glad about that, but thought, "I guess we will soon be trading the dangers of the Woods for dangers of the North." He worried about what they would encounter when they left the forest. He couldn't speak Freelandan, and they had no idea how the Northlanders would react to a Deep Woods Woot and an escaped bound-servant girl.

Then, after several hours of walking, they came upon a set of huge tracks that crossed the trail. The tracks were of an animal with massive paws – paws almost two feet across. On both sides of the trail, where the creature had pushed its way through the woods, a wide strip of grass and bushes was completely destroyed, and even small trees had been broken and mashed beneath its feet.

Panni didn't know what animal the tracks were from, but Circles thought they had to be those of a Brarrie, a huge Deep Woods creature that was known to the Talkers. Brarries were also Talkers, but they never spoke much. They preferred to remain quiet and just let others do the talking. Circles said they were extremely large and powerful, and could be dangerous, but would not attack unless they were made angry.

"If we meet any Brarries, I'll be very polite," promised Window. Circles explained about the animal to Panni, and she nodded in agreement. Window was thinking that maybe this was one Deep Woods danger that he would be happy to trade for a smaller danger outside of the Woods. They continued on their way north.

By the middle of the afternoon, as Window looked up the path, he could see the bright blue of the sky peeking through the trees, not above them, but directly ahead. The end of the Deep Woods path was in sight!

They hurried the last quarter mile as the path continued right up to the edge of the Woods – but not completely out of the trees. They pushed past the last few branches, and from beneath the trees, and out into an open area of grass. Window had made it through the Deep Woods and to the Northlands! He had done it! "I guess that now I can be in somebody's story," he thought to himself. "I have done more than walk to the river!"

Window looked up above at the broad blue sky. "Welcome to the Northlands," he offered to his companions. Smiling happily, Panni hugged both him and Circles. Circles replied, "I am happy to be here – very happy to be here." He spun around, and his fur flew out from his arms and body.

Window looked back to the Woods. The entrance to the path was completely hidden just as it was on its southern end. Unless he marked the location of the path somehow, he would never be able to find it for the journey back home. He certainly did not want to have to go completely around the eastern edge of the Deep Woods to get back to the south, as Breeze's mysterious traveler had been forced to do.

Several hundred feet from the edge of the Woods, alone in the grassy open, were two, tall oak trees, growing close together. Window thought that he would be able to recognize those trees again if he was searching along the edge of the Woods. To be sure, he walked to the trees, took his knife, and sliced three small diagonal stripes in the bark of one of them. Then he added a star in the center of the stripes – well, it was supposed to be a star – just like on his medallion. Maybe today, he would find out where the medallion came from.

Then they were on their way! Calisay awaited the three travelers – kites, towers, and many unknowns. It was a beautiful spring day in the Northlands. The sky was clear and the sun was warm – another perfect day for an adventure

According to Grandpa's map, to reach Calisay, they needed only to continue straight north. That would be the easy part. Window remained greatly concerned about how the Northlanders would greet the three of them, and how they would get food with only the few Windlands coins he had brought from his grandparent's house.

They continued their journey to the north, across rolling hills of tall grass and scattered groups of trees, many of types Window did not recognize. And, while they walked, scattered groups of birds soared above them, and, as with the trees, Window could not identify many of them. It was as though they were in an almost entirely different world from the one in the south – and they were.

Panni explained to Circles that, after the Wars, the Northlands Kingdom collapsed and lost all contact with Freeland and the other Old Countries. The Northlands deteriorated into a small, isolated world of its own. Literature, education, science, and the arts all regressed terribly, and the lands were now, perhaps, only as advanced as the Old Countries had been several hundred years before.

The part of the Northlands where they were now, and where the city of Calisay was located, was called the Calisenne Province. Outside of the city, just as in the Province of Traepellen, where Panni was from, Calisenne was separated into hundreds of small estates ruled by landowners, who kept much of the lower class bound as laborers and serfs. These estate nobles controlled the lives of almost all of the local farmers and traders, and taxed them heavily.

Panni had never been to Calisay, but knew that to reach the city, they would have to pass though many such areas. Calisay itself, she thought, was large and wild, only under partial control of a self-proclaimed ruling prince. He was Prince Martellan, a descendent of a nephew of the former king. Few people respected his authority, so he used his soldiers to attempt to control the population. The soldiers were cruel and indiscriminant. The Prince was widely hated by the Calisay commoners, who did their best to live their lives and take care of their families in spite of his domination.

After a few hours of walking over gently rolling hills, accompanied by a pleasant breeze, the travelers saw their first sign of civilization. Circles pointed excitedly. "Look! There's a road up ahead! And beyond those trees it turns to the north!"

Window checked his grandfather's map. It was the road they wanted – the road to Calisay! Then he remembered the children's rhyme "All Roads Lead To The King". He thought about singing a few verses, but changed his mind. Being in the Northlands was a lot different than singing about it.

The travelers reached the road, and followed it as it wound though the Calisenne Province countryside, passing scattered woodlands, a few small, poor-looking farmhouses, and poorer-looking fields of wheat and clover. They saw a fenced-in field of a dozen or so very thin cattle, and another that held a small flock of dirty, matted sheep.

After several miles, the travelers passed a small spring-apple orchard and decided that it was time for lunch. Window held Circles up to reach three of the bright green fruit. The apples were not quite ripe yet, but they ate them anyway as they walked along, hoping they would not encounter anyone.

As they continued along the road to Calisay, deep white clouds slowly gathered across the wide sky. Then, when they stopped for a rest, Panni lay on her back, on a slight hillside, and looked up at the mountains of clouds overhead.

"Lae renne tallofenzae," she said to Circles, as she pointed up at a towering formation of billowing white above them.

"Oh randenen see kefrae," replied the Woot. Panni grinned and closed her eyes, the midday sun warming her face as she rested.

Circles turned to Window. "Panni sees her future in the clouds, Window – running free on a sunlit hill."

"I hope so, Circles, I hope so."

The three travelers kept steadily on their way up the road to the North, Window remaining quiet, Circles and Panni sometimes talking, sometimes singing. Circles tried to teach Panni "Back To Calisay" in Atlandan, but was not very successful.

They walked for several hours without incident. Panni's new shoes, and the flat dirt of the road, made the trip easy on the bottoms of her feet. The road was not rough, mud-rutted dirt, but was packed and smooth, and finished on the edges.

Window wondered to Circles why the road would be in such good condition. Circles had an answer to that question. Panni had told him about a large clan of Northlanders who kept the roads in repair. They were simply called the Builders.

The Builders worked on the roads in the Calisenne lands all through the province. They had no permanent homes but lived in large wooden, covered wagons, and continuously traveled the roads, repairing and expanding them. When they repaired roads in one of the estates, the nobles would pay them in food and clothing. The Builders spent their entire lives working on the roadways of Calisenne. Because of them, the roads were one of the few things in the Northlands that were kept in good condition.

The travelers met no Builders, or anyone else, as they went on – just a few field rabbits and a sleeping grass hen. Then, as they were passing through a slightly wooded area, Circles heard something.

"Quick, someone is coming," he warned suddenly. Circles left the road and motioned for the others to follow. Window pulled Panni by the arm as the three of them ducked behind a group of big bushes off to one side. From there, Window could hear the clopping of horses, and soon, through the bushes, they could see two horsemen approaching up the road.

The riders appeared to be soldiers of some type. They were wearing light grey armor on their chests, arms, and legs, and carried long swords from their belts. Their horses carried light armor as well. The rider's clothes were colored brightly in red and white and they seemed to be going somewhere in a hurry.

As the soldiers passed closely by the hidden travelers, Window could see the military symbols on their shields that hung from their saddles – two red stripes under a red rising sun. He thought of the medallion in his pocket and wished that the soldier's shields had carried the same symbols as the medallion.

As the horsemen disappeared in the distance, Window realized that it was too dangerous for them to be seen by anyone – especially armored, sword-wielding horse soldiers. In fact, he didn't know what they would do when eventually they did meet someone. But they would need to be more careful now. They decided to stay off of the road for the rest of the day, and traveled through the grass and trees off to one side, still in view of the road, but not on it.

The northern road continued to wind on – past small farms and two colorless villages. Twice, ox-drawn wagons carrying wheat or rye passed by them on the road, but the travelers kept out of sight. All the while, as they walked, Window was feeling excited that tomorrow – on Panni's birthday – they would probably reach Calisay.

They stopped for the night in a small group of trees at the base of a hill. It was well past suppertime, but again the three travelers had nothing to eat. A few miles before, Circles had tried the leaves of a big field flower-bush that he thought looked pretty good, but found the leaves to be bitter.

Window did have the one last springcookie in his pack, but Circles had suggested, "Let's save it until we reach the kites." Window didn't mind that idea, but had no idea of where to find the kites, or anything else in Calisay – if only he had asked Grandpa Windowen for a map of the Northlands city.

Just what they would do when they got to the city was uncertain. Window's plan was simple – try to keep from attracting any attention. Somehow, they needed to get clothes and food. Window knew it could be dangerous, but he was still excited to be going there. The three of them would just have to make smart decisions about whatever came up. He felt comforted to have friends to help make those decisions.

Window was sure of one thing. Before reaching Calisay, they would have to disguise Panni. Certainly, she could not be seen

wearing only her night skirt, and, of course, her ankle band had to
be covered.

Before they lay down to sleep, Window took what remained of
his blanket and made a slit in the center of it. He slipped it over
Panni's head, so she could wear it as an overcape. Her head stuck
up through the hole, and her body and legs were completely
covered. Then he made two more slits for her arms, and trimmed
the bottom of the blanket a bit. It was almost ready. He finished
the cloak with a belt, cut from the light rope he had in his pack.

They didn't know what the local young women's fashions were
in Calisay, but perhaps Panni could be mistaken for a poor farm
girl rather than an escaped bound-servant.

The bigger question was how the Northlanders would react to
Circles. Window couldn't think of any way to disguise him, so
they would just go on, hoping that Northlanders, who were
familiar with some of the Talkers, had seen Woots before, and
would not pay Circles too much attention.

As the last of the sun disappeared behind a treeline far to the
west, the air became very cold. Window didn't want to chance
lighting a fire for fear of discovery, so the three travelers spent an
uncomfortable night together. Panni wore the blanket-cape and
she and Window both huddled against Circles to try to stay warm
in the cold night.

Window's thoughts jumped back to the night he and Mary had
fallen asleep on her living room sitting couch. He had awoken in
the middle of the night, and just remained quiet, lying against
her, listening to her breathing. That was the moment when he
first knew he was in love with her.

Now, even as he enjoyed achieving his goal of reaching the
Northlands, Window missed Mary terribly. He didn't want to
think about being separated from her, and about how he would
probably not see her again until she returned to Windtown in the
spring a year from now. He tried to push those thoughts from his
mind.

As he lay awake, Window listened to Panni breathing next to
Circles. He wondered if Panni had ever been in love, or had ever

even had a man as a friend. It made him sad to think of how she
had been forced to live in servitude – making no decisions for
herself – being kept away from family, friends, and freedom. She
was free now – but not really. She had nothing – and no one but
two odd traveler friends. He would help her if he could, but what
could he do?

Window slept very little that night. He was cold, and troubled
by thoughts of Mary, and fears of uncertainty and possible
dangers they might face in Calisay. He wondered, as he had
before, if maybe his journey to the North was a bad idea. Even
when he finally did fall asleep, he dreamt of terrible creatures
chasing him, and of Mary being stolen from him by fierce pirates.
At last, Window's cold, restless night came to an end.

+++++++++

He was awake as the sun came up, and watched it shoot its
early morning tongues of fire over the eastern horizon.
Immediately, Window's spirits lifted – it was Panni's twentieth
birthday and – they were going to Calisay – and he had suddenly
realized – it was the first day of May, the fifth month of the
Windlands year.

Back in the Windlands, May was called the month of flowers,
and the first day of May was a special day – a holiday called
Flower Day. Window could picture the townspeople back home
this very morning, preparing for the annual spring flower festival
in the park – finishing their best floral arrangements and
readying their displays for the competitions. There would be
flowers of every size, shape, and color. Window especially enjoyed
seeing the giant, wild-looking flowers grown by the gardeners
from White Top, the town on the other side of the Near Woods.

And he thought back to when he was a boy, when, for Flower
Day, his mother would create a new, beautiful arrangement of her
best windflowers and heartflowers. Those two flowers were her
specialty – and several times, she had won a prize for her work.

But here, on the road to the North, Window and his friends would be preparing for something quite different – today they would reach the Northlands' once-glorious ruling city!

Window hoped they could find a market where he could buy Panni a gift for her birthday. Maybe some shopkeeper would like to have a couple of Windlands coins in exchange for a fancy scarf or something. Then Window reminded himself, Panni needed more than a scarf. She needed all new clothes. They all needed food and supplies. He had no idea how to get them.

As Window called to the others to wake up, he had a fanciful idea. Maybe, as they walked, they would find some treasure lying along the side of the road, so then they would have money when they got to the city. He glanced down at the ground, as if expecting to find something of value beneath his feet. "Well," he smiled to himself, "They probably have all the dirt they need."

"Good morning, Circles," Window spoke to his friends as they opened their eyes. "Happy Birthday, Panni. I am so glad that you are with us on your special day. And I hope that this year brings you all of the joy you deserve."

Panni seemed to understand what Window was saying and looked at him fondly, her eyes bright and direct. She thanked him again for his help and friendship. *"Sae laeselle fasenne, Window. Trae marette mayevaer."*

Panni's birthday started the same way as the day before – without anything to eat, and with just a few sips of water. Then the three travelers started off once again. Panni wore her overcape, and this time, they stayed on the road. They thought that they may as well meet their first Northlanders now as later, but, as they continued, they passed no one on the road.

Their spirits grew higher and higher as they anticipated reaching the city. As they went along, Circles sang a Woot birthday song for Panni, and she sang a Northlands birthday song for him – although he didn't know when his birthday was. Panni's song was the one her mother always sang to her when Panni was a little girl.

Circles and Window each knew many songs, but Panni knew even more. As part of her duties at the castle, she and the other young women in the servant's chambers had to pay special attention to holidays. They learned many songs for each holiday, as well as hundreds of other songs, to be used to entertain the nobles. Panni hated her captivity, but fondly remembered her evenings spent with the other dancers, wearing delicate lace and silk, carefully grooming, and singing. Panni enjoyed singing immensely, and was pleased to be able to share songs with her new friends. Window enjoyed her voice – she sang as softly and as carefully as she spoke.

As they passed through a slight valley, they noticed a patch of wildflowers far off to one side of the road. Circles waded through the tall grass and picked the brightest pink flower he could find, and presented it to Panni for her birthday. She stuck it through her hair on one side of her face. It accented the blue of her eyes and the soft tone of her skin.

After another hour, two other roads joined with theirs. A rough hand-painted sign marked the intersection. It read:

Kinae ah Calisay – 5
Kinae ah Torenne – 21
Kinae ah Laselle – 60

They would reach the city in an hour!

Still more roads intersected with theirs as the walkers happily continued to the north. They began to see other people on the road – ahead of them and behind them, but all of them also traveling north. They were apparently commoners, a few pulling handcarts or walking beside horses loaded with wares. Everyone they saw was traveling toward the city. Perhaps something special was going on in Calisay today.

Then, off to their right, they passed a small castle that must have been the noblehouse of one of the Calisenne estates. The estate's late morning workers were nearby, in a side field, cutting clover for their unattended cattle.

Two more miles passed beneath their feet. Window's heart was beating fast in anticipation of reaching the city. He glanced at Panni and her eyes met his. They both looked towards Circles, who had hurried ahead a bit, and noticed how, every once in a while, he added a skipping step to his regular stride.

Suddenly they heard horses approaching from behind. There was no time or place to hide, so they could only move to the side of the road as the riders grew near. There were seven soldiers – dressed in blue and white. Their armor was black and their shields carried a symbol of two bright blue arrows on a white field.

Window was sure he and his companions would be challenged or arrested or something, but the soldiers just passed by them, and paid them no attention. Even a bright white Woot didn't seem to interest them. Window felt a great relief. At least this time, they were okay.

Window watched as the riders followed the road up a wide hill ahead of them. The city must be on the other side of the hill. The riders disappeared from his view as the road wound through a final grove of trees as it reached the top of the rise.

Window, Circles, and Panni followed the road up the hill and had almost reached the top as they stepped from beneath the trees. And, there they saw them, high in the deep blue sky above the spring-green grass of the hill – bright colors of red and blue and green and pink and gold – hundreds of fluttering and flapping colors, filling the sky above them – their multi-colored tails trailing down and away in the strong mid-day breeze.

They would not have to search for them after all – only open their eyes. Flying in the sky above the three travelers were the wonderful kites of Calisay!

CALISAY

CHAPTER SEVEN

IN THE FAIR CITY

Window, Circles, and Panni ran up the road to the crest of the hill. In the wide valley far below them was a fantastic sight of color and shapes and movement. Calisay was spread before them – nearest, at the base of the hill, was a great, grassy field of hundreds of kite flyers – behind the flyers, a wide bridge over a twisting river. Beyond the river were more open fields of colorful tents and flags and people and movement. Every tent seemed to be of a different shape and color, and every tent was topped with a flag of different design – all flapping and fluttering – like a wildly moving rainbow. Past the fields of tents was the city itself. Calisay was a huge city of low, dark buildings and near its center – a dozen white towers reached high into the bright blue sky.

Panni stood still with Window and just looked in awe at the world below them. The kites were such a joyous sight, the towers so beautiful. Circles held his hands and arms above his head, and smiled happily as he squinted to see as far as he could across the field of color. Then he left the road, and ran in the grass along the hilltop to their right, sometimes jumping and hopping, and otherwise celebrating their reaching the city.

Panni watched Circles running across the grassy ridge, then pulled her blanket-cape off over her head and, without saying anything, handed it to Window. She looked straight into his eyes for a moment, with an expression of thanks on her face, and a hint of tears on her cheeks. Window's heart joined with hers until she slowly closed her eyes and slowly turned away. Then Panni wiped her cheeks, and with a smile on her face, ran after Circles.

It was an odd, happy sight – the Woot living up to both of his names, running and circling and sometimes falling down – Panni chasing him, and pretending to catch him, only to let him go again. They laughed and laughed some more.

Window quietly watched as his friends celebrated – Circles so pleased that his dream of going to Calisay had come true, and Panni celebrating her freedom and her joy of life that was so long buried deep inside her.

As he ran, Circles' fur flew out behind and around him. Panni followed him, her body moving smoothly and easily, her training as a dancer having given her perfect shape and form. Window watched the girl as she ran. More than ever, her beauty was clear. Panni's slender bare legs and arms flashed in the reflected sunlight, as the blue stripes of her skirt added moving color. Her long light-golden hair trailed behind her, as Window thought, like the tail of a kite flying freely in the wind.

Window applauded as the two runners returned, out of breath and still laughing wildly. Panni happily kissed Window on the cheek, and then hugged Circles, and kissed him where she thought his cheek might be.

Then the three travelers became quiet and thoughtful. Panni took her friends by the hand and led them to a spot under a tree a bit farther along the crest of the hill. She sat down with them to rest, and they all just quietly watched the wonderful scene in the broad valley below them.

The kites filling the sky before them were beautiful and mesmerizing – so many colors – so many kites – scores of them so high they were just dots in the deep blue above. The wind was blowing from the west and carrying the kites off to their right. Window took a deep relaxing breath, leaned back against the trunk of the big tree they were under, and let his mind fly up and join the kites filling the sky.

Above him, he could see colorful windsails, cross-wings, tri-frames, round-spinners, long-frames, and step-kites – and every other kind of kite Window had ever seen back home – plus uncountable more types, some of which were of shapes so odd he could not even guess how they were able to catch the wind and stay aloft. Some of the kites had tails that must have been hundreds of feet long. Those tails seemed to just be hanging in the sky, as the kites they were attached to were now too high above him to see.

In the grassy field below the three travelers, the kite flyers of Calisay were spread out from the base of the hill to the riverbank. There were a few small hills and rises in the mostly flat field and those, too, were covered with flyers. There were men and women and children of all ages, mostly in groups of two or three or four. The flyers were milling about, visiting with others, and looking overhead as need be. Only a few people seemed to still be trying to get their kites aloft.

Window happily noticed that Panni's cape would fit right in with the clothes the flyers were wearing – simple and drab and colorless. It seemed that the flyers were probably poor peasants and city dwellers, and that the only color in their lives was that of their kites.

To their left, the road curled down the hill and ran through the great field of flyers. At the river's edge, the road reached the Calisay Bridge. The bridge was low and wide, and spanned the river for maybe two hundred feet. Along each side of the bridge span was a wide, flat-topped, stone railing. More flyers were standing on the bridge railing and flying their kites from there.

Window's memory flashed for a moment, and he quickly dug into his pack for the last springcookie. He pulled it out and held in up at arm's length in front of his face. The picture on the cookie was cracked and somewhat crumbled away, but it was the same – exactly the same. The bridge on the cookie was the same bridge – the Calisay Bridge!

Window showed his friends and they both looked out at the bridge and back at the cookie, then back at the bridge. Circles sharp eyes looked beyond the bridge as he excitedly remarked,

"Look at that tallest tower on the left, Window. I think that that
is the same tower, too!"

Circles was right! Window was sure. The tallest of the towers
of Calisay was the same tower as on one of the other cookies
Circles had eaten. Its crown was the same – its sidespires were
spaced just as on the cookie, and the lower roofline of the base
building matched his memory perfectly.

Window could hardly believe it. He quickly tried to remember
all of the pictures on Grandma's springcookie board. He recalled
that her board had twelve different carvings on it, the twelve
carvings arranged three across and four high – with double
straight lines separating the carvings into rectangles.

Window named them out loud, as he thought of the different
pictures. "The bridge, the tower, the kite..." He was amazed at, in
his excitement, how much trouble he was having remembering
them – even though he had been eating those same cookies at his
grandmother's his whole life. "Oh, yeah – the windmill, the
flowers, the sword and shield... the Angel... the Silkie..."

"The flag, and the ship..." offered Circles as he thought of two
others that he had eaten.

"That makes ten," counted Window. "The row of cannon – that
makes eleven."

Try as he could, Window was unable to remember the twelfth
carving on the board. But, it didn't matter right now – the bridge
and tower were enough for him. Grandma's Amerand cookieboard
not only had a carving of a Northlands Silkie, but the Calisay
bridge and tower as well! But, Window's grandmother had gotten
the board from her grandmother, who had come to the Windlands
on a ship from Ameran. How Window's great-great-grandmother
had gotten such a board was impossible to guess.

Window gave up trying to remember the last carving, for it was
time for the travelers to finish their celebration. Window took his
boot knife and cut the bridge cookie into three pieces. They each
took a piece, and taking small bites, slowly ate it – the last of their
food. It was time to go on into the city.

Panni touched Window on the shoulder, as he was about to get up. He could tell by the look in her eyes that she wanted to wait a little longer. It was the perfect place to rest before they went on down to the city. Window leaned back against the tree and closed his eyes. He wished that instead of being hungry, he had just finished a good lunch – like the ones his Grandmother Breesian used to give him when he was a boy in school. Even now that he was grown, he still had lunch with her sometimes, when he picked up his carpentry tools or dropped them off at his grandfather's workshop. He still fondly remembered his boyhood days with her, years ago.

+++++++++

[ACROSS FROM THE WINDTOWN SCHOOL]

Miles and miles to the south, the Windtown School midday bell was ringing. Teresa Breesian stood on her front porch, and looked across her large yard to the narrow, old, two-story, red brick building that stood at the back of the school grounds on the other side of the alley. The bell was clanging happily, and the town kids were happily pouring out of the front door of the school, and streaming to their homes for lunch.

"Hey, Johnny!" Teresa called, as a young boy, about ten years old, came running across the alley and into her yard. The bubbly, brown-haired boy came racing to her house and bounded up the four front porch steps and hugged her. Johnny was her grandson, and just like Johnny's cousin Window often did when he was a boy, Johnny sometimes came to her house from school for a quick lunch.
Johnny loved to eat lunch with his grandmother. He loved what she fixed him to eat. It was the same thing every time – scrambled eggs and toasted bread. Grandma had even let him cook the eggs a few times, but they didn't turn out

*nearly as good as when she made them. And, there was
always milk, and for desert – sugarcookies – always too sweet
and always too soft, but Johnny didn't mind. Many of his
schoolmates were sitting back in a crowded lunchroom eating
cold sandwiches, but Johnny was having a real meal.*

*And, besides the food, Johnny especially liked that when
he came for lunch from school, he had his Grandma all to
himself – not like when he came to visit with his family. One
time Grandma Teresa had even let him feed the ears of hard,
yellow corn to the two squirrels that came down from the big
oak tree. They waited on the wooden shelf that Grandma had
nailed to the back porch post, chattering until they were fed.
She had showed Johnny how to make a clicking sound with
his mouth, so the squirrels would know that it was time to
eat.*

*His grandmother loved to watch the squirrels, although,
once, one had gotten into her back porch room and chewed
into a lot of bags and boxes. She was pretty mad about that!*

*Grandma Breesian was tall and thin, and wore her long,
straight, grey hair in a bun. Johnny remembered how
surprised he was the first time he saw her take it down. She
was sitting in the big, soft, living room chair, unpinned her
hair, and unrolled it in front of her. Her hair was so long
that, as she combed it, it reached down with the ends of it
lying in her lap. He had never imagined that his
grandmother would have such long hair.*

*Since his Grandfather Breesian's death a few years ago,
his grandmother Teresa began to rely a lot on visitors to keep
her company, and so Johnny's visit was a fun time for her,
too. He always had a story to tell about what he had been
studying that morning – sometimes it was Windlands
history, or spelling, but today it was something about lines
and intersecting circles that she didn't understand too well.
She hadn't understood it too well it when she studied it
herself, in school, many years before.*

*And, today Teresa had a special treat for Johnny. She
had decided to use a package that her son Ernest had sent*

+++++++++

The breeze brushed against Window's face. He opened his eyes
and glanced towards the others. Panni had been watching him.
She was ready to go.

They looked knowingly at each other and stood up. Panni slid
the cape back over her head and the three travelers returned to
the road. In a couple of minutes, they were at the bottom of the
hill and following the road across the field of kite flyers.

They left the road and wound though the crowded kite field.
Some flyers were fixing lunch and eating. Others were working on
their kites – some were sleeping – so sure that their creations
would be fine without their attention.

No one paid any attention to Circles at all. Apparently, Woots
were common enough in Calisay that, as with Panni, he wouldn't
attract any unwanted notice.

As they passed by them, Circles overheard a group of men
discussing the day. It happened that, as on the Windlands

prairie, the first day of May was a special day in the Northlands.
It was a holiday to celebrate the coming warmer months and the
beginning of what they called the Season of the Sun. It was
commemorated with games and races and music and, of course,
kites. Farmers and peasants and city folk were all invited to
participate. So the city was filled with Northlanders from far and
near – merchants, families, and, of course, kite flyers. Later in
the day, the award-winning kites would each earn a Northlands
silver coin for their builders.

Suddenly, among the hundreds and hundreds of people they
were passing, Circles spotted two Deep Woods Talkers – Owts.
They stood on their hind legs and were a bit shorter than Circles.
They had very long snouts, short, stubby legs, and short grey-
brown fur.
The Owts were standing, holding a giant kite between them.
The kite was bright green in color – and much taller than either of
them.
"Lae Owter!" Circles called to the two Owts as they readied
their kite. They looked over to him, surprised.
"Lae Wooter!" one of them called back. *"Hae raemet trasonne."*
"Ree daeloewene," Circles returned the greeting.

Window turned to Circles. "How are they going to get that big
kite into the air? It looks much too big for them to handle – and
the sky is already crowded with kites."
"I don't know," replied the Woot. "But, Owts are very
resourceful. Let's watch and see what happens."

The Owts were named Frazzle and Locker. Frazzle reached
behind him and grabbed on to the handle of a woven basket that
was sitting there. Then he opened the hinged lid and out flew
seven big grey birds.
"Flickers!" cried Circles. "They brought Deep Woods Flickers!"
The three travelers all watched in amazement as four of the
birds hooked their claws along the top of the kite and, flapping
furiously, flew upward, carrying the kite with them. The other
three Flickers grabbed onto the kite's tail as it hung down, and

flew holding on to it, following the kite up into the air. It was a magical sight watching the kite rise into the sky. Several people nearby pointed, and alerted their friends to watch, as the bright green kite was lifted high and higher.

As the wind caught the kite, the Flickers let go of it. The strong midday breeze carried it quickly away, with Locker letting out the string as fast as he could. One of the Flickers holding on to the tail of the kite, though, didn't let go quite soon enough, and was flipped upside down in the air as the kite jumped upward. But, the bird quickly recovered, and in just a few moments, the Owt's massive, green creation joined the myriad of others high in the Calisay sky.

Window, Panni, and Circles all applauded. Frazzle and Locker smiled and bowed deeply in their direction.

"Raleenne sae mekan," Circles yelled at them, as he waved goodbye.

"Tae Wooter," they replied, as the three travelers turned and continued through the field.

Then, in the crowd of flyers, Window noticed a second pair of creatures that must have also been Talkers. They stood on their hind legs and were about as tall as the Owts. But unlike the Owts, who were very pleasant looking, these creatures were just the opposite. They had ugly rat-looking faces and beady red eyes. Their long twisting tails twitched behind them as they stared in Window's direction.

"Hey, Circles, look. There are a couple of other Talkers. Shall we go over and say 'Hello'?"

Without adding any details, Circles replied, "No, let's leave them alone. Marrents aren't very friendly."

"Okay," smiled Window, and let it pass without any further explanation from Circles.

The travelers rejoined the road as it started over the Calisay Bridge. It was a low, wide bridge, and not very high above the water. Years before, it was an important commercial link to the southern areas of Calisenne Province. Now it was mostly being used as a footbridge to the Fairgrounds.

Today, the bridge was full of townspeople and country folk all enjoying the sun and the day, some of them simply walking across the bridge, but many others just sitting on the sidewall, or standing on it, flying their kites. Window hopped up on the wall and walked along it for a few steps. He looked back toward the kite field and noticed there were now flyers even on the side of the hill he and his friends had come down earlier. It was a wonderful sight!

Window glanced down into the water passing under the stone arch beneath him, and thought of the river bridge back home, at Lowpoint. He had once climbed up to the top of its high, wooden frame and tossed rocks into the Windlands River. Maybe the next time he was there, he would try to fly a kite from its top.

As Window turned and looked across the bridge to the other side of the river, he heard distant cheering. It was coming from a mass of people who were standing at the top of a slight hill, across the river and far off to the right, beyond one of the many areas of tents. The hill appeared to be a grass-covered ridge of ground, sticking up from the flat field surrounding it, and stretching several hundred feet off to the east. The crowd covering the hill seemed to be looking down its other side, and cheering wildly. Something exciting was happening over there

"Let's go see what's going on," Circles suggested. Window nodded in agreement.

The three travelers passed over the bridge and worked their way through the crowds of people on the other side. They wound through one of the fields of colorful tents and admired the flags as they passed. They watched jugglers, and listened to strolling musicians. They dodged running children and barking dogs. They glanced at merchant-tables of tools and wares and food. They were very hungry, but, of course, had no Northlands money.

To reach the hill, they also had to pass through an area of larger tents that held groups of soldiers and their horses. The tent-flags bore designs that signified the estate or palace of the owners. A few of the soldiers looked carefully at Circles and Panni as they went by, but no one said anything to them. Window examined each flag carefully, looking for the design that was on his medallion, but could not find it.

When they finally reached the base of the hill that held the cheering people, Window could see that Panni was reluctant to push her way through the mass of Northlanders. He took her hand and led her up the side of the hill, and through the pressing crowd. Circles took Panni's other hand and followed them. When they reached the top, they stared in surprise at the sight on the other side.

The hill was actually only one side of a ridge of high ground that, except for a narrow passageway far to their left, completely surrounded a huge, rectangular field inside the higher ground. The field was a huge competition field, marked with white stripes that ran across the field from left to right. It was a racing field!

Down and to their left, near the open end of the high ground, they could see several groups of soldiers in bright colors, each walking their horses in a resting area. The horses would be racing next.

Farther across the grassy field, near a massive, dark rock at the start of other racing lines, a group of runners were lining up for a foot race. Circles jumped up onto Window's back, put an arm around his neck, and looked over Window's shoulder, so he could see better. Panni pushed next to Window, held on to his arm, and looked on. The clamoring crowd waited in anticipation for the race to begin, and cheered wildly as the starting flag was dropped. The runners started across the field, following their racing lanes, towards the finish far to their right.

Panni and Window looked on in complete surprise. Along with the men racing, they could see the huge, dark, shape that had been near the starting line, moving across the field with them. It wasn't a rock at all. It was a huge, four-legged creature, much taller than a man, and at least five times as wide – and it was racing the men! It looked so odd to see the huge shape moving across the field, and – it was winning the race! The crowd squealed its approval.

"I hope you are feeling polite today, Window." Circles called to him above the noise.

Window looked at him inquisitively. Circles answered his unasked question. "That big, brown, furry, hump moving along the ground is a Deep Woods Brarrie – the animal you don't want to make angry!"

And so it was. Racing with the men was one of the massive creatures whose tracks they had seen on the path. The crowd was going wild. The Brarrie was still ahead in the footrace! He was lumbering and galloping on his four, thick legs, ahead of everyone else.

Panni squeezed Window's hand in excitement, *"Ou sae tolasenne!"* she yelled excitedly. *"Ou sae, ou sae!"*

They watched in awe as the race finished in a celebration of noise. The Brarrie crossed the finish line well ahead of the other racers, and the crowd roared with pleasure.

Panni leaned close to Circles' ear and spoke excitedly to the Woot.

Circles dropped down to his feet and repeated Panni's request to Window as the cheering died down. "She wants to go down and talk to him."

"Talk to whom?" Window replied.

"The Brarrie. She wants to talk to him."

Panni looked pleadingly at Window *"Faelanae, Window? Please?"*

Window didn't answer, not knowing what to think.

Panni spoke again to Circles, quickly and excitedly.

"She says that she would love to meet such a powerful creature – a creature that no one ever tells where to live – or what to do. She wants to meet him – and she promises to be polite!"

"Please, Window? Please? Jae tou fornenntee." Panni's eyes were alive with hope.

Window couldn't disappoint the pleading girl. "Okay, we'll go down there, but just be careful – both of you. Don't do anything to attract attention to us."

"Don't worry about me, Window," answered the Woot, smiling sheepishly.

"Yeah, right," Window replied with heavy skepticism, hoping that he was not making a mistake by agreeing to the request.

Window looked into Panni's eyes and nodded "Yes" to her. She reacted immediately.

Panni began pulling Window by the hand to go down the hill towards the racing field. She was so excited about meeting the massive Deep Woods creature, that the quiet, gentle, servant girl was willing to push through the crowd ahead of them. It was very clear to Window how important meeting the creature was to the girl. Her captivity had had a profound effect on her. She needed to connect with this animal of strength. She needed to feel its security just by being close to it.

Panni led her friends down the hillside towards the runners and the crowd surrounding them. At the bottom of the hill, they brushed past a group of horse soldiers and their squires. One soldier eyed the girl and her Woot friend as they went by. Window realized that they had certainly better not give the soldiers any reason to talk to them.

The runners from the Brarrie's race were all gathering back at the starting line to collect their overclothes. The Brarrie followed them and stood quietly by himself.

The Brarrie was a gigantic creature. Its back was taller than Window as it stood on its four thick legs. It had the body somewhat like that of a black ice-bear, but it wasn't a bear – it was a Deep Woods Talker, with an intelligent face and deep, sad looking eyes. It had floppy, dog-like ears and a huge mouth of silver-yellow teeth. In fact, everything about the creature was huge. Its deep brown-black fur hung thickly and loosely from its body, and the creature looked as though it was wearing a blanket across its back, as the fur hanging from its body moved when it walked. Window noticed that around each of the creature's huge legs, just above its feet, and almost hidden by his dark fur, was a thin ring, about as wide as Window's hand, of white fur.

The Brarrie sat down on his haunches and panted dog-like. No one came near the beast. Apparently, everyone knew better than to approach it. His eyes were surveying the crowd as Panni walked right up to him and bowed.

"Tae, Brarrie. Sae lotren oh felinon." She addressed him calmly and gently.

The Brarrie turned, and his deep eyes looked directly at the girl, but he did not respond to her.

"Sae na meree Panni," she introduced herself. Several people nearby noticed what the girl was doing.

Window was still worried that something might go wrong. Circles felt the same way. He moved closer to Window and touched his arm as a warning. More people started to notice the girl, and gathered around, getting closer and closer to Panni and the Brarrie, listening to their one-sided conversation.

"Ka naeten so fenee," Panni complemented him on winning the race. There was still no reply from the beast.

"Ka tou trissensae, Brarrie. Ka tou trissenne," she continued.

Then, as though there was nothing odd about being approached by the girl, the creature spoke back to her. His voice was deep, but clear, and his words almost as carefully spoken as Panni's.

"Sae na meree Rings. Lae fonamintae."

The crowd grew quiet – everyone was watching and listening. Window was fearful. Panni was getting too much attention.

Panni turned to her friends. *"Wae meree, Rings. Trevel tou non."*

She turned back towards the Brarrie and asked him in the most polite manner she knew how, *"Sae maelle tou trentae? Ka maseene?"*

Surprising even Panni, the Rings creature agreed to her polite request. He flopped down on his belly and put a massive paw-foot out towards the girl. Panni stepped right onto his big, shaggy leg, and, grabbing on to a handful of his fur, pulled herself onto his back. The crowd burst into cheers.

Panni smiled as she straddled across the creature's back. Several soldiers came over to see what was going on. They were wearing black uniforms that bore the symbol of a single black sword on a white field – they were the soldiers of Prince Martellan, the cruel ruler of Calisay!

The crowd backed away a bit as the soldiers approached. Panni didn't notice them. Window wanted to tell Panni to climb back down – but he didn't dare say anything in Atlandan.

One soldier moved closer to the Brarrie. *"Nen sonne retae!"* he shouted at the Brarrie.

Rings looked at the man and the Brarrie's sad eyes turned suddenly menacing.

"Nen sonne retae!" the man angrily repeated.

The Brarrie started to stand up. Panni was surprised by the unexpected movement and lost her grip on Rings' fur. She slid partway down the side of the creature, and as she did, her cape slid up, revealing her legs – and revealing her ankle bracelet!

Several people gasped. The midday sun struck the jewels on the bracelet, and flashed gleaming rose and purple, sparkling against the dark fur of the Brarrie. Everyone could see that Panni was the property of a nobleman!

"La sonelle oh sensae!" the soldier shouted at Panni. She jumped down from the creature and started to run to Window.

Three other soldiers came quickly, two of them drew their short swords, and the third one of them grabbed Panni by the wrist. He pulled her roughly and Panni cried out in terror, *"Taena! Window! Window!"*

Window was frantic also. He reached out for Panni's other arm. One of the soldiers struck down on Window's hand with the butt of his sword handle. Window grabbed his hand in pain, as Panni was pulled further away from him. Window had to get to the girl! "Panni! Circles!" he cried out.

Now the attacking soldier held his sword blade towards Window and shouted angrily. Window thought of his boot knife, but it would be of no use. Panni was being pulled away into the crowd. "Circles! Circles! What can we do?" he cried wildly.

Window's desperate eyes met with the glance of the little Deep Woods animal. The soldiers were not paying any attention to Circles, and Circles knew that he had to try something.

He ran between two of the soldiers and right up to the huge, brown Brarrie. Circles shouted something to the creature, not in Freelandan or Woot, but some other language.

Immediately, the creature stood completely up on his massive legs, and let out a deafening, angry growl, directly at the soldiers. For an instant, everyone stopped, frozen with fear and surprise. Then everything happened very quickly.

The frightened soldier holding Panni dropped his grip on the girl. Window slammed himself into the man as hard as he could and knocked him into a group of people. Then Window grabbed Panni by the arm and pulled her into the crowd. The massive Rings creature roared even louder and the people moved away in a panic. The soldiers tried to follow Window and Panni, but the crowd was too thick. They shouted orders above the noise but no one moved out of the way so they could chase the girl.

Someone grabbed onto Panni's cape – but she pulled free. Others started cheering again as the soldiers angrily tried, without success, to follow the fleeing strangers.

Window didn't dare stop long enough to look back for Circles. He didn't know where to run, but they had to escape! They couldn't wait for him! They had to run! Circles was lost to them now! Circles was lost to them!

Window knocked into people as he desperately led Panni though the crowd to the open end of the racing field. They pushed out of the field and into the massive area of tents and merchants and families. Together they ran, frantically pushing past townspeople and farmers, dogs and horses, children and cooking fires, small merchant's carts, and table of food sellers.

They could hear shouts behind them. Someone was still chasing them. Window didn't look back. Panni was frightened and pleading, *"Senne traenne, Window! Window!"*

Panni stumbled and fell. Window pulled her up – and on they went. They pushed past more tents and tables and curious families who watched as they frantically hurried by. Panni's sore feet screamed with pain but she held on tightly to Window's hand.

At last they reached the edge of the tents and broke into an open area of grass. But, ahead they saw more soldiers, on horseback, who were riding in their direction, so they turned and ran down an embankment and up the other side. One of the soldiers called out to them but Window and Panni just kept going without looking back. The outer buildings of Calisay were in sight. They had to reach the safety of the buildings where they might find someplace to hide.

They gasped for breath as they finally reached the northern edge of the giant celebration field and entered the city. They ran past low buildings and down narrow streets, past stores and stables. They slowed down a bit. They could see nor hear no one behind them. Finally, Window and Panni stopped running, but continued on, deep into the streets of the city. They had escaped the crowd, they had escaped the soldiers, but they had left their only friend behind. Circles was gone – and Window and Panni were lost in Calisay!

The two walked on through the streets of Calisay. The buildings were all old, rough, wooden buildings – drab and dark, with no color. Only a few had glass windows. None had been built with any of the skill or care Window used when he built a structure back home. Back home – he could only think of it for a moment. Then he heard something behind them. Someone was still following them. There were running footsteps behind them!

They hurried around the corner of another building, down a narrow alley, and ducked behind a high porch on the side of a deserted store. They waited. Panni's breathing was wild – she was so frightened. Her face was bright red with exhaustion and fear. Window was sorry that he had let her come into such danger.

Window tried to let go of Panni, but she held too tightly to his hand. As she trembled and tried to calm herself, they could hear the footsteps still coming nearer. Panni looked back at Window and into his eyes. He returned the look and they both knew that they could not escape this time. They were caught!

The footsteps stopped. Panni pulled herself tightly to Window's arm. She buried her face against his chest. Window couldn't think of anything else to do. They stood up from behind the porch, expecting to be facing a soldier's sword or a sheriff's wrist-irons.

But facing them was a small boy, of about age eight. He was wearing rather ragged clothes, but a clean face. Panni relaxed her grip on Window's arm a bit. Window didn't know what to think. Perhaps he should knock the boy down and run again.

Before Window could decide, the boy walked up to them, and spoke to them in perfect Atlandan, "Follow me, I know where you can hide."

Window could hardly believe it. It was impossible! Who could this be?

He tried to comfort Panni, and she seemed to understand that the danger was over for the moment. The boy started walking, and spoke again, "Come this way. Quickly!"

Window and Panni had no idea who he could be, but they also had no idea of anything else that could offer them a better chance of safety. So, they put their trust in him. Window and Panni followed the boy through the dark, narrow streets of old Calisay.

"Who are you?" Window asked, as they hurried down a crooked, dusty street. "How did you find us?"

"My name is Rook. My grandfather saw you run from the soldiers at the Fair, and sent me to find you. I have been behind you the whole time, since you ran from the Fairgrounds."

"But why did you follow us? Who is your grandfather?"

"My grandfather's name is Rayard Oldsmith. He is a metal-smith by trade and is also, sometimes, a horse squire for the Matenne Palace. He was caring for the Matenne horses at the Fair today. We were watching as the soldiers approached you, and we heard you call out to your friend in Atlandan. When you ran from them, Grandfather told me to run after you and to try to keep you safe from the soldiers. That is all that I know. You really did run pretty fast, but I was able to push between the crowds of people, and, I know how to get around this part of the city."

Oldsmith! – Grandpa Windowen's Oldsmith – from his Northern Expedition – Rayard Oldsmith who returned to the

Northlands with Revell to search for treasures – this boy was his grandson!

Oldsmith was still alive and Window had found him. Well, Oldsmith had found Window. Either way it was fantastic! Window could only wonder where Rook was leading them. But, wherever it was, it had to be better than being alone and lost in the Northlands city.

Panni and Window followed the lad through winding streets and narrow back alleys. Once they had to hide as a group of sheriff's men came up the street, but they seemed to be out of danger from the soldiers. After about twenty minutes of sneaking through the city, Rook lead them to a stable-barn that was attached to a small low house. The sign above the large stable door read "Rayard Oldsmith – Treaman."

Rook took a key from his pocket and opened the door to the house. They stepped inside.

Window glanced around the room they were in. The small house was really mostly just this one room. There was a small table with three chairs, and a bench by the single front window. The table held a lantern, a jar of sugar and a pipe and tobacco tin. Rook pulled the simple window curtains closed.

On the left wall, there was a fireplace, a wall cupboard, and a small cooking board. On the far wall, there was a single bed, a door leading to a small back room, and an overflowing bookshelf.

In the wall to their right, was a third door that opened to the stable-barn and smithy-shop. A highly polished, silver military longsword hung on the far side of that door. On the near side of the door – and Window's heart leaped when he saw it – was a large piece of black cloth, framed in wood, and hanging like a picture. And attached to the cloth were military patches – Windlands patches – Atlandan patches – Northlands patches – colorful stripes of blue and silver and white and faded red. And there were ribbons, and metal pins of all sorts. Window was in the home of his grandpa's lost army partner!

The young boy invited Window and Panni to sit down, and went to dip them each a cup of water from a bucket that hung by the cupboard. Window sat down on one of the wooden chairs at the table, and Panni sat on the bench in front of the window.

"Grandfather will be here soon," Rook explained. "He had to return the racing horses to their own stables. Then he will come right away, I am sure." Rook also explained to Panni in Freelandan that they would not have long to wait.

Panni pulled off her cape. Her thin underblouse clung to her skin, wet with perspiration. Her legs and chest ached. Her feet were almost numb and useless. She took a sip of water, leaned back against the wall, and closed her eyes. She was exhausted. Window watched her, so happy that she was safe.

Every few minutes, Panni would open her eyes, lean over and pull the ragged curtains apart, searching the street for a sign of Oldsmith. On about her tenth look between the curtains, she excitedly turned to Window, *"Lae sorae. Yes. Yes!"*

He was here. The door opened and in came Oldsmith – rather tall and rather older looking than Widow expected. He was standing straight, but looked tired and worn, as did his clothes. He removed the only color he wore – a black sash with a stitched design on it – a bright silver horseshoe, opening upward and crossed by a silver arrow. He pulled the sash over his shoulder and hung it on a hook by the door.

"Hello, my good Visitors," he spoke to them in Atlandan.

"Hello, my kind Host," returned Window. "And greetings also, from my grandfather, William Windowen."

The old man looked carefully at Window. He glanced at Panni and back at Window. Then Rayard Oldsmith sat down, surprised and smiling. It was the beginning of another friendship for Window on his trip to the Wilds.

+++++++++

Window and Oldsmith spoke for hours that afternoon and evening. Oldsmith offered to speak in Freelandan, but Panni declined his offer. She would be happy to wait to hear all of the details of the situation later, but for now, she was thrilled to be in a friendly home, and with people she wanted to be with. The house was old and poor and worn – not a silk-draped castle dancer's quarters – but it was clean and friendly and safe, and she was free. Panni was comforted in a way that perhaps they could not understand.

Window's first concern was for Circles, alone in the Fair city. Oldsmith sent his grandson out to look for him. "Don't worry, Rook will find him," Oldsmith assured Window.

Apparently, Rook was a member of a large band of children who belonged to a sort of secret underground organization in Calisay. These street boys and girls regularly did things for the adults, such as delivering messages, warning of the coming of soldiers or sheriff's men, and otherwise ran around the city gathering information and doing anything that needed to be kept secret from the Prince. In the rare instance that the Prince's soldiers came upon these kids, the soldiers could never catch them. The children would quickly run away between buildings and over fences and would escape. And today, Rook would put this small army of kids to work looking for Circles.

Panni just listened quietly as Window and Oldsmith spoke at the table. She offered to make them something to eat and Oldsmith had agreed. She had eaten almost nothing for days and she had not cooked in more than a year, but remembered well what she had learned in her servant's duties. This time, however, she was happy to cook. As the men talked, she relaxed greatly, chopping potatoes and carrots, and dividing the old bread she found in the cupboard. Then she spent a long time preparing and cooking, at the fireplace, a piece of beef that Oldsmith retrieved for her from the smokehouse behind the stable-barn. Panni had never before been so happy to prepare a meal.

Window noticed that, as she worked, Panni was whistling softly to herself, just as his Grandma Windowen did when she worked in her own kitchen. So, as Panni worked at the small cutting and mixing board, it was just as comforting and relaxing for Window, too.

Oldsmith explained to Window why he had sent Rook to help them escape from the soldiers. Oldsmith said that, just like most other people in Calisay, he hated the Prince's soldiers and was happy to help anyone in trouble with them. And, he was especially happy to help someone who had been enslaved as a servant.

Also, he explained, the Matenne Palace, that Oldsmith had squired for today, was not really a palace, but had only been one in the years before the war. Now, it was just a small group of horsemen who enjoyed racing and caring for their animals, and displaying their ancient colors and banners. Oldsmith did all of the shoeing and harness making for them in his stable-barn.

As the day went on, Window answered all of Oldsmith's questions about the lands in the south, and Oldsmith told of the nearly fifty years he had spent here in the Northlands. But for now, Oldsmith just briefly explained to Window how his Grandfather's army expedition member happened to be alive and well and living in Calisay.

When Oldsmith and John Revell were dismissed from the army in the Windlands, they decided to return to the North to find the coins hidden in the Battleplain graveyard. Then they would look for the lost gold and jewel mines in the east.

At the graveyard, they couldn't remember behind what stone Captain Near had buried their slain expedition member, Private Rails, and the Freeland coins they had been forced to abandon. So, they dug behind about a hundred grave markers, but didn't find anything. They felt that, perhaps, someone else had already beaten them to the treasure.

Window told Oldsmith that his grandfather's notes said that the gravestone they were looking for was that of Captain Page. Oldsmith couldn't remember if he and Revell had looked behind that stone for the coins.

"Anyway, we never found Rails' grave. We never found the hidden coins."

Their failure to find the coins had made Revell very angry, and he blamed Oldsmith for their lack of success. The two men fought about it for days.

Then, on their way to search for the Eastern Mines, Oldsmith and Revell were attacked by Northern wildmen. Oldsmith was struck by an arrow, and Revell's horse was killed. Revell, fearing for his own life, took Oldsmith's horse, and abandoned his partner, who was left badly injured and helpless, and apparently dead by the side of the road.

Fortunately, the injured Oldsmith survived the attack, and was discovered hours later by a local village woman, who took him to her home and cared for him. The woman nursed Oldsmith back to health. He ended up working in the village as a blacksmith after he recovered, and eventually, he and the woman's daughter were married. Oldsmith decided to stay in the Northlands to live, having never found any treasure of coins or gold or jewels, but the treasure of the love of a woman.

Surprisingly, three years later, Revell returned looking for Oldsmith. He had heard stories of a Windlands man living in the village, and was thrilled to find Oldsmith alive and well. Revell had gone east to search for the mines but didn't say if he had found them. He expressed his sorrow for having abandoned Oldsmith, but said he had to leave again immediately. He was being chased by someone, but he wouldn't say who or why. Revell shoved a silver key in Oldsmith's hand and left saying, "Hide this for me."

"Did you ever see him again?" asked Window

"No, I never saw him again – but after more than forty years, I do still have the key. I don't know what it will open, but I guess that it might be a key to something valuable."

Window looked up at the display of patches and medals on Oldsmith's wall. He pulled the medallion from his pocket and asked the question that he hoped, at last, would lead to the discovery of its origin. "Have you ever seen this before?"

Oldsmith took the medallion and examined it carefully. "No, I don't think so, but it looks like an ancient Windlands or Atland army insignia," replied the old man.

"Well, yeah, I guess it does," answered the disappointed Window, with a shrug. Even Oldsmith didn't know where the rusted piece of metal had come from. Window's great medallion search would have to continue.

Panni politely set the table as the two men continued their conversation. She lit the lantern, as it was beginning to get dark outside. Then, it was time for their dinner. Soon they were all enjoying a meal of beef, vegetables, and sugared apples for desert. Panni ate more than both of the men – but, as always, she ate slowly and carefully. Window and Oldsmith thanked her repeatedly. She smiled with each comment. Window smiled with almost every bite. He could hardly believe his good fortune of finding Oldsmith – and Circles – and Panni.

As the three of them were finishing their last bites of sugared apples, there was a knock on the front door. Oldsmith open it and there stood Rook with Circles at his side!

"Hey, you guys," said Circles kiddingly, "Where did you go? You missed all of the fun!"

Window and Panni beamed with delight at his safe return. The girl hugged Circles until he begged for air.

After recovering his breath, Circles sat down on the bench next to Panni and told his story. Apparently, Rings had caused quite a lot of trouble before he left the Fair. Soldiers were knocked down – people were scattered – tables and booths were destroyed. Several soldiers were seriously hurt. One had drawn his sword and pointed it at Rings. The Brarrie didn't take it too well. He simply kicked his giant front leg against the man, who was sent flying, and helped off with a broken leg and arm. Soon, another soldier's face was badly bleeding as he retreated to a safer distance from the angry beast.

That set the crowd cheering again, and more soldiers were called in to try to get things under control. Three more soldiers were sent sprawling before things quieted down, but Rings wouldn't leave until he got his prize for winning the race. Finally, a race official retrieved the prize and tried to give it to him, but the Brarrie's giant paws couldn't hold it. Circles volunteered to carry the prize for Rings, and they left the Fair together, with Circles riding on the beast's back. The people cheered again as the two Deep Woods creatures made their way through the parting crowd. The still angry Brarrie kicked and walked over everything in his way.

Window and Panni sat and listened in amazement as Circles finished his story. Then Circles reached into a cloth bag he was carrying and held up a long, shiny, metal tube with curved glass lenses at each end. Proudly he announced, "And Rings gave his prize to me – a far-looking scope! Now I can see farther than ever."

"And look what else I brought with me." Circles walked to the door that opened into the small attached stable-barn. He opened the door and let everyone look into the barn. There, sitting in Oldsmith's stable and smithy-shop, and almost filling up the entire room, was the massive Brarrie. Circles had brought the gigantic Rings along with him!

CHAPTER EIGHT

AT THE NORTHLANDS HOUSE

That evening was a happy time for everyone. More stories were told, and Circles had plenty of apples and cheese and dried berries to eat. Oldsmith's big, dark grey cat, Trix, came out from his hiding place in the small back room and was introduced to the visitors. Panni held out her hand to him and he let her pet him for a moment before he went and lay down in front of the fire.

Oldsmith sent Rook out again and he returned in about twenty minutes with the boy's mother, Oldsmith's daughter, Sara. Sara and Rook lived not too far away. She was a tall, slender woman who worked as a baker. She brought with her, from her bakeshop, a sugar cake that she had covered with pale pink and blue frosting, and topped with twenty small pink candles.

Panni beamed as the candles were lit and everyone sang her a Northlands birthday song. Well, Window sort of hummed along. He was a pretty good singer but, of course, didn't know any Northlands birthday songs.

Rings sat on the dirt floor of the stable-barn and stuck his giant head through the door into the house. It was an odd sight – and sound – as even he tried to sing along. But his singing was more like a low rumble.

Panni closed her eyes and made a birthday wish. Her face was calm and smooth and confident. Window didn't know just what she was wishing for, but he joined her in hoping that all of her wishes came true.

Smiles and laughter were everywhere as Panni blew out the candles on her cake. As everyone cheered, she looked around the room at her new friends, and saw in their faces the caring and friendship she so desperately needed. Then tears of happiness and relief flowed down her cheeks. Her years of living as a prisoner and servant were over. That terrible part of her life was forever behind her.

Quickly, Panni wiped her face and recovered her smile. Oldsmith reached into his pocket and took out a small package and handed it to the girl. It was wrapped in grey paper – but tied with a bright green ribbon. *"Tou tenda verin soenae, Panni,"* he again wished her happy birthday.

Panni slowly and carefully opened the gift, trying not to rip any of the paper. Finally, she unfolded the last bit of inner-paper and held up her gift for all to see. It was a small, gleaming, five-pointed, silver star on a long, silver neckchain. The center of the star was cut out so that only the star-shaped outline remained. It glistened beautifully on Panni as she hung it around her neck. The light from the fireplace reflected from the star as it lay against her chest.

"Lenne sae touone maitelle," Panni thanked the wonderfully generous man.

Oldsmith spoke again to Panni and then explained to Window, "The star belonged to my wife. I gave it to her on <u>her</u> twentieth birthday. I know that she would be happy for Panni to have it."

Then Oldsmith turned back to Panni and told her that, in the morning, he would remove the servant bracelet from her ankle.

Panni expressed her thrill at the prospect of being cut free from her slavery. *"Mae tonne lae nen realle!"* Then she repeated as Circles often did, *"Mae tonne lae nen realle!"* as she reached for the man's hand and kissed it.

Rook presented Panni a gift also. He would help her learn to speak more Atlandan. It had been that Oldsmith, to keep from completely giving up the Windlands life of his youth, had taught his daughter, and then his grandson, to speak the language. When Rook came to visit at his house, all of their conversations were in Atlandan. Now, Rook spent time teaching the basics of it to his friends in the band of street children that he was part of. Understanding some Atlandan had become a requirement to join the group of young boys and girls and they used it as their own secret language, if ever they wanted to talk without anyone else understanding them. And, because they could speak some Atlandan, the group had started calling themselves the Atters. Panni loved the idea of learning Atlandan immensely. She felt as if her whole life was opening up and she wanted to experience all that she could. And, of course, she wanted to be able to talk more completely to Window.

But for tonight, the celebrating and the learning and the eating were almost over. Oldsmith had no wine, or other special drink, to share as a toast, so he removed the silver longsword from the wall, and held it out toward Panni, his hand wrapped around the hilt, and its sparkling blade pointed up toward the ceiling.

"Kasaelle wenne torsae, Panni," he wished her, then repeated for Window, "Peace and beauty in your life."

"Now and always," added Window.

"Now and always," echoed Circles.

Panni, happy, but exhausted from her day of adventure, was so tired she could only give a quiet reply, an expression of her deep appreciation. *"Non soe towenne lafanne."*

Then Panni managed a hug for everyone, even for Rings, although she could hardly reach her arms halfway around his massive head. Then the Brarrie left the house for a sleeping spot where he had been staying near the western edge of the city, but promised he would return in a couple of days. Sara and Rook said their goodbyes and went home as well.

Oldsmith remade his bed with fresh linens, and then pulled some old, ragged quilts of his wife's from a chest in the back room. These he spread in front of the fire. Panni would use the bed while the others would sleep on the floor. Trix would join Panni, and sleep at the foot of the bed as he always did.

Panni was too tired to do anything but slide under her covers, and after one last, comforting look around the friendly house, she closed her eyes to sleep.

Window went over to her and quietly spoke, "You have had quite a birthday, Panni. Sweet dreams tonight." But she didn't hear him. She was already dreaming of running in the grass across the top of a sunlit hill. He gently touched her face and wished her the best forever.

The next morning, Oldsmith was up long before the tired travelers. They awoke to the smell of griddlecakes and cheese. The cakes were hot and sweet as Oldsmith covered them in butter and sugar. It was the first of many mornings together at the Calisay house.

As Panni enjoyed her breakfast, she thought back to her Traepelle Castle and how the dancers would be at their late-morning meal without her. She wished them a good day and dreamt, that someday, all of them could be free to have breakfast wherever they wished.

Between the griddlecakes and milk, Oldsmith and Window talked of plans for Window and Circles to travel to the Battleplain cemetery. Oldsmith, of course, had been there twice, and knew exactly where it was located. Also, in that same part of the Northlands lived Oldsmith's second child, a son named Dawson. Dawson had remained in the Northway village where he was born, when the rest of the family moved to Calisay.

As the two men spoke of their plans, Panni listened, but couldn't understand most of what they were saying. She wondered what Window had in mind for her – if he wanted her to go along, too. And that had been her birthday wish – that Window would ask her to come with him.

After breakfast, they all went into Oldsmith's smithy-shop, at the back of the stable-barn, to watch as he removed the metal band from Panni's ankle. Oldsmith lifted a large metal-cutting scissors tool from the wall near his iron-working anvil. Panni sat on the worktable and held her left leg out and rested it on the anvil. She was shaking with excitement as Oldsmith slipped one of the blades inside the bracelet next to her leg and closed the other blade under the bracelet against the anvil. It only took one blow of his giant iron hammer on the scissors blades to cut through the band neatly. Another cut and the band fell free – and Panni was free as well!

Panni rubbed her now-naked ankle again and again. Everyone smiled and shared in her joy of freedom.

Then Oldsmith carefully heated the severed pieces of the ankle band in his smithy fire and, using tiny pincers, gently removed the jeweled stones. There were six stones in all – three rare, purple aqua-stones and three beautiful rose-diamonds. He polished them with a soft cloth and dropped them into Panni's hand. She wiped a few tears away from her eyes with her other hand as she held the jewels tightly to her chest. Panni was thrilled beyond words. She carried the jewels with her the rest of the day.

+++++++++

It was the first day of several weeks that passed at Oldsmith's Calisay house, as the three travelers rested and Window planned for their trip to search for the Battleplain treasure of Northlands coins.

On some of the days, in the morning, Panni would help Sara in her bake-shop. Sara taught Panni how to bake zell-bread, and Panni taught Sara several recipes for fancy evening breads and party cakes. They enjoyed each other's company, and Sara told Panni, that if she decided to stay in Calisay, she would be welcome to work in the bakery with her. Sara had never heard of springcookies, but tried to bake some, using the ingredients Window remembered from helping his grandma bake hers. The cookies didn't turn out like springcookies, and, of course, Sara had no picture pressing board, but they did taste pretty good.

Circles wanted to see the Calisay towers close up, so he and Rook went out on several expeditions into the center of the city. Circles was thrilled to have a friend that was about his own size, instead of having to look up at Window and Panni all of the time. The two small adventurers returned home with happy stories of their days – including a story of being chased away by some sheriff's men when they tried to sneak into one of the towers. Circles was thrilled to see, up close, the towers he had dreamed of for so long.

Window mostly stayed in the house. He got to shave for the first time since he left home, and he enjoyed that. His beard had grown just long enough to start to bother him, and he was glad to be without it for a while.

Everyday Window spent time writing in his notebook and just relaxing around the house. Sometimes he helped with the cooking and also cleaned the stable for Oldsmith. One afternoon, he went with Oldsmith to care for the Matenne horses.

Window also spent hours studying the patches and medals in the frame on Oldsmith's wall. He asked Oldsmith a hundred questions, until he knew all about where each one had come from, and what it signified. Window thought that his medallion would look good up on the wall with the other military insignia.

While looking around the house, Window found two Atlandan books in Oldsmith's bookcase. One was an Atlandan-Freelandan dictionary and the other was full of maps and was the history of *The Continent Wars*. Oldsmith had brought them with him when he came to the North with Revell. These were the two books that he used to teach Rook to read Atlandan. Window spent a couple of afternoons with them, trying to teach himself some words in the Northlands language.

Trix spent most of his time eating, and sleeping in the sun on the wide front windowsill. He didn't seem to be interested in doing much else. But sometimes he would jump up in someone's lap and sleep there for a while.

Rook and Circles also spent several afternoons building kites in the workshop at the back of the stable barn. Circles made one of bright red paper that Sara found for him in the paper drawer, back at her house above the bakery. The next afternoon, everyone went to a field at the west edge of the city, near where Rings was staying, and watched as Rook helped Circles fly the kite. It flew pretty well and Circles was thrilled. He called his creation the "red monster," although, except for its bright color, it was a very tame looking kite.

Panni insisted that some of the jewels from her bracelet be used to buy clothes and supplies for the travelers, and for Oldsmith and his family, too. She decided to keep two of the three rose-diamonds and one of the purple aqua-stones and to sell the others if she could. Sara put on her best clothes, which really weren't very good, and took the gems to a jewelry merchant in an upper-class area near the heart of the city. The merchant eyed her rather suspiciously, but didn't ask any questions about how a poor working-class woman came to have three beautiful gemstones. Sara came back with enough silver coins to solve the traveler's immediate money problem and to have some left over.

With the money from the stones, the next day, Sara took Panni out shopping to buy clothes for her, and also, a few things for Window. For him, they bought two long overshirts, a second pair of longpants, underclothes, and socks.

Panni, of course, needed all new clothes. She had already thrown her night skirt and underblouse away, and had been wearing an old, but happy, sundress that Sara had found for her.

For Panni, the women bought soft white underclothes, two thin lace underblouses, a short, light teal-blue walkingskirt, and a pair of soft leather shoes that tied over her feet and high around her now unbanded ankles. To go with her skirt and new shoes, Panni was thrilled when they found several pairs of brightly colored, patterned, leggings that reminded her of the dancer's leg warmers she often wore at the Traepelle Castle.

Panni also bought a long-sleeved overshirt, a thigh-length tunic with designs stitched into its front panels, and two, loose over-blouses that had very slight over-the-shoulder sleeves and low, scooped necks. The last clothing they found for her was a pair of heavy longpants, for walking in the woods or tall grass or brambles.

Panni enjoyed the search for clothes quite a bit. In her life at the Traepelle Castle, all of her clothes were provided, so she had never been shopping before.

Lastly, Sara helped Panni buy grooming items – a hairbrush, a washcloth and soap, and several clips and ties to help keep her extremely long hair from flying wildly, as it had been doing since she left the castle. Sara had already given Panni and Window, each a cloth shoulder bag that she had made, in which to carry their personal items.

Panni also chose to buy a small mirror. She enjoyed seeing herself in the looking glass. Back at her castle, the dancers' rooms had many mirrors they used to groom themselves. Panni missed that part of her days with the other young women.

Later that same day, Oldsmith came back from a market near the horse stables with a side-sword for Window. It was about a foot and a half long, with a simple silver hilt and blade, in a brown leather sheath. Window had never used such a weapon, but reluctantly agreed that it might be necessary.

For Panni, Oldsmith bought a small dagger – the blade not much longer than the handle, but thin and pointed and exceedingly sharp. Panni had requested it. She was determined to never again be helpless as she had been in her captivity. She had never held a dagger before, but, even around Oldsmith's house, she wore it in its silver, metal sheath, on a light grey, cloth belt against her hip.

The Northlands days were warm and getting warmer. Some mornings, just to relax, Panni would wash her hair with water she pumped from Oldsmith's well, and heated in a big pot at the fireplace. Then she would sit in the sun on the low, uncovered porch behind the house, and comb and brush her hair – and sometimes braid it. She knew many beautiful braiding styles. The Traepelle dancers had often spent afternoon hours combing and braiding each other's hair. And, Panni's hair was so long that she could braid it in a different fashion every day.

Panni also spent many of her afternoons sitting in the sun at the back of Oldsmith's house. She would lie back in the big lounging chair there, place a cloth across her eyes, and let the sunlight kiss her legs and chest and arms for a short time. Living with the dancers, she was forced to stay mostly indoors, and so she enjoyed being in the sun now, wherever she wished. Her skin was very fair, however, so she never stayed as long as she would have liked.

As Panni relaxed in the afternoon sun, Oldsmith would let his chickens out of their pen behind the barn. They would run around and peck at the corn he threw to them. Panni enjoyed talking to the chickens and telling them stories of when she was held at the castle. Sometimes Trix would join her, and she would talk to him, too. And, she was very happy to show everyone, after a week of resting, how her injured feet were almost completely healed.

One afternoon, Panni even went along with Oldsmith and helped him milk the cow that he kept in the small shared-pasture up the alley a bit. She laughed so much that it seemed to bother the cow. It took them a long time to get enough milk for supper.

In the evenings, after supper, Oldsmith would fill his pipe from the tobacco tin on the table and relax with a smoke. Window remembered the tobacco smell from when he was a boy, and would visit a neighbor man who lived up the street. Window loved the smell of the burning tobacco – strong and sweet, and somehow comforting.

One cool night as Window and Oldsmith were talking at the table, Circles curled up in front of the fire.

"What do you think happened to Revell?" Window asked, as he tried to find out still more about the Northlands.

"I guess that he went back to search for the Eastenne Mines."

"What about the mines – haven't others looked for them?"

"Many have looked for them, but they have never been found."

Oldsmith continued, "A few years after I came to the North with Revell, there were great tremors and quakes in the Eastern Mountains.

"Since then, many people have searched for the mines but no one has been able to find them. People say that the lands are changed. So I guess that the mines are lost and are still waiting to be rediscovered."

"I'll bet we could find them, Window," spoke up Circles, who had been pretending to be sleeping by the fire.

"I thought that you were sleeping, Circles."

"I've been planning," responded the young Woot. "I've been planning."

"Well, plan something that doesn't involve traveling to the unknown Eastern mountains, will you? We have enough to do to get to the Battleplain Cemetery."

"But, Window, wouldn't you like to find a really big treasure, not just a few Northlands coins?"

Window started to answer, but then didn't say anything.

Oldsmith interrupted Window's thoughts. "If you really want to search for treasures, Window, there are many treasures to be found here in the Northlands."

Window remembered that the traveler to Uncle Breeze's tavern had spoken of "many treasures" in the North.

Oldsmith went on to explain that there were three treasures lost in the Northlands. They were called the Old Kingdom Treasures. During the Continent Wars, when the Northlands King, Alezan, knew that his kingdom was going to be lost, he had a plan to protect his massive treasures from being captured by the Atland armies. He separated his wealth into three parts – his gold and silver coins, his crown, jewels, and golden chains, and his golden plates, urns, statues, and large castle ornaments. He trusted each part to one of his three sons.

One part was taken by wagons, west to the Atlandic Ocean port city of Meriselle. One part was taken east to the mountains to be hidden. The third part was hidden somewhere in Calisay, but no one knows where. Some people think that it was just buried near one of the towers, or built into the stone wall of a building. No one is sure which treasure went with which son, but everyone is sure that the treasures where hidden and have never been found.

Suddenly Window remembered a Windlands rhyme:

> Treasures hidden by the king
> But where can treasures be
> Treasure hidden in the woods
> Treasure by the sea

Treasure high and treasure far
Treasure underground
Oh, the King's a pauper now
Treasures never found

Towers tall and flags of blue
Treasures rare and...

Window couldn't remember any more of the rhyme, but like so many others, the rhyme was true – there really were three treasures of Calisay hidden in the Northlands!

"Do you think that maybe Revell went looking for those treasures too?"

"I wouldn't be surprised. He really was driven to get rich somehow. That's why he was so upset when we didn't find the Northlands coins in the Cemetery."

Window thought silently to himself for a few minutes. Circles got up from the floor and walked over to him and quietly spoke.

"I'll bet Panni is good at finding treasure, Window," he said with a smile.

"Go to sleep, Circles. You are already dreaming."

"I'll bet she is," repeated the Woot as he flopped back down on his blanket by the fire. "I'll bet she is."

Window had, of course, been wondering if Panni wanted to remain with them and travel to the Battleplain. At first, he had thought that she might want to go with Circles and him, but then he also knew that she enjoyed working with Sara and might choose to stay and work in the bakery, and live in Calisay. He only wanted what was best for her, and he didn't have to wait long to find out.

Early the next evening, politely and sweetly, of course, Panni, asked Window if she could come along with him. She had spent two entire afternoons with Rook, preparing to speak with Window, by having Rook teach her, in Atlandan, the exact things she wanted to say.

Panni spoke to Window alone on the back porch, *"I would like to come with you, Window. May I please come along with you and Circles to look for treasure? I would like to find a treasure, too. And I would miss you if you go without me."* Her eyes were bright and hopeful – her voice was clear and her pronunciation careful and exact, like everything else she did.

Window smiled at her. He knew what his answer was going to be, but he asked, "What will you do, if I say that you may not come with us?"

She understood his question and softly replied, using more words she had been practicing, *"I will follow you."*

Window looked into her eyes. She repeated even more softly, almost whispering, *"I will follow you."*

He took her hands and squeezed them as he nodded, "Yes." Panni hugged him tightly and replied, *"Sae touone maitelle. I mean, thank you, Window, thank you. My heart is with you!"* Then she ran inside to tell the others.

And Window now knew that Panni was a permanent part of his adventure.

That evening was another happy one. After supper, Oldsmith revealed a small secret about himself – he could play the violette. He got out his instrument and played happy dancing songs as Circles hopped and twirled in front of the fire. The violette's strings sang sweetly as he raced the bow across them. Window chose to just watch and so did Panni. She was not yet ready to dance. It would take her time to overcome her reluctance. But she and Window did clap along with the music. Trix, as always, showed his appreciation by sleeping on the hearth.

The next night, Rings came back for a visit. Like all Brarries, he was usually a pretty solitary creature, but he had quickly grown fond of Circles and the others. He appreciated that they were not afraid of him as most people were. And like Woots, Brarries understood Atlandan, so conversation with him was easy. As before, he sat inside the stable-barn and stuck his giant head through the door into the house.

Panni decided to tease him a bit and went over and twirled a long hunk of the fur on his face around her fingers. The big animal liked the attention and just sat and panted loudly. Finally, Panni stopped playing with his fur, and scratched the top of his head for a while. Rings had never experienced such attention. He liked it a lot. His panting changed to a growling purr. Being cared for by Panni was a long way from being hated by Deep Woods creatures who were all afraid of him.

Later that same night, Window asked Rings why he was racing against the men at the fairgrounds when they met him.

"I like to win," he replied. "I don't care what it is. I just like to win – and I hate to lose."

He went on, "But I get bored, because I nearly always win at anything I do. So I keep looking for a new race to win or something else to try."

Circles had an idea. He jumped up and joined the conversation, "Have you ever gone looking for treasure? That is what we are going to do."

"But I don't want any treasure," answered Rings.

"Have you ever found a treasure? It could be exciting."

"Why is finding treasure exciting?"

"Because you get to beat everyone else to finding it. You get to win the race to find the treasure," Circle continued. "I will race you to the treasure, Rings."

"What treasure?"

"Any treasure."

Then Circles thought that he had better check his idea with Window. "Would that be okay, Window, if Rings came along with us?"

"Sure, I would love to have you join us, Rings. You would be a fine treasure hunter."

Rings loved the idea, too. He was tired of running and fighting and would enjoy a new challenge. "Well, okay," he answered. "I will go with you. But, I don't want any treasure. I only want to find it."

"That sounds good to me," spoke up Circles with a twinkle in his eye. "I will be happy to take your part of the treasure for my very own." Window gave Circles a friendly, irritated look.

"What will you do with the treasure you find, Window?" the Brarrie asked.

Window chuckled as he answered, "I have never thought of that, Rings. I have never thought of that. I don't know what I would do with it. I guess that I don't really need any treasure either."

So it was decided that Rings would accompany the travelers in their search for the Northlands coins. Oldsmith would make a large leather harness for Rings to wear, and packs that would hang from the harness. Rings would carry all of the food, clothes, and other supplies to the Graveyard, which he could easily do, and didn't mind doing at all. And, he could carry the coins back to Calisay, so they would not need to take a horse with them to do that.

Rings had never before been part of a group doing anything, and he liked the idea of being included. Brarries rarely had any friends, but Rings did like the others and felt a loyalty towards them all.

The next morning, Oldsmith started, in his stable-barn, making the leather harness for Rings, and the several leather and cloth packs that would be hooked and tied to it. He was a skilled leather worker, and quickly fashioned a beautiful-looking device of smooth straps, buckles, and hooks.

Window and Oldsmith went to the markets and bought some equipment to take with them. They got a shovel, a pickaxe, and prying bar, and some heavy rope. They also bought a pair of gloves for Window and two blankets for Panni and Window to sleep under, and a pair of heavier shoes for Panni, "just in case." Then they bought more matches, a compass, and two metal roasting sticks for small game they might catch along the way.

And, of course, they bought lots of food for the trip. Most of the food was for Window and Panni, but Circles asked to have a few things brought along for him, too. Rings would eat any grass or leaves, so he would not have to be provided for.

There was much discussion about bringing more weapons than Window's sword and Panni's dagger. Oldsmith thought that there were still probably savage wildmen who lived in the hills beyond the Cemetery, and that the travelers needed to be very careful. They might also encounter dangerous animals, although they would certainly be much safer with Rings along.

Finally, it was decided to include a long military spear that Oldsmith borrowed from a horseman friend of his. It was very old, but still was strong and sharp. It was from the time of the Northern Wars. Oldsmith made a special leather sheath that would hold the spear along the side of Rings' body with the other equipment.

Two nights later, Rings came back to try on the harness Oldsmith had made for him. After making a few adjustments to the harness, Oldsmith invited Rings to stay and enjoy the evening with everyone.

The night before, Oldsmith had gotten out a deck of very old playing cards he had brought with him when he came to the North with Revell. He used to play cards with his wife, but since her death, he had only played them with Rook and Sara a few times.

Oldsmith taught Window how to play his favorite game, Northdraw, and Window reminded Oldsmith how to play Diamonds. Window liked how the soldiers on Oldsmith's cards were wearing the insignia of the early Atland army. And, the Arrow card was bright blue like the one the Windlands soldiers wore. They played long into the night after the others had gone to sleep.

Tonight, Sara and Rook were coming over and they were all going to play. Rings wanted to play, too – well, he wanted to win. Of course, Rings had never seen playing cards before and neither had Circles. Panni had played cards with her dancer friends, but the Northlands card deck she was familiar with was different than the one Oldsmith had.

Circles didn't want to play, but only to watch. Panni also chose
not to play, but sat by Window and watched his cards as he,
Oldsmith, Sara, Rook, and Rings began a game of Northdraw.
After a while, Window sometimes let Panni choose which of his
cards to play. She quickly became pretty good at the game. She
especially liked winning a double trick by playing the Red Ace.
Oldsmith laughed a lot as the games continued. He hadn't had
such fun in a long, long time.

Rings, of course, couldn't hold any cards, but he talked Circles
into holding the cards for him. They had pulled the table over by
the door to the barn, and Rings again stuck his giant head into the
room. Circles held his cards up so Rings could see them.

Rings was fascinated by the game. He had never even heard of
playing cards before and was thrilled to find another thing he
could try to win. But, he warned everybody not to intentionally let
him win. He said that would just make him angry, and, of course,
nobody wanted him to become angry, so they were very careful
that they played fairly. Rings never did win a game, but he did
win several matches and that made him very happy. And Circles
loved being Rings' partner.

When they finished the game, Rings politely thanked everyone
and asked if they might play again soon.

"I would like it if you could play cards with my Uncle Breeze
someday," Window told him. "I think that you and he would get
along well."

Two more sunny days and one rainy one passed in the friendly
Calisay house, and then it was almost time for the travelers to
leave. Their last night with Oldsmith had arrived.

Rook, Sara, and Rings all joined the group again for one last
evening together. Oldsmith played the violette again, and
everyone sang along as best they could. Circles danced with Sara
and Rook, and this time Panni moved her feet as she sat on her
favorite bench in front of the window. Trix lay by the fire and
cleaned his fluffy, grey hair.

Oldsmith surprised Panni with another gift. She had given
him the two rose-diamonds from her bracelet as her gift to him for
his kindness. She knew that he was a poor man, and could surely

use the money the stones would bring. Oldsmith had reluctantly accepted her generous gift, but had plans of his own.

For almost a week, he had worked late into the night in his smithy-shop after Panni was asleep, melting and forming the pieces of her ankle bracelet into a comb that she could wear in her hair. It had three slender blades connected by a flat bar between them. The blades were wide and would hold the comb securely in place. And, embedded in the silver bar, was one of the two rose-diamonds that she had given him. It was a beautiful addition to her hair as she sat in the firelight. Of course, her smile was joined by a few tears that ran down her face.

With Rook at her side to help her choose the words, Panni said to him, *"It is beautiful, Oldsmith. I will treasure it always."*

Circles spoke up, "It looks like you have found your first treasure, Panni."

"Oh, this is not my first treasure, Circles," she replied, as she looked around the room at her friends. *"I already have more treasures than I deserve. Tresenne sae laetreielle."*

Tears were about to come to everyone's eyes as Oldsmith had one more gift to deliver.

"This is for you, Window." He held up the key that Revell had given him all of those years before. "I want you to have it. Maybe you can find the lock it will open."

The key was brightly shining silver-blue in color, and, although very old, was not a bit rusted. It appeared that the key itself might be a treasure. Window thought that it was made of some metal he had never seen before. And, its handle-end was heart-shaped. "Maybe it is the key to someone's heart," thought Window wistfully, as he held it up for all to see.

"I thank you, Oldsmith. I thank you for everything. And I will tell my grandfather about all of your kindnesses. You have been very generous with us. We will never forget you." Window paused, and then added, "You are a treasure to all of us."

So their last evening together came to an end. In the morning, Rings would return, and after putting on his harness and loading

it with their clothes and supplies, which were all prepared and
ready in the barn, they would leave for the Battleplain.

Rings said his goodbyes first and soon after that, Sara and
Rook also left for home.

The fire crackled quietly as everyone else lay down to sleep.
Window wished that there were some wind chimes hanging
outside somewhere that he could listen to for a while, but there
were none. He was left to his quiet thoughts and memories. His
thoughts and memories were of Mary, so far away from him now.
He could hear Circles breathing as Window closed his eyes for the
last time that night.

+++++++++

[AT NEWTOWN]

*Julie Page couldn't sleep. She didn't know why. There
was nothing in particular on her mind. She sighed to herself,
"Five thousand people in Newtown, and I'll bet I am the only
one not sleeping." Well, she <u>was</u> thinking of her boyfriend,
John, at the University.*

*But, she would see him in a couple of days when she
returned from her visit home. It was just by chance that her
cousin from Coastown had been able to bring her home from
New Laws for a few days. It had been a long trip by wagon
through the central Windlands.*

*Julie had spent most of her days at home, sitting by the
river, watching a barge being loaded with the famous
Newtown bricks for their trip to Summerland. The brickyard
was built right at the source of the peach-colored, mud-clay
used to make the beautiful bricks highly preferred by the
Summerland mansion builders. Julie had sat, watching the
river flow by, thinking of nothing in particular. Well, she <u>was</u>
thinking of her boyfriend, John, at the University.*

176

+++++++++

"Window! Window! Wake up! Wake up! The soldiers are here!" Circles was shaking him and frantically shouting. As Window opened his eyes, a loud pounding of a sword hilt on wood shook the front door of the house.
"They found out. The soldiers found out that Sara sold Panni's jewels. They have come for Panni. Window!"

Oldsmith ran to the door and checked the latches as he desperately said something in Freelandan to Circles. The pounding came again, accompanied by the angry voice of the Captain of Prince Martellan's city forces. Oldsmith glanced out of the window – in the early morning light he could see them – five soldiers, dressed in black, and each carrying a silver sword. The

Captain was standing at the door on the small front porch platform.

Oldsmith quietly shouted at Window, "You have to go, now! I will keep them as long as I can."

Oldsmith repeated, "You have to go. Now! – Out the back of the stable!"

Panni was up and frantically dressing. She threw the rest of her things into her shoulder pack, took a quick look at Oldsmith, and pulled Circles into the stable through the side door.

Their equipment and supplies were all packed and sitting on the ground waiting to be hung onto Rings harness. Rings! He was still at his sleeping spot. They would have to pull and carry everything to him. But the soldiers would surely catch them!

"Nae son tevae pareinne!" cried the Captain. *"Nae son pareinne"*

"Sentousae trerisse!" called back Oldsmith, pretending to be just waking up, and pretending to be looking for the key to the door.

Window picked up his shoulder pack and took one last look at the eyes of the wonderful old man, whom he had grown to care for so much.

Oldsmith returned the glance, and they both understood what they meant to each other. Window stepped into the stable-barn and Oldsmith quietly shut the door behind him.

Inside the barn, Window reached Rings' harness down from some hooks and threw it toward Circles. "Go!" Window spoke quietly for fear of being heard. The Woot dragged the straps of leather and cloth behind him as he went out the back door.

Oldsmith knew that he had to open the front door or the soldiers would break it down. He unlatched the door and slowly pulled it open a bit. Outside, on the low wooden step, the Captain of the Guard grabbed at the door, and tried to push it all the way open. Oldsmith stood in the doorway to keep the soldier from entering the house.

Twenty feet and two walls away, Window and Panni each grabbed three packs of food and clothes and supplies from the floor – Panni quickly followed Circles out the backdoor. Window took one last look around. The shovel, pickaxe, prying bar, and army spear were all still leaning against the wall. They would have to leave them. They were too heavy to try to carry along with all of their other things. Then, at the last second, Window grabbed the spear and pulled it behind him as he forced his way through the small back door.

Oldsmith's chickens noisily flapped and squawked as the three ran past them and down the alley towards the edge of town where Rings was sleeping. Dust flew everywhere, as Circles dragged the harness and hooking straps behind him in the dirt. They would have to find Rings! They would have to escape from the soldiers, who would certainly be right behind them!

The Captain of Prince Martellan's city guard roughly grabbed Oldsmith, and tried to push him aside so he could get into the house.

"Tiena see enn matarin solelle," he angrily demanded. *"Tiena see enn matarin!"* Oldsmith did not move.

"Has tinne tras delenden, whensae falnasae!" the officer angrily continued, but Oldsmith offered no explanation of where a smithy's daughter had gotten a handful of jewels.

Behind the Captain, the four other soldiers stood ready to enter the house as soon as they were given the order. Oldsmith knew that his friends needed more time to escape. He would have to do something – anything!

He reached into his pants pocket. Hidden deep in the pocket was the second rose-diamond Panni had given him. It was the only chance he could give to his friends.

Oldsmith didn't say anything, but just held the gemstone up in the morning sunlight. All five of the soldiers were stunned into silence and inaction. The diamond sparkled brightly against the drab boards of Oldsmith's house.

He let each of the soldiers get a good look at the jewel. They kept their eyes on it with great interest. Then he did something they did not expect. Oldsmith took the jewel and threw it over the soldiers' heads, across the narrow street, and into the tall grass growing on the other side.

The soldiers quickly forgot about everything else. Even the Captain no longer cared about chasing a run-away servant girl. They only cared about a chance to have the diamond as their own. All five of the men turned from Oldsmith and ran to the spot where they thought that the stone had disappeared into the grass. They dropped to their knees and started wildly scrambling and searching the grass, each determined to be the one to find it. They pushed each other, and cursed, and pulled grass and weeds aside in a frantic search for the stone.

Oldsmith had done it! He had saved his friends. By the time the stone was found by one of the soldiers and they returned to their duty, the travelers would be far away. Oldsmith had saved his friends, but lost the rose-diamond. But he really didn't mind too much. The stone would have bought him a little easier life for a while, but his new friends were all he really cared about now.

As the soldiers continued their unsuccessful search in the grass, Oldsmith looked down the street to the west, "Goodbye, my friends. May the Angels be with you." His voice sounded tired but happy.

Just then, Trix came out from behind the open front door and jumped up into Oldsmith's arms. The old man scratched the big cat's head and spoke to him, "That's right, Trixy, they are on their way. And I hope that someday we see them again."

The cat purred in agreement.

A mile or so to the west, beneath a small grove of trees at the edge of the city, Window and Panni were throwing the harness straps over Rings' back. Panni finished tying the straps together as Window hung the packs and bags of supplies from the side hooks.

Then Window lifted Circles up and pushed him atop the Deep Woods Brarrie. Rings yawned, and was ready. Window lightly took Panni's arm and turned her to go. Panni stopped, and looked back towards the city.

Quietly, she spoke for all of them, *"Goodbye, Oldsmith, Sae lan touelle. Sae lan faresse. We keep you in our hearts."* Each of them held the rest of their thoughts to themselves.

The four travelers turned towards the west. The road was clear before them. The day was just beginning.

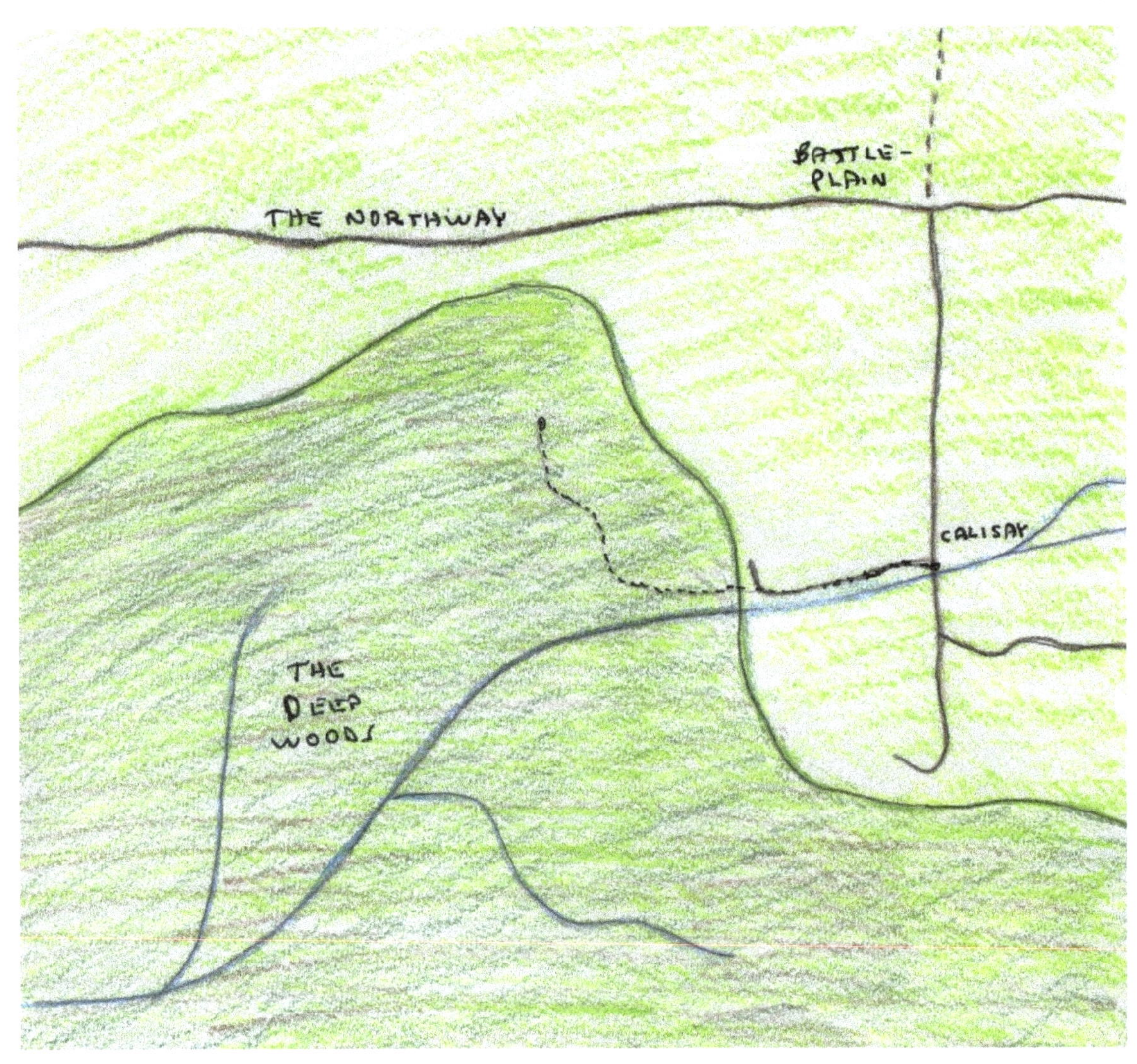

THE NORTHWAY
BATTLE-
PLAIN
CALISAY
THE
DEEP
WOODS

CHAPTER NINE

TO THE FOREST WORLD

The road ahead led to the west, not north to the Battleplain Cemetery, as the travelers wanted to go. They had decided earlier that if they took the road north from the city, the sheriff's men or Calisay soldiers would be sure to find them. It was impossible to hide the massive Rings, so their plan was to travel west where there were no villages and few farms, briefly enter a corner of the Deep Woods, and come out on the north side of the Woods. Then they could approach the Cemetery from the west, rather than directly from the south. This way they would be much less likely to be discovered by any of the authorities that may be looking for them.

Although the day had started out frantically, by noon things were very relaxed and calm for the travelers. The four of them talked and laughed as they walked. Well, Circles didn't walk much. Most of the time, he rode on Rings' shoulders, and held on to one of the pack straps across the Brarrie's back. And, I guess that you couldn't really say that Rings could laugh. But he did growl in agreement when the others did.

Once the four of them were several miles from Calisay, they stopped for a while and assessed the equipment and supplies that they had. When they were forced to leave Oldsmith's in such a hurry, besides the larger tools in the stable-barn, they also left behind a lot of food and a few other things that they had not yet packed for the journey. But, they did have all of their clothes and personal items, which were packed the night before.

Circles had the only two things he owned, the far-looking scope that Rings had given him, and the kite Rook had helped him build. He had taken the kite apart and rolled it up carefully before sliding it into the sheath that was supposed to be for the spear Oldsmith had given them.

Among the items they had left behind was an archery bow and a quiver of arrows for Circles. Rook was going to bring them over from his house in the morning before the travelers left. It had been decided that besides the sword and dagger for Window and Panni, Circles should have a weapon as well. Rook had spent two afternoons teaching Circles how to shoot the bow, and he had learned quickly. Circles enjoyed shooting and his padded hands could hold the bow quite firmly, while his keen vision helped him see the most distant target. Besides shooting at trees and bales of hay behind Oldsmith's house, he and Rook had sneaked back to the fairgrounds and practiced on the real archery targets there. But, now, Circles had no weapon.

Rings, of course, couldn't hold a weapon or anything else, but he had his own size and strength to protect himself and his friends.

The spear that they were able to bring was hung from the straps from Rings' harness and, as they walked, seemed to be pointing the group in the direction they were to go.

The road they were on was called the West River Road. It went from Calisay along the northern bank of the Calisay River. As they walked, the river was on their left and mostly just open ground on their right. They did pass some poor farms and a few small forests, but mostly they just enjoyed the walk. They were an odd-looking group of travelers, but few people were there to notice.

The mid-spring sun warmed them as they marched along. After several hours, they stopped again for a rest and sat in the grass under the shade of a big tree by the side of the river.

Circles was thinking and planning, as he loved to do. "Let's go to the ocean, Window. Let's go see the ocean."

"We are not going to see the ocean, Circles. It is too far away."

"Then let's go to Meriselle and look for the King's Treasure."

"You know very well that the city of Meriselle is at the ocean, Circles," Window replied, pretending to be upset with his friend.

"I have another idea," continued Window, glancing at a shallow area along the riverbank. "You say that you can run on wet rocks. Let's see you run on some of those rocks."

"Even though you didn't get us any money in Calisay, which, as you will remember, was your job to do," Circles reminded him, "I will do my job."

Circles popped up from the grass and ran directly towards the river. He didn't slow down as he got close to the water, in fact, he sped up. At the water's edge, he just kept on running. He stepped on dry rocks, he stepped on wet rocks – rocks of all shapes and sizes. Some were sticking out of the water, some were buried beneath the surface. He twisted and turned and ran in circles, jumping and hopping from one stone to another. When he stepped on rocks that were just under the surface, it looked as if he were running on top of the water. It was an amazing sight. His sticky padded feet kept him steady and he never slipped or wobbled even once. His balance was steady and his grip on the wet stones was flawless. He hopped and jumped and turned from rock to rock, then stopped on top of a big rock and bowed to his amazed audience.

"Wow, that is really something, Circles!" called Window. Panni applauded and started laughing so hard that she couldn't stop. Rings made a sound that really was almost a laugh.

"That's nothing. Watch this," Circles instructed. He ran across the tops of a few more rocks and jumped into the water. Well, let's say, he jumped on the water. Circles special fur only let him go down into the water a few inches and then immediately lifted him up. He bobbed and floated high in the water like a duck. Then he rolled over on to his back and floated like a log, never even getting his face wet. Circles was a natural floater. It seemed that he could not sink in the water even if he wanted.

Rings was really enjoying the show. He made a strange
hooting sound that caused Panni to start laughing all over again.
Finally, Panni recovered enough to call out to the Deep Woods
floater. *"Come back, Circles, I will fix you something to eat."*
She opened one of the bags hanging from Rings' side and pulled
out some sweet rolls that Sara had packed for them. Circles loved
sweet rolls. Of course, he had never had any before he got to
Calisay, but one bite of Sara's sugary bread at her bakeshop and
he was hooked forever. So the travelers had a sweet, late lunch
before they continued. While the others sat and had rolls and
berries, Rings wandered over to a patch of tall river grass and ate
by himself.

The rest of their afternoon was uneventful. Circles even went
to sleep while riding on Rings' back. Window and Panni walked
together. Sometimes, Panni would reach up and hang on to one of
the straps on Rings' harness for a while, just to feel even more
connected to the powerful beast.
Later, as the sun started to go down, Rings told the others that
they were almost at the home of a friend of his. It seemed that
whenever Rings would leave the Deep Woods to visit places in
Calisenne Province, he would stop and visit with a shepherd who
tended a flock near the edge of the forest.
The shepherd's name was Royal. He was a quiet, but friendly
man, who, like Rings, preferred to keep mostly to himself. He led
a simple life, with only a small shed used to care for his animals
and to sleep in. Royal enjoyed it when Rings would stop to visit.

As darkness was falling, the travelers reached Royal's place.
His shed was in the open grassland, surrounded only by a few
trees, and hundreds of fluffy grey-white sheep. Circles had never
seen sheep up close before and wanted to ride one. Window told
him he didn't think that was a very good idea. Panni had had a
pet lamb when she was very young and lived at home. Seeing the
sheep reminded her of the happy days she had as a child in
Traepelle. She wondered if she would ever have days like those
again.

Royal was pleased to see Rings and his friends and offered the travelers some soft ground near his fire to sleep for the night. Window was surprised that Royal was able to understand and speak Atlandan somewhat.

After everyone shared greetings, Window and Panni pulled the harness from Rings' back and unpacked a few things. They opened a package wrapped in white paper and treated Royal to some cheese they had brought along. He enjoyed it immensely. Royal hadn't had any cheese since his goat had died the year before.

The group sat by the fire late into the night and talked of nothing in particular. Window told of the time when he was a boy and had tried to catch a bird using a loop of string. With Circles' help, Panni told a funny story about her lamb, Ginger, eating carrots.

Royal explained how he had spent most of his life as a soldier at the Calisay Palace. After years of an unhappy life there doing the bidding of Prince Martellan, he left his position and came out to the western edge of the province to live by himself. He hoped that he could one day return to Calisay and somehow make up for the hardships he had helped place on the people there while he was following the orders of the hated Prince.

Then Royal told stories of his only other visitors – Owts from the Deep Woods. Several of them enjoyed stopping to see him occasionally, and would recite their latest rhymes for him. He had tried to make up a few of his own rhymes but was not very successful.

It was from the Owts that Royal had learned to speak some Atlandan. He wanted to be able to understand all of the rhymes the Owts brought to him, no matter what language they were in. And since he lived by himself and had plenty of time to practice, he spent a lot of that time reciting Atlandan rhymes to his sheep. He thought it kept them calm and happy. He also knew some Woot and some Mallen.

Besides Rings and the Owts, Royal had two other very odd friends – a couple of triple-winged prairieflies that lived inside of an old tree near his shed. In the evening, the buzzing creatures would come and join him by the fire. They were large – almost as long as his hand – and with their dark, but shiny skin, were beautiful to watch, whether they were flying or just sitting. Tonight, they came and quietly perched on a log and didn't do anything – just sat there enjoying the fire in their own insect way. Circles thought that it was kind of sad that a man would have to have bugs to keep him company, but Royal thought that, along with his sheep, they were all of the company that he ordinarily needed.

Royal did tell his guests, though, that some nights when he sat by the fire rolling up new strings of wool yarn into balls for storage, the prairieflies would play a game with him. He would tie a long string of yarn into a small ball about the size of a walnut. The flies would fly over by Royal's shed and then head back across the fire pit as fast as they could. When they passed overhead he would throw the little ball of yarn high into the air towards the tall grass.

Buzzing furiously, the two flies, who Royal called Wilie and Rilie, would race after the yarn ball to see which of them could catch it before it hit the ground. Whichever reached the yarn ball first was the winner, and would hook it with his feet and struggle to carry the ball back to Royal and drop it in his lap.

Once while they were playing that game, Wilie had dug his little claws into the ball of yarn when he caught up with it, but the ball was too big for him to control and it just kept going, turning Wilie over and over and over as it spun through the air. Wilie was finally able to let go just before the yarn ball hit the ground. Otherwise, it could have been a dangerous landing for Royal's insect friend. But, when it happened, Royal thought that Rilie's wing-buzzing almost sounded like he was laughing.

Tonight though, "The Boys" as Royal also called the prairieflies, didn't feel much like flying and chasing. They did, however, hum along with their wings as Royal sang a Northlands shepherd's song for his guests.

"Tellemae trenne sae ahlessnon. Naetouon laeselle," Royal quietly sang in the peaceful prairie night. It was a song of the joy of the rain falling gently from the sky.

Eventually the talking and singing and buzzing faded to a sleepy finish, as everyone felt ready to end the pleasant evening on the grasslands of western Calisenne.

That night, the travelers slept by the crackling fire with Circles again lying on top of Rings. Rings didn't mind. He could hardly tell that Circles was there.

Panni and Window used their new sleeping blankets. Window went to sleep, listening to the soft bleating of about a hundred spring lambs. Their smooth, steady sound was comforting. He thought to himself that it was the quietest noise he had ever heard.

In the morning, after a breakfast of bread and more cheese, the travelers said their goodbyes.

"Selren tousae," Royal told his visitors. "You are always welcome."

"We will see you again," Window replied, hoping it would be true.

Panni gave the friendly shepherd a hug, then she and her friends were on their way again. They would reach the edge of the Deep Woods by mid-day and when the road turned north along the Woods, they would leave the road to enter the forest.

As the travelers walked along, a small flock of about ten forest birds flew overhead. Rings let out a high-pitched whine and the birds came over to him and perched on a big fallen tree trunk by the side of the road.

Rings sat on his haunches in front of the birds and spoke to them in a language that Window didn't recognize. Circles told him that the birds were called Rilli-birds, and were not really Talkers, but could understand Talkers, and could repeat things to other animals. Circles said that he had always wanted to learn to talk to birds, but had never had the chance.

Everyone waited, and pretty soon the Rilli-birds nodded their heads in understanding, and chirping loudly, took off and flew towards the Woods. They flew together, side by side, and then, all at once, split from each other, spreading out like a fan, flying in different directions.

Rings explained to the others. "I have sent them to announce our arrival. They will tell everyone that we are coming and to meet us for a celebration. Tonight, there will be a gathering of forest creatures in your honor. I want you to experience the hospitality of the forest world.

Panni was very pleased. She continued to be thrilled by her freedom. She went up to Rings and gave a big tug on his harness. The creature raised a giant paw and very carefully rubbed the side of her face. She held on to the paw for a moment.

It wasn't too many more miles, when the sun was high overhead, that Rings announced, "We are here." The road was turning to the north, but straight ahead of them, they could see the wide green of the Deep Woods in the distance. Without any further discussion, the travelers left the road and continued across the grass and through the prairie weeds and flowers towards the wall of trees before them.

In about half an hour, they reached the edge of the Woods. It appeared as dark and dense as it was south of Calisay where Window had been on the path from the Windlands. Rings explained that there were forest paths in this part of the Woods too, although not like the wide, straight path that Window had followed. Here the paths were narrow and winding, just wide enough for one animal at a time to pass.

Window felt much more secure approaching the Deep Woods this time than when he was about to enter it at the beginning of his adventure. Having an adventure with friends, especially with one as big as Rings, was certainly better than having one alone.

Rings led them to the edge of the trees, right to an opening, where a path came out into the grass. The sun had been warm on them as they walked, and so now, they were looking forward to the cool of the forest.

Rings led the way as they approached the path. Circles walked next. Panni took Window's hand as they entered beneath the heavy shade. The cool of the Woods refreshed them all.

And as the travelers passed into the trees, but unseen by any of them, peering out from behind thick bushes off to their left, were two pairs of eyes. Not friendly eyes, but menacing Deep Woods eyes. It was another dangerous day in the Woods.

+++++++++

Rings continued to lead his friends though the thick forest. They followed the winding path for a while, then turned on to another. Window quickly lost his sense of direction. He knew that without Rings to guide them, they would never be able to find their way out.

They trekked on. Sometimes scaring birds or small animals that scurried off, unseen, into the dense underbrush.

Rings was too big for most of the paths, so he just stepped on bushes and knocked down small trees as he forced his way deeper into the woods.

On one part of the path, the walkers had to step over big apple-size holes in the ground. "What are those holes from?" Window asked Rings and the Brarrie replied, "Those are ground-dog burrows. You will meet some of them tonight."

"How many Talkers will we see tonight, Rings?" Window wondered.

"More than you can count, Window. Many more."

"Are you sure, Ringer?" Circles jumped in, smiling. "He can count pretty high."

"Thanks for your support, Circles," Window jokingly answered. "You are a real friend!"

"And so are you, Window," Circles seriously assured him. "And so are you."

Rings was leading the group to a Talker meeting place – a large clearing where the animals could gather and rest. There were such places in various parts of the Woods and this one was the closest to the northern edge. After about three hours of twisting through the trees, they arrived at the forest meeting place.

It was a big opening in the trees, with those trees at its edge providing a sort of ceiling above them, although not nearly as high or as complete as the towering trees where Window and Circles found Panni. Near the left edge of the clearing was a slow-moving stream, and straight ahead, on the far side of the opening, another path led off to the north.

The Rilli-birds had done their job well. Already there were dozens of Deeps Woods creatures waiting for the travelers. Window immediately recognized Frazzle and Locker, the two Owts who had been flying their kite in Calisay. Also in the clearing, standing about or seated on one of the many logs around the huge fire pit, were many different types of small animals. Circles introduced himself and his friends to each type of creature. There were several other Owts, some Zeeters, who were tall, skinny otter-looking creatures, and at least thirty Wommies, who were the little ground-dogs that lived in burrows like the ones they had seen. Rings said that they could expect many more of the forest creatures by the time the sun went down.

Besides the Talkers, a lot of other Woods animals began to arrive. Chatty grey squirrels, tree-hares, and water-rakes as well as some birds with extremely long legs – almost two feet high. Circles called them Tay-leggers. They just walked around the clearing pecking at bugs on the ground. Then they sat down with their rumps on a log and pulled one scrawny leg up and crossed it over their other, like a man might do. They really looked comical to Window.

And still the animals came – more Owts, more Zeeters, more Tay-leggers. Five fire-red Stone-foxes arrived. Then, just before the travelers had something to eat for a quick supper, three man-size, furry-ball Talkers walked into the clearing. They were mountain Tree-bears who claimed that they were distant relatives of Rings, although he wouldn't agree that it was true. Window didn't know that there were any mountains in the Deep Woods, but Circles confirmed that there were some far in the western interior. That was the part of the Woods where Rings was from.

Just when Window thought that certainly no more animals would be coming, the night creatures began to arrive. There were long-necked Snackers, long-armed Xaypers, a lumpy, raspberry-looking Treenob, a greenish leafy-looking creature who didn't say anything but just sat on a log and watched everyone else, and, scores of little wild woods-mice, and fuzzy-furred ground-wigglers. Panni started to pet the Treenob, and soon she was surrounded by a sea of rub-seeking creatures. It wasn't until the head Owt, Duster, called everyone to attention that they left her alone.

There was a great feeling of celebration in the air, but Circles was disappointed. As everyone assembled, he saw that there were none of the friendly paw-creature Fire-claws he and Window had encountered on the Deep Woods path. Also, Circles had hoped to see some little forest creatures called Jammies. But none arrived.
Years ago, when Circles was a New-Woot, he used to play with Jammies near his home, but they all disappeared one summer and he hadn't seen any in a long time. Rings told him that they had apparently been chased from their burrow-lands by some Woods monsters and no one knew where they had gone, or even if they survived.

The Owts, who were in charge of the celebration, had decided that there were so many different Talkers, who all spoke different languages, that to keep confusion to a minimum, everyone would be speaking in Atlandan tonight, or at least trying to. Circles would stay close to Panni to interpret, and everyone else would just do the best they could.
Because tonight was a special night, to welcome the travelers to the forest, it was to be a Talker sharing-night. Every creature was invited to perform – sing, dance, tell a rhyme or story, or do a trick for the others. It was going to be a fabulous evening of fun and sharing.
 Several of the Owts gave directions to some of the other creatures, and soon a roaring bon-fire was ablaze in the center of the clearing.
Circles, Window, and Panni sat in the seats of honor, which were just logs to sit on like everybody else. Panni sat between

Window and Circles, and held two of the cute little Wommies in her lap. She petted them gently and they purred their appreciation.

Rings sat on his haunches way in the back of the clearing. He couldn't sit any closer because none of the smaller animals would be able to see over his giant body. All the while, above the clearing, on the branches in the trees, hundreds of night birds were quietly waiting for the show to begin.

"Line up for introductions!" Duster yelled, and the animals started to group together.

"Who's here tonight?" Duster yelled at the huge crowd of creatures.

"We are!" responded the first group of animals, who proceeded to the north side of the fire where the evenings performances would take place.

This process continued. As each group replied to Duster's "Who's here tonight?" they would move as a group and line up across the edge of the clearing. A lot of scuffling and scrambling took place, as the animals in each group were to line up from tallest to shortest in height.

It was quite entertaining to watch as each bunch of creatures moved to their proper place in line. When each line was complete, Duster would again call out, "Who's here tonight?"

This time the answer would be by group name such as, "The Owts are here," or "The Snackers are here." Then each group would add another line, something polite like "And we are glad to be here," or "It is so nice to see you." Then the entire line of creatures would bow together, and everyone would cheer them.

After every group was introduced, which took an amazingly long time, even though some of the more bashful creatures decided to just stay seated and not join in the introductions, it was time for the performances.

One by one, the groups returned to the front of the gathering and shared a presentation with the happy crowd.

The first group to perform was the Snackers. They sang a song about chasing a ground-cat up a tree. Everyone laughed, especially when four of the smaller Snackers acted out the story and ran around wildly.

Next, several of the Owts sang an old Woods song about themselves and their good forest friends, the Woots. They invited Circles up to sing it with them. He sang from his seat. It went like this:

> An Owt and a Woot went out for a walk
> For an Owt won't walk alone
> And a Woot won't walk without an Owt
> As far as it is known
> So a walk about without an Owt
> Is a walk a Woot would do without
> And without a doubt an Owt about
> Is better with Woot than without

The animals loved the song, and the Owts were having such a good time that they refused to give up the stage. They sang another song. This one was simply called The Owt Song.

> Slicker – Skiffer – Babble – Fratz
> Standing in their traveling hats
> Slicker – Skiffer – Babble – Fratz
> Each upon a pair of legs
> Slicker wondering, Skiffer too
> What a Babbling Fratz will do...

It went on for many verses, each one more ridiculous than the last. Many of the animals in the audience knew the song, and soon almost everyone was singing along.

The next performance was of another song most of the creatures knew. Even Window recognized it, although back in the Windlands, the kids sang it as "Monsters in your bed!"

> Monsters in the woods you can bet can bet
> Monsters in the woods will get you yet
> You can go in but you won't come out
> Monsters in the woods no doubt

Monsters in the trees will grab your toe
Monsters in the trees won't let you go
You can cry and you can yell
But you will not live to tell

On into the night, the songs and poems continued. Window knew a few more of them and quietly sang along to himself.

For their sharing, the Wommies put on a little play about planting seeds and then trying to pull big vegetables out of the hard ground when they were grown. It really was more entertaining than it might sound.

When it was their turn, the Tree-bears tried juggling, but they were not very good at it. They were hooted at, and ended up throwing pawfuls of dirt on some of the animals in the front row. Everyone really enjoyed that.

The most exciting performance was given by the strange looking Xaypers. They took thick sticks in each of their boney hands, which were at the end of their long, boney arms, and stood behind the hollow log on which they had been sitting. Then they knelt behind the log and beat on it with their sticks in the most captivating rhythm. The sound of the whacks and thumps of their drumming shot out of the end of the log and filled the clearing.

A couple of the drumming Xaypers then stood up and spun around while they kept the rhythm going. Creatures all over the clearing got up from their seats and danced, and clapped, and shook with the music. The sound echoed across the Woods. When the stick-beaters were finished, the cheers were everywhere. And, it is really something to here cheers coming from scores of different animals, with scores of different voices, in scores of different languages.

Circles was next to perform. As a special guest, he wasn't expected to, but he was happy to share one of his songs with everyone. Since he was the only Woot at the meeting place, he sang alone. He stood on a log and sang clearly and brightly. It was another sweet song, like the one he had sung for Window when they first met. This one was about a mother Woot putting her children to bed and singing them to sleep. All of the animals were very still and quiet as Circles sang. When he finished, they went crazy with applause.

Panni was glad that she was not expected to perform. But when a group of big Dilly-bugs buzzed a humming song, she closed her eyes and moved her feet, as she pictured herself wrapped in smooth silk and on stage with her dancer friends back in Traepelle.

About half way through the evening, the clouds, which were thick overhead, briefly parted, and the entire clearing became brightened by light of the late-night moon. The silver moonlight shined down and gave the performers a real look of being on a stage. It was fortunate for the animals that the night was such a beautiful one. Window thought that it was an almost perfect night. Then, for him, the night did become perfect.

Circles, who was now sitting next to Window, scooted over close to him and tapped his shoulder. When Window turned to look at Circles, the Woot nodded his head in a direction off to the side of the log where Stone-foxes were sitting.

And there it was – the Watcher! It was the dark, shadow-creature that Window had spent an evening talking to when he first entered the Deep Woods. At least, it probably was the same one. The creature was quietly doing what it seemed to do best – standing, watching, and listening.

Window was thrilled. He gently touched Panni's hand. She turned to him and he pointed out their new visitor. No one else had apparently noticed the creature. Panni's heart took a little jump. The creature was charming and magical. It drifted out of shape a bit and then returned to its man-like form. It was fantastic! Panni immediately shared in Window's wonder and delight.

And Panni knew how important the creature was to Window. He had told her all about it. She knowingly squeezed his hand. She loved her friendship with Window and was deeply pleased to share his reconnection with his mystical Deep Woods friend.

As Window continued to look towards the shadow, it raised one of its wispy arms and held its shadow-hand up towards him. Window returned the greeting. It <u>was</u> his shadow friend from before! It was his Watcher!

Through the remainder of the evening of performances, Window regularly glanced back to check to see if the Watcher was still there. As long as the moonlight remained, so did he.

Little by little, though, the heavy clouds returned, and with them, the shadow-man disappeared, returned briefly, then, disappeared again. Window had hoped to talk to his shadow friend after the performances, but realized, with such thick clouds filling the sky, that it was unlikely he would see the Watcher again tonight. But, he felt assured, that certainly, someday, they would meet again. It was a treasure he would look forward to.

With a happy sigh, Window turned his attention to the group of Slack-lizards that had somehow sneaked onto the stage area and were trying to balance themselves into a tall tower of lizards. It was really funny to watch.

Then Window realized something else. He had been holding Panni's hand the entire time since the shadow-man appeared. He gently released his grip. Panni softly slid her hand from his. She reached down to the ground in front of her and picked up a little long-tailed Doh-squirrel to hold. She looked straight ahead to the balancing lizards. The light from the fire reflected in her eyes.

It was a wonderful evening of joyous celebration that lasted far into the dark of the night. One by one, each of the other groups performed. There was more singing, more dancing, more storytelling, until everyone had had their chance. Finally, Duster asked if anyone else had anything to share.

Frazzle and Locker, the kite flying Owts, decided to end the evening with a couple of verses of a happy song they had written. They stood on a big log on the far side of the fire, and loudly sang it for the – by now – sleepy crowd. It was a nonsense song with a bunch of nonsense words that were easy to learn. Everyone started to sing along with the chorus and the two Owt friends really hammed it up as they hit the big final note. Their faces were shining in the fire light, and everyone was on their feet, stamping along. Then it happened.

As Locker raised his head high, singing the final note, something very confusing happened. It took a moment for everyone to realize what it was. As he raised his head and sang, suddenly something dark appeared on his up-stretched throat. At first Window couldn't see what it was – then he realized the terrible truth.

Sticking from Locker's throat was an arrowhead and part of an arrow shaft. Locker had been shot from behind with an arrow through his neck! His bright fire-lit blood shot out from his neck as his face tighten in agony.

Next to him, Frazzle fell forward, an arrow piercing his shoulder from behind. Then Locker fell forward – a second arrow buried in his back.

Window grabbed Panni's hand. The Deep Woods monsters were attacking!

The terrified cries of hundreds of Talkers and their friends filled the clearing. Another dozen arrows flew into the crowd and several more animals fell dead – a Zeeter, a Snacker, two smaller animals.

Most of the animals turned to run away from the direction the arrows were coming. When they reached the back of the clearing near the relative safety of the trees, the second attack came.

Pouring out from their hiding places in the trees, came ten or twelve of the hideous Teeth-monsters that Window had narrowly escaped from on the Deep Woods path. Along with the Teeth-monsters were another twenty or so wild Ashdogs, and four vicious Nakes. The Nakes stood on two long legs and had wicked split tongues that slithered from beneath their snake-like eyes. The monsters grabbed any forest animal they could reach and attacked them fiercely – their monstrous teeth and claws ripping the smaller animals to pieces.

Death was everywhere. The Ashdogs had killed one of the Tree-bears and had attacked another.

Window pulled Panni back towards the spot where they had

put Rings' harness and their packs of equipment. His sword was there. He had to reach it to have any hope of surviving. He lost hold of Panni's hand and she fell to the ground behind him.

Window turned to help Panni, and was knocked violently forward – he caught himself on one of the big, sitting-logs. He felt something behind him and then pain as he had never experienced before. His mind screamed in agony but his breath was gone and his body was frozen. A Teeth-monster had grabbed him from behind with his filthy, matted paws and had sunk his four rows of jagged teeth into Window's shoulder and back.

Window tried to stand up straight, the monster's giant mouth still attached to his shoulder, his jacket keeping the monster's teeth from being buried even deeper into his back. Just as suddenly, the monster let out his own terrible cry of agony. Window spun around as the monster released his grip and his teeth from Window's back. Window was looking directly into the creature's face as its ugly black eyes seemed to lose their focus and go dim.

The monster fell to the ground. Standing behind it was Panni – her blood-drenched dagger in her uplifted fist. She had just pulled the dagger from the back of the monster. She had saved Window. She had killed the deadly creature!

Panni's face was filled with horror. Her face and blouse were covered with sticky, deep red blood. She heaved a massive sigh of relief as tears came to her eyes. She had been frightened beyond imagination. Never before had Panni ever been close to anything like this. She would be lost without him. Window was being killed. She had saved her Window.

There was no time to think about it anymore. Attacking monsters were everywhere. The monsters with the bows and arrows had entered the clearing. They were Marrents, the ugly, rat-faced animals that Circles had not wanted to speak to on the Calisay kite field. But Marrents were Talkers. They must have joined forces with the monsters.

Chaos was everywhere. Many smaller forest animals and scores of the Talker animals were dead on the ground. There were cries of pain and terror echoing across the clearing.

Above all of the noise, Window could hear Rings roaring.
Window spun around and saw his giant friend at the back of the
clearing. Teeth-monsters and Nakes were dead at his feet. An
Ashdog went flying through the air. Arrows stuck out of the
Brarrie's side and legs. Another Ashdog was tossed into the air.

Window noticed something he hadn't known about Rings.
Hidden inside of his massive paws were long claws. Claws which
were now extended and being used to slice at the attacking
monsters. Five Ashdogs were trying to bring down the great
beast, but Rings was fighting them off.

All around them the injury and death continued.

Circles! What about Circles! Panni pulled at Window's sleeve
and turned him towards the Woot. Circles was on the ground
near the fire, struggling with one of the Marrents. The creature
was on top of Circles and was about to bring his elbow down on
Circles' face. Panni screamed out a plaintive *"No!"* as Circles was
nearly struck by the creature. Circles slid free and rolled away.
His silky fur had allowed him slip from the grasp of his attacker.

Circles ran towards the spot where they had stored Rings
harness. The wild Marrent ran after him. Circles reached the
harness a few seconds before his attacker, grabbed the army
spear, and slid it from its ties.

Just as the Marrent reached him, Circles turned around to face
him. The charging creature could not stop in time. He ran
directly into the sharp metal blade on the spear's end. Circles fell
backward but the damage was done. The spear had entered the
chest of the attacker. He fell to the side – his eyes and face filled
with death. Panni ran to Circles and pulled him to his feet. They
were both covered with blood and filth.

As the trio looked back to the fire pit, they saw the little
ground-dog Wommies had mounted their own counterattack.
Bunches of them were attacking different monsters, biting and
nipping at their feet and legs. They were tiny animals, but they
really did do quite a lot of damage. Others of the very small
animals joined in. Many of them were killed by the slashing claws
and teeth of the monsters – but those that survived fought on.

Slowly the tide of battle began to turn. Rings moved around the clearing, kicking and stomping and cutting any monster he could reach.

More and more of the smaller animals returned to the clearing and attacked the monsters in mass. A group of Owts had taken down two of the Nakes. Another Nake was tripped and pushed into the fire by some very brave Zeeters.

Window pulled his sword from its sheath on Rings' harness and headed back into the battle. Panni desperately grabbed his arm to hold him there, to somehow keep him safe from the danger. He turned toward her and looked into her terrified eyes. In a pleading voice, she simply cried, "Window!" He turned from her and went on.

Window tried to use his sword, but he had no strength in his right arm. He shoved the sword into his other hand and charged the two remaining Teeth-monsters. They turned to meet him, but it was to their bad fortune. Window wildly swung the sword out in front of him, and sliced into the chests of both of his attackers. Blood sprayed all around him, as he continued toward the monsters, swinging his sword without stopping. Before he realized just what was happening, he had killed both of the creatures. They fell at his feet, hissing and clawing at his legs as they died.

Suddenly the clearing was quiet. The surviving monsters had had enough. They retreated to the trees and pulled a few of their injured with them.

Rings chased them a short way but soon returned, seriously limping on a bleeding hind paw.

There was death everywhere. Snackers, Zeeters, Xaypers, Owts, Wommies, were all dead and dying. Some of every type of Talker and their friends were lost. Locker had died. Frazzle was killed as he lay injured. The ground was covered with lifeless forest animals.

Window turned to Panni. She was uninjured, but crying
deeply. Circles' legs were not only covered with the blood of the
Marrent he had killed, but some of his own blood as well.

Window's right shoulder and upper back had been brutally
sliced. His jacket had saved him from being hurt even more
seriously. And, of course, Panni had saved his life. Window
turned to her and threw his sword angrily down on the ground.
She ran to him and embraced him, squeezing him as tightly as she
dared. Blood from his injured back ran down her arm.

Window and Panni went over to Rings. He had collapsed on
the dirt in injury and exhaustion. Panni hugged him. There was
great pain in his sad eyes.

All around them, forest animals were caring for their injured.
Many had survived, but so many had died. The ground was
seemingly covered with their bodies. They had fought bravely, but
the cost was high. Panni stumbled back against the body of one of
the Tree-bears. She caught herself from falling, but again broke
into tears she could not stop. Window held her against his chest.
Comforting her briefly took his mind off of the pain screaming
from his still bleeding shoulder.

Circles was wild in his anger at what had happened. He made
his way around the clearing, gathering spent arrows, and then
finally picking up a Marrent bow that was not damaged. He
would have his weapon now, even if it was taken from his
attackers. He would have his weapon now!

Rings pulled himself to his feet, and started dragging the
bodies of lifeless monsters to the fire pit. The sickening smell of
their burning corpses made the task of retrieving the bodies of
their dead friends all the more difficult.

The animals worked until dawn, caring for the injured, and
collecting the bodies of those who had died. It was a long and very
sad night. Everyone agreed with Duster that the dead would be
buried in the morning, at the edge of the clearing. No one wanted
the vicious Caw-birds to be able to feed on the remains of those

who were killed. Rings worked tirelessly, even with his injured
paw, and his many arrow cuts, scraping out the necessary shallow
graves with his giant claws.

As the morning sun filtered through the trees overhead, the
preparations were complete. The graves were dug. Next to them,
the bodies were washed and lying in long rows.
It took several hours to complete the burials. As the bodies of
friends and loved ones were gently placed into the ground, each
group of animals sang its own special burial song of love and loss.

"Ohh lay saedenfae, Ohh lay saeenfae," mourned the Owts, in
their sad song of lost friends.
"Nae careen sol Fastulen," cried the Zeeters.
On and on the sadness continued.

Window stood with Panni and Circles. Rings joined them.
Window's back and shoulder and Circles' leg had been washed
with the juice from a den-berry bush. It wasn't the best of
treatments, but it was all anyone could think of at the moment.
Window could feel a lot of pain, but he wasn't thinking about his
pain at the moment.
Window thought back to the last burial he had attended. It
was that of his Aunt Elaine, Breeze's wife. He remembered the
sadness in his uncle's eyes – and the ache in his own heart.
Window wondered if he would ever forget the sadness of that day,
or the overwhelming sorrow of this one.

+++++++++

[AT THE FIELD ROAD CEMETERY]

*Far to the south, Bill Breesian was slowly walking down
the row of gravestones. At the end of the row was the one
stone he came to see – but the one stone he didn't want to see.
The clouds overhead matched his mood perfectly. They*

pressed down on him like a weight on his heart. It had been another lonely night for Window's Uncle Breeze.

Before he was ready for it, he was there, standing at his wife's grave. The smooth, dark stone seemed quiet and comfortable. The inscription hadn't changed since the last time he was there. It still simply said "Elaine Breesian, W.Y. 110 – 145."

Bill remembered the day Davis had asked him what he wanted the stone to say. His mind was in a whirl. He couldn't think of anything to express his love for Elaine – anything that could explain to cemetery visitors what the woman meant to him. So, he just kept the inscription simple. And, in the year and a half he had been coming here to visit, he still hadn't thought of anything more that he wished were on the stone.

Bill reached down and ran his fingers along the deep carved letters. He started with the "E" and continued until he had traced all six letters in her name. "What a beautiful name," he thought. "What a beautiful woman."

Like he often did, Bill Breesian sat down on his wife's gravestone. He didn't know if anyone else ever did that, but he was sure that Elaine wouldn't mind. He hoped that he was not the only one who ever came here to visit her.

Then he remembered – Window had told him that he stopped by sometimes.

His thoughts jumped to another sorrow. "Window – What has happened to Window? He should have been back by now. I should never have told him that story about the traveler who stopped at the Inn. I should never have told him about that path through the Deep Woods. I should never have let him go looking for adventure with that medallion he found. Please be alright, Window. Please be careful. Please come back home soon. I couldn't bear to lose you, too."

In the distant sky to the north, there was a flash of lightning. "Well, Elaine," Bill spoke aloud. " I'd better get going before I get wet."

+++++++++

The burials were complete. Rings pulled the dirt back over the
graves, carefully covering each of the bodies. Panni turned away
in tears. Circles took her hand, his head down on his chest.
Window closed his eyes.

The morning wind had brought some rain clouds. As the final
graves were covered, a light sprinkle started to fall. Everyone just
stood there and let the rain fall on them. Then, by ones and twos
and threes, the forest creatures slowly turned and drifted away.
Rings raised his giant head high above him, and cried for the first
time in his life. It was a terrible howl of loss and sorrow. It
echoed for miles through the trees of the Deep Woods.

TAESENNE RIVER
RYELAND
SELLETENNE PROVINCE
THE DEEPWOODS

CHAPTER TEN

ON THE NORTHWAY

The rain lasted for most of the morning. The forest Talkers and other animals drifted away from the clearing graveyard and returned to their homes and burrows. The four travelers were left all alone, except for a couple of Rainjays that were out for a wet morning search for worms and crickets.

Panni removed her bloodstained blouse and angrily threw it into the bushes. Then she took Window's damaged jacket and washed it in the stream behind the clearing. His shirt had already been used for bandages for two of the injured Zeeters.
The light rain easily washed all traces of the night's battle from Circles' silky fur. Rings waded around in the stream for a while and sat down in the water. He seemed to feel better after that.

Window's injuries were the most serious. His shoulder and back were severely cut. The monster's teeth had reached through his skin and torn into the flesh and muscle. Window had great difficulty lifting his arm. Panni used a bar of soap from her pack to wash his wounds as best she could. Circles found more den-berries and Panni gently rubbed his cuts with them, their purple juice stinging as it cleaned away the poison of the dirt and germs.

The others' injuries were not as serious. Circles had a cut on his head from being thrown against a large rock, and a long cut on his left leg.

Rings' left front paw had been badly hurt by the Ashdogs, but he said that it would be fine in a couple of days. He hardly mentioned his arrow wounds. He had been struck by at least a dozen arrows, but most of them didn't do much damage. His thick fur and skin protected him from serious harm. Most of the arrows were fairly easily removed, except for one that had gone deep in his left rear leg and broken off. It took Panni almost twenty minutes to dig it out and clean the wound. Rings didn't make a sound while she treated him.

While Panni was washing Rings' arrow wounds, Circles saw something familiar behind some trees at the edge of the clearing. What he discovered were the destroyed remains of the giant, green kite that Frazzle and Locker had flown at the Calisay field. Its bright paper and its tall frame were ripped and broken beyond repair.

Pushed under some bushes near the kite, and hidden from the eyes of the attacking monsters, Circles found something else. It was the woven basket that held the Deeps Woods Flickers that had helped the two Owts get the kite into the air in Calisay.

Circles opened the basket – the birds were still inside. They didn't try to get out or fly away. It was as though they didn't know what to do without Frazzle and Locker. Probably the Flickers had been friends with the two Owts since the Flickers were born. Circles reached into the basket and took them out, one by one. He whispered something into the ear of each one, and then tossed it into the air. Each big, grey bird flew up and perched, in a row, on the same branch above. When the last Flicker had joined the others, they looked down at Circles, chirped loudly, and then took flight together. Circles sadly watched as they disappeared above and beyond the trees.

Finally, with a deep sigh, Circles pulled the multi-colored tail from the Owt's broken kite frame and carefully folded it. When he got back to the others, he shoved it into his pack, which was on the ground near Rings' harness. Then it was almost time to go.

Fortunately, the travelers' clothes and supplies were kept dry in the heavy canvass packs Oldsmith had made for them. Rings insisted that he could still carry everything, so Panni and Window again attached his harness and hung the packs and bags from it.

Panni dug a clean blouse from her pack and carelessly put it on. She ran her comb through her hair and let it drip and hang down her back. They started on their way.

Circles carried his bow and slung a quiver that he found, and had filled with arrows, across his back. He had washed every arrow carefully. Window noticed that Circles took only those that he had found on the ground or imbedded in trees, not any arrow which had killed or injured any of the forest creatures.

Window's sword dangled from Rings' harness. Panni's dagger, thoroughly cleaned and sparkling again, rode against her waist.

They were to head to the north from the clearing and should reach the edge of the Woods later that day. As they left the once-happy meeting place, no one said anything. They had not slept. They had not eaten. They had only cried and buried the dead. The travelers kept their thoughts to themselves. Well, except for Rings. As he walked past it, Rings kicked one of the sitting logs and sent it rolling half way across the clearing.

Unlike the paths that took the travelers to the meeting place, the path to the north was straighter and much wider. They walked quietly. Rings limped a bit. Circles also favored his injured leg. Panni held on to one of Rings' harness straps when there was room for her to walk along side of him.

By the middle of the afternoon, they reached the edge of the Woods. The rain had cleared, and as they burst from the trees and into the Northlands again, the sun was starting to peek through the clouds. Their spirits lifted as they left the Deep Woods behind them. Still not saying much, they continued north across open lands through what was known as the Selletenne Province. This area of the Northlands was only thinly populated. The former ruling city of Sellette had been abandoned after the Northern Wars, and most of the Sellettes went to Calisay to live.

The travelers' goal was to reach the Northway. This was the
main east-west road, which stretched all the way to the ocean
several hundred miles to the west. The Battleplain Cemetery was
to the east of where they were now, so they would be following the
Northway to the right, once they reached it.

Window's shoulder ached terribly and his head felt no better.
The others were dragging themselves along as best they could.
They would need to stop and rest soon. After a few miles through
the open country, they found a gentle hillside with a few trees,
and decided to camp there for the night. The sun was still fairly
high in the sky, but they could go no farther.
There were not enough trees nearby to provide wood for a fire,
so they just pulled the harness from Rings' back and opened a food
pack. Rings didn't eat, but wandered off a bit, and collapsed in
fatigue under a tree.
Panni spread an eating cloth on the grass and tried to make a
nice little meal for herself, and Window, and Circles. They sat on
the ground and finished a loaf of rye bread and the rest of the
white cheese. Circles had a few berries and the other two each ate
a strip of dried meat.

After the quiet meal, Window and Circles spread one of the
blankets on the ground, up against the equipment packs. Panni
lay down and closed her eyes, the sun still shining directly on her
face. Circles went over and lay next to Rings.
Window sat on the blanket next to Panni and leaned back
against a big canvass pack. He looked over at Rings and Circles.
Window could hear Rings breathing. The Brarrie's massive body
rose and fell as the warm, late-afternoon air filled his massive
lungs and left again. Circles slept silently.
Window looked down at Panni, lying next to him, just as she
briefly opened her eyes. His eyes met hers for a moment. Her
face relaxed for the first time that day. She closed her eyes again.
Window watched her until he, too, was lost in sleep.

The weary travelers slept all through the rest of that day and night. The early morning sun woke them refreshed, and somewhat recovered from their terrible ordeal.

Breakfast was quick, and before long, the group was back on its way again. It was an uneventful trek north to the road. They saw no people and few animals. Rings' injured paw didn't bother him too much, but Panni had to wash Window's cuts again when they came to a field-creek.

Window thought ahead to the treasure of Freeland coins waiting for them at the cemetery. He realized that he didn't seem to care about them much anymore. The attack at the forest clearing had so affected him that he had lost interest in adventure and treasure hunting. He just wanted to keep his friends safe, and couldn't think of anything else. And, besides, he told himself, those few coins weren't really a treasure, and they may not even still be there.

But mostly, he thought that he really didn't want to go to the Cemetery right now. He had enough of death for a while. He was sure that seeing rows of graves of slain soldiers would be difficult for him. He wondered if the others might feel the same way.

The weather remained pleasant, and the travelers walked on most of the day. Rings limped a bit but never complained. Panni was worried about Window's injuries, but never mentioned it, even when she, once again, cleaned his wounds.

By late afternoon that day, they could see the Northway up ahead. Off to the left and right, the road stretched across flat land and wound through low hills. They saw no one on the road, but decided to wait until the next day to approach it. They would camp for the night just this side of the road, and then get a fresh start towards the Battleplain in the morning.

In this part of the country, there was plenty of firewood available, so Window and Circles built a nice campfire while Panni took out some items for supper. Rings wanted to help, but his paws were too big to hold anything.

"I wish there was something I could do," he offered.

Panni had an idea. *"Why don't you tell us a story while we fix things to eat?"* she suggested, speaking as carefully as she could.

"Yeah," Circles agreed. "Hey, tell us a story about the Silkie. Window says that maybe we can go see the Silkie."

In his entire life, Rings had never been asked to tell a story. He was thrilled by the idea.

"All right, I will," he agreed. "I will tell you a story about the Silkie."

He sat back on his haunches and thought for a moment. The others continued with their chores. Then Rings began.

"Many years ago, there was a terrible storm in this part of the country. Rain and lightning filled the sky for days and nights and the vicious wind blew down all the trees. The birds and animals lost their nests and burrows. The waters flooded the lands. Only the Silkie had necks long enough to reach out of the water. They rescued all of the other animals who hung to the Silkie's necks while they were carried to safety."

"Wow," Said Circles. "Where did you hear that story?"

"I didn't hear that story," Rings replied. I made it up just now."

Panni let out a little laugh. Circles responded, "Oh, come on, Ringer. Don't you know any real stories about the Silkie?"

"Well, the Owts tell a story about Angels that ride on the Silkie in the bright moonlight, but I don't know if it is true."

"I wouldn't count on it," Window jumped in, wondering if Rings knew any other stories about Angels.

Circles wouldn't give up, "I wish we could go see the Silkie."

"Rings, do you know where the Silkie are?" asked Panni. *"Senne trae oepan tuecut..."* Then, thinking carefully, she added, *"I would like to see them too."*

"I know that they are somewhere to the west of us, in Ryeland. At least, that is what I have always heard."

Circles look at Window. "Hey, Window, if we are going to see the Silkie, we should do it now, before we go to the Cemetery."

Window didn't say anything. It was an interesting idea. He really did want to delay their trip to the Battleplain.

"What about finding the Freeland coins, Circles? Don't you want to find the treasure?" Window finally responded.

"We can do that later. Let's go find the Silkie!"

Window liked the idea of putting off the cemetery visit for a while. "Rings, how far do you think it might be to the Silkie?"

"I don't know where they are, Window. It could be half way to the ocean."

Circles saw his chance. "Let's go to the ocean, Window! Let's go to the ocean! Let's go find a big treasure, like the treasure of King Alezan! We could go to Meriselle and find the King's Treasure."

Again, Window didn't reply right away. He looked at Panni. He looked at Rings. On their faces where expressions, not of disagreement, but of excitement and hope. Well, at least on Panni's face. Rings didn't say anything, but just looked at him, waiting for his answer.

"But it is very, very far," Window responded. "It would take us weeks to get there."

"It would take us weeks to get there, even if we didn't go," Circles argued.

Window smiled. He couldn't think of a single thing to say in response to that statement.

Rings spoke up. "And, after we see the ocean, and find the Treasure, we could go to the cold far north. I have always wanted to go there. That is where my Brarrie ancestors lived before they came to the Deep Woods."

We could go to the Battleplain Cemetery on our way back," Circles repeated. It will be right on our way back."

"You realize, don't you, Circles, that we have no idea where to find the King's Treasure? It could be anywhere in the city. It would be impossible to find."

"Impossible to find, like you found me and Panni and Rings? That kind of impossible?"

"Well, not that kind of impossible, but a different kind of impossible."

"Like the kind that – Hey, wait." Circles thought of something else. "Panni is supposed to help you find a treasure. That was the agreement when she joined us," he exaggerated. "And, we already know where the Battleplain treasure is. She needs to help us find a different treasure – like the King's Treasure."

Window looked deep in the eyes of his dancer friend. "What about you, Panni, do you want to see the ocean?"

She immediately replied as clearly as she could, again using words Rook had taught her, *"I can't go back home, Window. I will go with you. I will go anywhere with you."*

Rings joined the conversation again, "I don't mind a long walk, Window. My paw will be just fine soon."

In desperation, Circles tried one more thing. "Maybe there are some Silkie by the ocean, Window. Maybe there are some Angels riding on them!"

Window looked into the eyes of his friends. There could never be better friends to share an adventure. Even the guys back home would never be this enthusiastic about just a simple trip, like going to the woods or to the lake.

He knew that he really didn't need to get back home anytime soon. Mary wouldn't be returning to Windtown until next spring. Everyone would worry about him, but – he thought again of what his grandmother had said about not coming home too soon.

Window smiled inside to himself, but the others could see it on his face. They would go to the faraway ocean. They would look for the King's Treasure. And although he had no idea of how they would get there, they would travel to the far north, as Rings wanted, too. It would be a grand, grand adventure!

Suddenly Window noticed that his spirits had lifted. He had broken free from the sorrow of the deaths in the Deep Woods. He had a new adventure to share with his traveler friends.

"We'll start in the morning," he smiled. Rings let out a happy howl. Circles turned a flip in the air, right where he was standing. Panni just looked at Window quietly. Inside she was thrilled.

And Meriselle will be easy to find," Circles excitedly added. "We just walk until we get to the ocean and we will be there! And, you will see, Window. We will find the Treasure."

Looking back at the little Woot, Window replied, "As Panni said at Oldsmith's house, I have already found a treasure, Circles. I have already found a treasure."

+++++++++

That evening around the fire was a happy one. Panni just sat and watched the flames flicker and jump as she quietly sang to herself. Circles cleaned his arrows again, and made imaginary plans to ride on a Silkie. Of course, nobody knew if you could actually ride a Silkie or not, even if you were an Angel.

Rings loved the idea of doing something challenging, but he decided that he had better rest up for the trip. After a meal of field grass and banti-leaves, he flopped down by the fire and hardly moved for the rest of the night.

As Window warmed his face by the fire, he thought of where they would be going on their new adventure. He knew that as the Northway went west from the King's mines, it passed through the northern edge of the Calisenne Province, then the Selletenne Province, where they were now, and continued west through the central part of the North, called Ryeland.

Window recalled the story he had been told in history class at school. When the first Freeland settlers arrived in the Northlands, they found that the weather was harsh and the ground was not very fertile for the several hundred miles from the coast to the Calisay inlands. When early explorers returned to Freeland to report on their discoveries, one said to the King, "I don't think that even rye could grow there." From that time on, the central part of the Northlands, which was officially named Taesenne, was known as Ryeland.

The travelers' goal was at the Northway's western end, the Atlandic port city of Meriselle. Meriselle had once been as large as Calisay, but was completely destroyed by the Atland army during the Continent Wars. It was probably just abandoned ruins now. Where a treasure might be hidden, Window had no idea.

The early morning sun found everyone in good spirits. Rings said that his foot was feeling fine. Circles' injuries were healing and he was ready to go. Panni again cleaned Window's cuts. He was very sore and couldn't move his right arm much at all. His back and shoulder, though, did seem to be beginning to heal.

They had a breakfast of crackers and apples before hanging the equipment onto Rings' harness. Before long, they had traveled the half-mile or so to the road and were soon standing on the dust of the Northway, looking to the east, the way to the Battleplain. "We'll be back," Window said, mostly speaking to the road itself.

They turned and began the long walk to the ocean. The road ahead was wide and clear and should be very easy to traverse. Circles suggested that they celebrate the beginning of their adventure with a couple of verses of, "The Marching Song," and so they did. After that, they took turns telling stories.

"I hope you all know a lot of stories and songs," Window expressed. "This is going to be a very long trip."

"If we run out, we will just make up some new ones," Circles responded. "It will be grand!"

Fast moving clouds passed overhead. The four travelers followed the Northway across wide fields, over gentle hills, and through thin groves of trees. The types of trees and birds seemed to change a bit.

Window enjoyed spotting new types of birds. He decided to keep track of the ones he saw and tell his grandmother Windowen about them when he got home. "I guess that I got my interest in birds from my mother, and she got hers from Grandma," he thought.

He was going to ask Panni if she had ever watched birds when she was younger, or if she could identify many different types, but he didn't. She had learned a lot of Atlandan already, but it was still difficult to carry on a regular conversation with her. "I wish she could understand me better," Window thought. "I would love to be able to talk to her about... all kinds of things."

The weather stayed mostly pleasant for the next couple of days. Only one brief rain shower sent the travelers under some trees for an hour. The rest of the time they walked on. They lost interest in telling stories and singing. Circles sometimes took his bow and would shoot an arrow as far ahead on the road as he could. Then he would count the steps until he reached the arrow. Eventually, he could send an arrow more than three hundred steps up the road. And, he only lost one arrow in the bushes, because, as he explained, "A surprise gust of wind blew it off to the side."

Evenings were quiet – their campfire the center of their world in the darkness. Panni sometimes walked off by herself for a while. Window never asked what she was thinking of.

Several more days passed. Only a couple of times, did they meet any other travelers on the road. Those other travelers looked with great suspicion at the group of four odd walkers. After a few pleasant remarks, they would pass by and disappear behind them to the east.

Most of Window's cuts were healing, but one part of his shoulder remained very red and painful. Panni continued to clean the wounds twice a day, but there was concern that something more needed to be done for him. Unfortunately, they had no medicine besides the berry juice that Circles continued to find. Panni was worried about Window.

After a week or so on their way to the sea, after many miles of open road, open sky, and sun above, the travelers came upon the first important landmark on the Northway. It was the Ryeland Bridge. The bridge passed over a deep ravine above the Taesenne River. It marked the eastern boundary of Ryeland. It was a beautiful, wide, bridge of metal and stone, that was built just before the Wars, when the Northlands was at the height of its power and development. The Atland army used the bridge to attack the inlands, so the bridge was not destroyed, as was most of everything else in Ryeland and beyond. The travelers stopped to rest and to enjoy the bridge for a while.

Panni enjoyed standing in the middle of the bridge and hanging her upper body over its wide siderail, looking straight down to the river far below. She told the others that she always loved to climb hills and trees when she was a young girl, and that being high above the river, like this, was a little like flying.

Circles got out his kite, and flew it from the siderail close to Panni – just as he had seen others do in Calisay.

Rings lay on the bridge and blocked the way when any of the others tried to cross. He demanded a toll from each of them but was completely unsuccessful in collecting anything other than a friendly kick from Circles.

Watching his friends, so happy and carefree, made Window feel much better than he had in any of the days since the attack at the clearing. As he watched Panni hang over the sidewall on the bridge, with her long hair flying in the breeze, while Circles' kite tail did the same thing high up above, he felt renewed and lifted. It was as though the Ryeland wind was blowing his sadness away. His spirits were recovering nicely.

The travelers decided to camp for the night next to the bridge. Late that night, as the others fell asleep by the fire, Window stayed up. He just didn't feel sleepy, so he threw a few more branches on the fire and got out his notebook. He hadn't thought much about his medallion or his grandfather's expedition for a while. He pulled the medallion from his pocket and rubbed his thumb over its raised surface a couple of times. The medallion was a real treasure to him. It was, after all, the reason he was on his adventure in the Northlands with his three traveling friends. He was so glad that he had found it. If only he could find out where it came from.

As he had done before, Window read down the list of names from the Northlands Expedition, "Gravand, Cassidan, Canette..." "How about Private Canette? Window thought. "Maybe he was the one with the treasure-hunting grandson. Maybe that grandson had stopped and camped by this very same bridge."

Window settled back against his pack, pulled his blanket over his legs, closed his eyes, and wondered, "Where might that grandson be hunting for treasure at this exact moment?"

[NEAR THE BRIDGE AT CALENNE]

Thousands of miles to the west, Katherine Canette had found the perfect spot. Not only was she living her dream of returning to the Old Country, from which her grandfather had originally come, but she had found the perfect shade to sit under as she painted the perfect picture of the most perfect bridge in all of Calenne. And she loved to paint above all else.

Back near her home in the Windlands, she had spent hours and days and weeks and months of her twenty-one years traveling along the Windcoast stopping whenever and wherever she could, to paint the most colorful sights of the beautiful hills and trees that followed the entire coastline.

Now she was the happiest she had ever been. Before her was the beautiful bridge at Calenne which joined the city across the Island River. It was built about O.Y. 750 during the time when the country was at its peak of wealth and style. During those times, King Marelle was determined that Freeland would be the "Jewel Of The World" and encouraged all Freelanders to construct buildings and other structures that were beautiful, as well as functional. Of all the cities in the world, Calenne was now held by many as the most beautiful.

Katherine carefully measured out the paints she would use today – bright blues for the sky and water, soft greens for the grass and trees, deep reds for the dramatically shaped bricks of the bridge. These days the bridge was used only by pedestrians, and there were many using it today, each in brightly colored clothes that dotted her view with patches of moving brightness that made the bridge seem alive.

Above the bridge, the sun shown on the whitest clouds Katherine had ever seen. And below, at both ends of the bridge, there stood massive, ancient, oak trees towering above the span and forming a roof over its endposts. But from this vantage point, the trees were on the other side of the bridge and did not obstruct her view at all, only added to the dramatic vista she held.

A gentle breeze ruffled her dark brown hair and caressed her bare arms and shoulders. Although the day was warm, she was very comfortable beneath the branches of the tall willow she was under. She surveyed the view before her again, once again reveling in her good fortune to be there. She quickly thought back to her trip across the Atlandic and the years she had dreamed of being in this exact spot.

It was time to begin. Katherine Canette took one more quick glance before her, and chose her starting point. She drew a satisfying deep breath and carefully dipped her brush into the lightest blue of her paints. Then her brush touched a spot near the top of her paper and moved in a blue arc, from one edge to the other. Although no one was near her to hear, the words quietly slipped out from her lips, "I love this place."

+++++++++

In the morning, the four travelers left the bridge and again continued towards the west. Circles often rode on Rings back and Panni would walk next to Window while holding on to Rings' straps. The countryside became bleak and barren as they passed through the heart of Ryeland. Days went by, but they met no one on the road, just a few scruffy squirrels and rabbits.

None of the travelers said much about treasures or the Silkie or about anything. They kept their thoughts to themselves as they pushed on. The sky was overcast for mile after mile and matched the Ryeland landscape. Slowly, their spirits were becoming as dark as the sky and the land.

Window's injuries refused to heal. His wounds became even more inflamed and he began to run a fever. Panni did her best to wrap Window's shoulder to keep him comfortable, but he had lost almost all use of his right arm and was in more pain than ever. He began to feel weak and had difficulty walking steadily.

Window rode on Rings' back for a while, but the shaking movement of the ride caused even more pain in his shoulder and he had to continue to walk, with difficulty. Panni was feeling desperate, and Circles became quiet and withdrawn. Window was becoming very ill.

Six days after they left the Ryeland Bridge, the travelers came upon a shallow stream that crossed the road. Near the stream, the grass and trees were much thicker and greener than any other they had seen in Ryeland. They decided to stop and camp here for the night. They crossed the stream and found a flat spot under the trees next to the road on the other side. It was getting dark by the time Panni and Circles had gotten a fire going.

Window sat on the ground and leaned against his clothes pack. After a light meal, Circles sat next to him and touched Window's arm. "It is my fault, Window, that you are hurt," Circles began. "It is my fault that everyone was killed."

Window looked caringly at his friend as Circles continued. "I should have heard the monsters coming at the clearing. If I had been a better friend, I would have been able to warn everyone." Circles began to cry. The tears rolled down his fur and onto the ground. "I am sorry, Window. I am sorry that I am not a very good friend."

Window's heart felt almost broken. "Come here, Circles," Window gently spoke to him. "Let me hold you close and tell you what a good friend you are." Window put his healthy arm around the little Woot and pulled him against his side.

"You are the friend who saved me on the path in the Deep Woods. You are the friend that knew how to talk to Panni so we could help her. You are the friend that led me to Calisay, and Oldsmith, and Rings. You are a friend forever."

Window continued while he hugged Circles close to him. "The terrors of the Woods are not yours. The death and injury are not yours. Even the Fire-claws would not have heard the monsters this time. They were too careful."

"Are you sure that I am still your friend, Window? Are you really sure?"

"For ever, Circles. And our friendship has really just begun. Even now, we are having a grand, new adventure. We are going to the ocean. We are looking for treasure. We have other friends to share our adventure. It would not be happening if it were not for you."

"But your arm, Window. What about your arm?"

"I can still do this with my arm." Window slowly reached up and wiped his hand across Circle's eyes. A few more tears dripped out onto Window's fingers.

"I don't know about my arm, Circles. But with you as my friend, I am not too worried."

Circles sighed and seemed to relax a bit. Window gave him another hug. "Let's go sit with the others by the fire," Window suggested. Circles silently nodded in agreement.

Window, Circles, Panni, and Rings sat around the Ryeland fire as the flames jumped high before them. Panni started singing a song about watching stars sparkling in the clear night sky. The others just listened and enjoyed her sweet voice. Her singing was very comforting to all of them. She sang softly and gently as her voice floated out across the grass and into the nearby trees.

But something more interesting than trees and grass was listening to her. Panni looked up. Standing near the road behind the others was a man. He was tall and thin – and seemed to glow all over with a soft blue light. Panni stopped singing.

"Reaselle venne tou lamanne," the man spoke in Freelandan. His voice was clear and precise as Panni's always was.

Everyone turned to him, and stared in amazement. Panni responded, *"Saenelle trae laevirenne. Kae onrae Atlandan?"*

"Hello, Dear Travelers. May I join you at your fire?" the man spoke again.

Window's friends all looked at him. "Certainly, you may join us." Window replied. "Come sit here by the fire."

As the man walked towards them, they could see him clearly —
not because of the firelight, but because of his own light. He was
wearing simple pants and overshirt, and smooth boots. His hair
was wavy, and pushed back on the sides. His skin on his face and
bare arms was silken and shiny light blue-grey. His face was very
angular, his blue eyes almost sparkling from within. All about
him was a glow of soft blue light.

And as the curious stranger walked over to join them at the
fire, tiny, bright paths of sparkling light followed each of his
fingertips in the darkness. It was as though the tips of his fingers
were each alive with bits of colored light. Each finger left a trail of
a different hue. The paths of light from each hand formed
rainbows of beautiful color that briefly followed his fingers before
fading away.

The man stopped in front of the fire and spoke to the travelers.
His eyes sparkled bright blue and white as he addressed them, "I
have come very far. Thank you for letting me rest with you."

"We have come a long way, too," Circles explained, "from
Calisay. Where have you come from?"

"I have come from up there," he answered, as he pointed
straight up into the air, his fingers leading a rainbow of light as he
did. Window noticed that the sparkling colored trails were not
coming from his fingertips, but from metal rings that he wore on
the first knuckle of each finger, and on his thumbs.

"You came from the sky?" Circles questioned. Window, Rings,
and Panni listened in amazement. "You came from the sky, like
rain?" Circles wondered.

"Yes, from the sky, like the rain, but from much farther away.
I have been traveling for a very long time, and would like to rest
for a while."

"Shall we call you 'The Rain,' " asked Circles, in an obviously
disbelieving manner. "Or do you have another name?"

"I have many names. My people are named by the worlds we
visit, and I have visited hundreds of different worlds. Part of my
name is Raenedejjreonne Trisaeleeusim Fasixannopin
Talenniditreelle, and you have guessed what others sometimes

call me. If you would call me Raine, as those closest to me do, I
would like that.”

The man’s voice was clear and commanding, not in a
demanding way, but in a strong and confident way. His shiny
blue skin reflected the firelight. Window noticed a small white
insignia painted into the skin on his right arm, just below his
elbow.

“Please sit down and join us, Raine,” Window invited. “Tell us
about your travels.”

“Thank you, my Dear Companions. You are kind to allow me to
your fire.”

“You are kind to join us,” Circles replied, as he shifted over
towards Panni, so there would be room for the visitor closer to the
fire.

“Do you really come from the sky, Raine?” Circles continued to
question their new visitor.

The strange blue-skinned man pointed again to the northern
sky. “Do you see those three bright stars in the shape of a
triangle? I come from beyond that one on the left, from a world
called Tessimaysan. It is a beautiful world of great cities, forests,
and seas. I was raised at a place called Moonfarm, near a forest
that has five moons in the late, night sky.”

“Are you an Angel?” Circles excitedly wanted to know.

“No, Circles, I am just a traveler – like you. I travel in a ship
that sails between the stars.”

“Have you ever seen an Angel? Circles persisted, totally
enthralled by the strange man from the sky.

“I have been to many places and seen many things, but I have
never seen an Angel. There are worlds where sky people live in
clouds, and I know winged men who live in trees, and other men
who ride giant birds, but they are not Angels.

“Do you really sail to the stars?” the Woot continued.

“Yes, I really do. I am a messenger. I sail the winds between
the stars and deliver important messages to important people on
many worlds. I speak to those who will speak to no other. But I
fear that I will never do that again.”

"My ship was damaged in a storm and I am lost. I don't know if I will ever find my way back home. My only hope is for others from my world to come and find me. But they may not be able to. I fear that I am lost here forever." Raine lowered his head and looked at the ground.

"Panni can't go home, either," Circles offered to Raine. "She has run away."

"I am sorry to hear that, Panni. It is a terrible thing to be lost and alone."

Panni had something else on her mind. "Our friend, Window, has been injured, and is ill," she explained, and then asked politely, *"Saetrene toufas coetae?"*

"I am sorry, Panni, I cannot get back to my ship, but maybe I can help Window without medicine. Window, let me see your wounds."

Panni carefully helped Window unwrap his bandages. Raine examined the infected cuts and then placed his fingers and thumbs against the skin around them. As the travelers all watched in complete amazement, silver sparks, mixed with bright red, traveled out from the rings on Raine's right hand, across and under Window's cuts, and into the rings on Raine's other hand. Window winced a bit and then relaxed.

"That should help you, Window. By morning you will be better."

"Will it really help, Raine? *Wae teefen toesae?*" Panni excitedly asked. *"Wae teefen toesae?"*

"Yes, Panni, it will really help."

Panni was thrilled that the starman might heal her dear Window – Window, who was so important to her. "Thank you, Raine, we have been so very worried. I thank you from all of my heart." She was happily stunned beyond any more words as she lovingly hugged Window.

Window nodded his thanks and closed his eyes for a moment. Panni wrapped his shoulder again and stayed close to him. Raine returned to his spot next to Circles.

Circles wanted to know everything about their amazing visitor. "Raine, how will you ever get home?" Circles continued to question, when the new traveler had sat down by him again.

"I don't know, Circles, I am lost here. I don't know how to get home."

"Well, you can stay here with us if you like – can't he Window? We are going on an adventure to the ocean."

"I would love to go on an adventure with you, Circles. I would like that a lot."

Window had been listening. He opened his eyes and looked at Panni and towards Rings. They both nodded, "Yes."

"Welcome to our group of travelers, Raine," Window announced. "We are glad to have you come along with us."

"I am fortunate to have been lost in such barren country," Raine replied, " – such barren country, with such wonderful travelers. It will be delightful to go with you."

Circles was completely fascinated by the man from the sky. "I wish that I could go to some of those worlds, Raine, like where you have been – to find some magical places."

"You don't have to go to other worlds, Circles. I am sure that there are magical places here in this world. You just have to go find them."

"Window, can we go to a magical place?" Circles turned and asked his friend.

"I think we are already there, Circles," Window responded with a smile. "I think we are already there."

EPILOGUE

+++++++++

[IN THE LAND OF MAGICAL PLACES]

"Window, can we go to a magical place?" Circles turned and asked his friend.

"I think we are already there, Circles," Window responded with a smile. "I think we are already there."

The mother of the twin girls put the book down on the clothes-stand. Veri was forcing her eyes to stay open. "I wonder what will happen to Window and his friends next, Mama."

"You know very well what will happen, Veri," her sister reminded her.

"Don't tell me, Tressi, I want to be surprised."

"Oh, alright, Veri. I won't."

"Time for sleep, Darlings," their mother quietly instructed the girls. "We can read some more of the story tomorrow night."

"I wish that I didn't have to wait, Mama," Veri spoke up from her pillow. "I don't like to wait for good things."

"I hope they find all of the treasure and lots more kites, too," Tressi shared from behind closed eyes.

"We shall see, Darlings. We shall see."

"Yes, we shall see," repeated Veri, as she pulled her light cover up over her.

The girls settled in for a night of quiet dreams. "Good night, Mama," they both softly spoke as their eyes closed tightly.

Then Veri added just as she drifted away, "And, someday, maybe we can go to one of those magical places, too."

Their mother stood up from the edge of the bed and shifted her white-lace night-dress. The bright light of the table lamp reflected from the jeweled pin in her hair and flashed on the ceiling like stars in the warm night sky.

She looked down at her beautiful daughters.

"I think we are already there, My Darlings," she quietly spoke to herself. "I think we are already there."

REFERENCES

**CHARACTERS, PLACES, AND THINGS
IN PART ONE
AND THE PAGE WHERE INTRODUCED**

+++++++++

Owt – A type of Deep Woods Talker that enjoyed visiting with
    men. Owts stood on their two stubby hind legs, and had
    very long snouts, and short grey-brown fur. p. 21

Panni [Pantine Tresette] – A beautiful Northlands young woman
    who had run away from her servitude as a dancer at the
    Traepelle Province Castle, and who joined Window and
    Circles in their search for treasure. p. 106
Park Street – The street near the Windtown Park. p. 27
Partridge Street – The Windtown street where Window's
    Grandmother Breesian lived. p. 9
Path (through the Deep Woods) – A wide path cut from the
    Northlands to the Wind Lands by the Northlands Army
    during the Northern Wars. p. 19
Paw-creatures [Fire-claws] – Small, sharp-clawed, ragged-furred,
    fire-loving Deep Woods creatures. p. 69
Piper [Tanding] – A boyhood friend, and hiking and camping
    companion of Window. p. 11
Prairie Hen – A wild, fast-running, non-flying, chicken-like bird of
    the Windlands Prairies. p. 34
Prairie Hen [P-hen] [Penny] – A small, copper, Windlands coin. p.
    44
Prairies – The Windlands east of the Windlands River. p. 12
Prince Martellan – The cruel, hated, self-proclaimed ruler of
    Calisay. p. 123
R. Hollen – A member of Grandfather Windowen's Northlands
    Expedition, from Ameran. p. 39

Ship's Harbor – A very small, very sheltered harbor town on the northern Windcoast. It was the first stop of ships coming down the coast from the north. Very little cargo was unloaded there. Its main function was to serve as a safe harbor for ships caught in one of the many storms to strike the coast from the North Atlandic. p. 9

Signal Hill – The hill built to the top of the trees just inside the southern edge of the Deep Woods north of Windtown, used, but not built by, the Northlands Army after completing the Path from the north. p. 54

Silkie [pl. Silkie] – Tall, long-legged, long-necked, silky-furred animals from the Northlands plains. p. 45

Slack-lizards – Long, slick-skinned, Deep Woods creatures. p. 198

Snackers – Long-necked Deep Woods Talkers. p. 193

South Continent – The huge, jungle-covered part of the Newlands Continent south of the Windlands. South Continent was settled by the Old Countries in only four places: Greyport – a wild, ungoverned city of pirates and other criminals, to the south, down the western continent coast from the Windlands – The Horselands – a large region of open grassfields and beautiful horses still farther down the continent coast – Sanarelle – a port used by traders who braved the jungle interior in search of exotic fruits prized back in the Old Countries – And South Cape – a region settled by Atland at the very southern tip of the continent. p. 139

South Corner – The intersection of the Windlands Road with four of the streets of Windtown. p. 8

South Range [Rangelands] – A region in the New South cattle country. p. 38

South Road Inn – An inn where the New South Road meets the Coast Road. p. 119

Southern Waters – The large ocean and islands region south of the Old Countries, populated by many colonies and small independent islands. p. 58

Springcookies – The rectangular, Amerand cookies baked by Window's Grandmother Windowen, using a carved, wooden cookieboard to press raised pictures on the top of the cookies. p. 35

explorer, John W. Near, was thought to have camped as he
came to the end of his inland journey in W.Y. 19. p. 29

Windlands Years [W.Y.] – Numbered from the year the Wind
Lands were first landed by ships from Atland in O.Y. (Old
Years) 801. Thus, W.Y. 1 was O.Y. 801. p. 13

Windmill Dollar – A large, sliver, Windlands coin. p. 44

Window [Windowen Ernest Breesian] – Young builder and
woodworker from Windtown in the Windlands Prairies who
travels to the Wilds and far beyond in search of treasure and
adventure. p. 3

Windport – A northern Windcoast town, where the winds from the
ocean were the strongest in all of the Windlands. p. 119

Windtown [Town] – The Windlands Prairies town at the eastern
end of the Windlands Road. p. 5

Windtown Journal – The Town newspaper. p. 27

Windtown School [Town School] – The school across the alley from
Grandmother Breesian's house where Window had studied
as a boy. p. 7

Wire – A small sea town south of Coastown on the Windlands
Atlandic coast. p. 119

Wommies [ground-dogs] – Deep Woods hole-digging mammals. p.
192

Woodmine – An Inlands city on the southern edge of the Deep
Woods. It was the only city in all of the Windlands to be
built into the edge of the Deep Woods. p. 6

Woodmine Bridge – The Falls River bridge at Woodmine. p. 102

Woot – A colorful, silky-furred, Deep Woods Talker. p. 77

Woot – The language spoken by Woots in the Deep Woods. p. 187

Xaypers – Long-armed, boney, Deep Woods Talkers. p. 193

Zeeters – Skinny, otter-looking, Deep Woods Talkers. p. 192

Zetani – Pirates preying on shipping in the Southern Waters. p.
58

Zumbler – A Deep Woods creature from several favorite
Windlands children's rhymes. p. 63

+++++++++

John Ernest Briggs

John has a Master's Degree in Mathematics and has spent much of his life as a Calculus Teacher, so he can deal well with complexity and detail, which he has written into the story in a delightfully entertaining and understandable manner. Plus, his creative and imaginative joy of wonder, excitement, family, friendship, loyalty, mystery, exploration and love are evident in every page.

Master's Degree in Mathematics
Mathematics Teacher - College and High School
Vietnam War Era Veteran
Singer, Songwriter, Guitarist
Music Producer, and Recording Engineer
Author and Illustrator of Fantasy/Adventure

johnernestbriggs@gmail.com

Window's adventures continue in:

The Adventures of Window Breesian

Part Two:
The Search For The Northlands Treasure